YOU'VE BEEN SERVED

KRISTEN ALICIA

Entangled Publishing, LLC
644 Shrewsbury Commons Ave., STE 181
Shrewsbury, PA 17361
rights@entangledpublishing.com

Amara is an imprint of Entangled Publishing, LLC.

Visit our website at www.entangledpublishing.com.

Edited by Gwyn Jordan and Alexander Te Pohe
Cover design by Elizabeth Turner Stokes
Interior design by Toni Kerr

ISBN 978-1-64937-394-6
Ebook ISBN 978-1-64937-415-8

Manufactured in the United States of America
First Edition June 2023

10 9 8 7 6 5 4 3 2 1

AMARA
an imprint of Entangled Publishing LLC

For Emerson and Desmond

PROLOGUE

"The asshole at table nine sent his plate back again. He said this time it just didn't taste right, whatever that means." Sam rolled his eyes. I was glad to see I wasn't the only one irritated at table nine's repeated requests for a new sauce. It was the third time our head waiter had brought the plate back to the kitchen with some kind of asinine complaint. First the sauce was too salty, then too sweet. Now it just didn't taste right. What the hell.

In the restaurant business, few things were worse than a customer that complained just for the sake of complaining, and I was starting to get the impression this guy was doing exactly that.

"You know what? Screw it. I'm going to talk to him. I want to see for myself what his problem is," I told Sam, rinsing off my hands and wiping them on my pristine white chef's coat. Sam raised his eyebrows before moving out of my way. He knew me well enough to know that now wasn't the time to ask questions.

"Chef," I called out to Jordan, the executive chef at Ipsa's, "table nine sent back his plate again. I'm going to talk to him. Cool?"

Jordan was busy reprimanding one of the new line cooks,

so I knew he wasn't paying any attention to what I said when he waved his hand and nodded.

Perfect.

I didn't want him to stop me from figuring out who this jerk was and why he kept dismissing my sauce. My bearnaise was outstanding, and I knew it. Hell, it should have been outstanding. I'd been working for three years to perfect it, and I could make it with my eyes closed. Literally. I tried making it once with my eyes covered at home, and it was surprisingly successful. The fact that an unsophisticated patron was insulting my hard work didn't sit well with me at all.

Slamming through the kitchen doors, I eyed the crowded dining room, scanning the tables until I landed on table nine. There he was. Older than the usual techies that frequented Ipsa's and dressed much nicer, the man looked harmless enough, but I didn't appreciate his gall. Working overtime to keep my composure, I walked over to his table.

"Hello, sir." The man looked up at me and smiled, but it barely registered for me.

"Hi there," he shot back. "What can I do for you?"

"I'm the saucier, and Sam, your waiter, has sent your meal back to the kitchen several times saying that you're not enjoying the sauce. What's the issue?"

"Exactly what I told the young man earlier. It didn't taste quite right."

And that was about the point I lost my shit on him. It had already been a long night, a long week, and, if I was being honest with myself, a long couple of years.

"Listen, I've never seen you here before, and I find it hard to believe that you would know whether my sauce tastes 'right' or not." I wasn't proud of myself, but I did the quote fingers primarily to be annoying. "And by the way, I tasted it, and it's perfect," I said, getting angrier as I spoke. "So if you don't like the sauce, order something else or leave the restaurant. I'm not making it again."

The shock and indignation on his face left me wanting to laugh out loud, despite my anger. Instead, I stormed back to the kitchen. Nothing irritated me more than overprivileged jerks coming into the restaurant and complaining about the food, and recently, everyone who came into the restaurant behaved like an overprivileged jerk. Or at least it seemed that way.

"Did you get it worked out?" Sam asked as I burst back into the kitchen, narrowly missing a server going through the exit door.

"Ugh, I'm so sick of this shit," I exploded. "Do you ever just want to get the hell out of this job and do something else?"

"Um, yeah. That's why I'm working here. To pay for my public health degree. I'm not doing this job for the fun of it," he said, then added, "no offense." He must have remembered that I was, in fact, doing it for fun. I mean, it was how I made a living, and I had been doing it a long time, but I did it because I enjoyed it. Except none of it seemed fun anymore. This was the third night in a row that service hadn't gone well, and over the last few months, I had started to seriously dread going to work. It seemed like I was never going to get the experience I needed to become an executive chef at Ipsa's, and at this point, I was pretty sure I didn't want to be an executive chef there or anywhere else. At only twenty-six, I felt like I'd lived a thousand lives, all of them overheating in a commercial kitchen.

I leaned my back against the counter, closed my eyes, and rested my head on the shelf behind me.

"I don't know if I can do this anymore," I said. "I've missed birthdays, holidays, skipped out on family dinners a couple times. I had to give my dog to my parents because I had no time to walk her, and for what? Slightly above minimum wage and the clout from cooking at Ipsa's? There's got to be a better option."

Sam nodded and asked, "Well, what else would you do?"

And that was half the problem. Cooking was the only thing I'd ever wanted to do, and without it, I had no clue what else I would do.

"Simone," Jordan's voice boomed, startling me out of my thoughts. Jordan had a nasty habit of standing way too close when he reprimanded his staff. Something about his diminutive figure made him believe that standing half a foot from someone was a reasonable way to address them. I took a step back, giving myself some room to breathe.

What now? I wanted to scream. It was always something with him.

"Do you know who's seated at table nine?" he asked. His voice had taken on a calm, eerie tone, and that's when I knew the shit was about to hit the proverbial fan.

"Some asshat who's never eaten at a Michelin-recommended restaurant?" I ventured. I suspected I was wrong when the vein in the middle of Jordan's head started to throb. The only other time I'd seen that happen was when one of the newer line cooks dropped an earring he wasn't supposed to be wearing in a dish and an unfortunate patron chipped a tooth. It was quite bad, and I couldn't imagine why my telling off a rude customer elicited the same vein-popping response.

"That 'asshat' is a restaurant reviewer for the *San Francisco Chronicle*, and you told him he has no taste," Jordan explained through gritted teeth.

Jordan had a tendency to take the most minor of infractions

and turn them into a federal case, but this time, he wasn't wrong. Not in the least.

I waited for the creep of embarrassment and guilt at jeopardizing the restaurant to flood my body, but it never came. Instead, I untied my apron, letting it drop to the ground, and uttered two words that rarely left my lips: "I quit."

B ack at my apartment, the high of quitting wore off as the gravity of my actions started to really sink in. I didn't have a job, and thanks to Ipsa's rich yet cheap patrons, I had very little money saved. Most of what I made went straight to rent, and sometimes that wasn't even enough. I didn't want to ask my parents for a loan again. I didn't even know if they would give it to me.

Wallowing on my couch and in self-pity, I called my best friend, River.

"I quit," I told her the moment she answered the phone.

"No, you didn't," she responded without missing a breath. "You'd never leave that place. You missed my last two birthdays and your parents' anniversary party because you had to work."

She was right, and now, it hardly mattered or seemed worth it.

"That's why I quit," I explained. "I didn't want to miss another big event with the people I love."

I ran through the events of the night with her, and when I finished, she was silent for a few moments before speaking.

"So?" she asked. "What now?"

My shoulders tensed, and I sunk deeper into the couch.

"I'm not sure," I responded.

After I hung up with River, I knew what I needed to do. I went straight to my closet and pulled down a box I used when I had questions I was only prepared to let fate answer. From what I figured, I only had two viable options.

As a kid, I used the Magic 8 Ball near constantly. Yes, the questions had been low stakes, mostly about boys I liked in class and whether they liked me back, but it always helped me to feel like the universe was giving me a nudge in the right direction. Now, the stakes weren't so low and the questions involved potentially life-changing decisions.

Shaking the toy I said, "Magic 8 Ball, should I ask Beckett for a loan?" Borrowing money from my brother was almost as desperate an option as borrowing from my parents so I was ecstatic when the toy told me, "My sources say no." Good. Beckett already thought I was wasting my life in the kitchen, and there was no way to ask him for another loan without confirming his suspicions.

Despite everything, the one good thing that had come out of working at Ipsa's was meeting Julian. He was an employment attorney at the nearby firm Emery Perkins, and he came into the restaurant multiple times a week. We crossed paths a few times at the restaurant and ended up going on a handful of dates.

On our first date, he took me to Atelier Crenn, a three-starred Michelin restaurant in San Francisco, and then to drinks at The Fairmont. Against everything I believed, I didn't even bother to offer to pay my half. I'd just paid rent and had approximately $37 left in my bank account. Contributing wasn't a real option unless I planned on also subsisting on rice and water for a couple weeks. On our second date, his firm bought a table for some fundraiser and he invited me to join him. My jaw had dropped when he picked me up in his black Maserati. Spending time with Julian reminded me that there were people my age who didn't have to borrow money from their older brothers to pay rent, and it had brought the idea of my long-shelved distant plan B closer to the forefront of my mind, especially as I started to grow wary of my desire for a future as a chef.

In college, I didn't think I really needed a plan B. I was going to be the next Edna Lewis, and nothing could tell me otherwise. I would have gone straight to culinary school, but my parents were footing the school bill and wanted me to get a more "traditional" degree first, so I majored in business administration and minored in philosophy. Many of my philosophy classmates planned to go to law school, and after a couple of classes, I understood the progression. Like practicing law, discussing philosophical concepts was basically the art of arguing two sides that were equally valid and convincing someone that one side was better than the other, and I was good at it. Very good. Writing papers arguing the validity of Sartre's theories on existentialism lit a gentle spark in me for the idea of law school, but it was never truly ignited. It stayed more of a very distant, break-glass-in-case-of-emergency plan B. And it didn't matter anyway because there was nothing in my soul that would have made me think I'd ever need a secondary plan. But here I was, dejected on my couch, cradling a toy and asking it if I should break the emergency glass.

Gearing myself up for its answer and promising that I would do whatever it said, even if that meant coming up with a plan C, I shook the toy before asking, "Magic 8 Ball, should I go to law school?" I closed my eyes as the cloudy liquid on the toy cleared.

"Please say no, please say no, please say no," I kept repeating. Kitchen to courtroom was a big change, and frankly,

I didn't know if I wanted it or even if I was ready for it. I opened one eye, then the other, and looked down. In plain-as-day writing, it said, "All signs point to yes."

Fuck. Fate had spoken, and I was going to law school.

CHAPTER ONE

When I decided to blow up my life into tiny pieces with two simple words, the thing I learned was that if you try to fit the pieces back together, you only end up with a jumbled mess. It's a far better option to hang onto the parts you loved, discard the rest, and hope fate threw you a bone in the process. Whenever the kitchen was short staffed, I occasionally did double duty as a baker, and truth be told, I was never much of a baker. It was too precise for my experimental, cheffy ways. With baking, even when you followed all the directions, sometimes you ended up with a flat, burned disaster and had to start all over again. Standing here, watching River drag my suitcase up the steps, I couldn't help wondering if my life's new ingredients would make something better than the toasted heap I left behind.

"You know, you could turn back right now, and no one would ever have to know we were here," River announced, stomping up the stairs with my suitcase clunking behind her.

I glanced back at my friend and shook my head. Leaving here wasn't a serious option, and she knew it.

"Fine, but did you have to pick the middle of nowhere to go to school? Couldn't you have chosen somewhere more glamorous like New York or Miami? They have law schools in Miami, don't they? Or even better, you could have stayed in California so we could be roommates."

I rolled my eyes at her, and when I reached the front door, I set down the bags I was carrying. "Rivvy, we both know why I ended up in East Lansing. Don't make it weird. Let's just get this stuff moved into my apartment so we can send my parents back to the hotel and figure out what this town has going on at night. If I have to be here for three years, I at least want to know what I'm in for."

River stopped at my front door and shrugged, waiting for me to open it so she could lug my suitcase inside. It was the last one I needed to bring in before we could start to unload the car my parents had rented for me to run the few errands I needed to get done to get my apartment in order. Moving across the country was hard, especially when you weren't that sold on the idea of moving in the first place.

"Simone, you don't *have* to be here for three years. You could always come back home and—"

I gave River a look, and she stopped. When you know someone most of your life, sometimes all it takes is a look to get them to stop in their tracks. I didn't want to talk about it anymore. I lived in East Lansing now, and that was that.

I opened the door to my apartment and found my parents lounging on the grungy, university-issued couch. They looked exhausted, and I felt bad for dragging them across the country. I told them River and I could manage, but they insisted on helping me, and secretly, I was relieved. I was nervous as hell, and their presence alone decreased my anxiety level from Xanax-required to almost manageable. Even though they weren't going to be here long, having them close by was comforting.

"Glad you guys made it back okay. I thought I was going to

have to grab an umbrella and float to find you, Mary Poppins style," my dad joked.

I looked outside as the trees whipped around, their thin branches occasionally hitting my window. There was only one person braving the storm, and if his curly hair was any indication, the gusts were getting stronger.

"I forgot how nice folks are in the Midwest," my dad commented as River and I unpacked my purchases and started putting them away. "Did you see that young man walking outside?"

"Yeah, what about him?" I asked.

"He lives a few apartments over. He came by to see if we needed any help moving in. Seems like a nice kid."

"And he's kinda cute," my mom added.

River ran to the window, craning her head to the side. "I don't see him," she said. I joined her to look, too, but I didn't see anyone outside anymore. Maybe he decided the wind was too much to handle. Or maybe I was projecting.

"Oh, honey," my mother said, interrupting my and River's attempts at spying. "This place isn't bad at all. It just needs a little air and some cleaning, and it'll be perfectly adequate."

I looked around. I guessed it could be described as perfectly adequate if that included scratchy carpet, a hard couch, and a weird stain at the door. But as "perfectly adequate" as my new abode was, I already missed my apartment in Oakland. I'd gotten lucky when I found the little gem in Temescal. Usually, those places were well above my pay grade, but the landlord owned too many properties to pay close attention to market rents, and she hadn't raised the rent in my building since 2001. It had pained me to give up those keys.

"I know. I'm not worried."

I didn't like to lie to my parents, but that one was a flat-out doozy, and I casually waited for the tornado threatening to touch down outside to scoop me up in retribution for the lie. I was indeed worried. Extremely worried and for a variety of reasons, first being that my "perfectly adequate" apartment had a perfectly inadequate—translation, shitty—little kitchen I couldn't imagine cooking a serious meal in.

"Why don't you and Dad go on back to the hotel? Riv and I can take it from here," I said, and when I looked over at River, she was nodding enthusiastically. "I'll be fine. I'll give you a call in the morning and we can meet for breakfast before your flight, okay?"

"All right, sweetheart," my dad said. "You girls be safe, and we'll catch up with you tomorrow." He leaned down to give me a peck on the cheek and a hug and gave River a squeeze of thanks on her shoulder.

"Take care of yourself, Simone, and we'll see you in the morning," my mom said after she hugged both me and River.

As soon as the door closed behind them, I remembered I'd left a few bags from my trip to Meijer in the rental car, and I needed to get them since my parents were taking it. I flung open the front door, yelled for Riv to come help me, and got to the car right as my parents were pulling out of the parking spot.

"Can you pop the trunk?" I asked my mom. "I left a few bags in there." She opened the trunk, and Riv met me at the back of the car. She pulled out a couple bags, and I grabbed the remaining three. I slammed the trunk down and knocked on the driver's side window to wave goodbye.

"Hey, you girls need some help?" a distant male voice asked as we crossed the parking lot of the complex.

"No, thanks," I said without bothering to look up.

At the same time, Riv said, "Sure." I wasn't in the mood to deal with some overly gallant dude while the wind ravaged my hair, but it seemed like the full day of moving had finally gotten to River. Manual labor wasn't really her thing.

"I can carry your bags, Riv. Give them here." I reached my hand out to take River's bags, and she slapped it away. I looked up at her, indignant at being smacked, and she jutted her head in the direction of the guy I assumed had been the one to ask if we needed help.

"What?" I asked her.

"Him," she said, nodding and smiling at the guy walking toward us. His curls made me wonder if it was the same person I'd seen from the window.

"What about him?" I asked, taking him in. From a distance, the only thing I could tell was that he was really tall and seemed to be checking out River, which wasn't atypical given her appearance. In her red leggings, black crop top, and hideous high-heeled sneakers, she made a striking figure, and I couldn't blame him for staring. River always made a splash wherever she went. She hated when people used the word exotic to describe her, but even trying my hardest, I had never come up with any other description that did her justice. She didn't look like anyone else I'd ever encountered, and that was part nature, part style aesthetic. She wore her long, wavy, dark brown hair shaved on one side, and her sleeve of tattoos was often on full display. She was tall, about five foot ten and wore heels anytime she left the house, putting her just over six feet. She had caramel-colored skin, and her light brown eyes reminded me of topaz. She was the embodiment of ethnic ambiguity. People often asked what she was mixed with, and since middle school, she'd always had the same reply: love—and that was the damn truth. Her parents had been Berkeley pseudo-hippies who were all about free love and "fuck the man" until they had kids and needed jobs that paid the bills, at which point her mom put her shelved law degree to good use at Legal Aid, and her dad taught comparative literature at Berkeley. Before that, her parents had divided their time evenly between protesting the Vietnam War and following Sly and the Family Stone on tour.

River's parents were both Cuban-American; her dad had dark, dark skin that looked polished to mahogany perfection, and her mom was a dead ringer for Gloria Estefan. Neither parent could figure out where River got her light eyes, and they always joked that their free love lifestyle may have had some unintended consequences. Though the Bazans often joked about River's parentage, there was no doubt she belonged to them. She looked exactly like a perfect mix of her parents, plus the Bazans might be the most in-love couple I'd ever encountered. They still mooned over each other like newlyweds, and when I was a kid, their constant displays of affection took some getting used to. (It grossed me out.)

"He's hot. Look at him," she insisted. He was still several apartments away, so I didn't know how she could tell he was hot because I sure as hell couldn't. From what I could see, he looked like a scruffy student. Probably an undergrad if his clothes told an accurate story.

"I'm going to introduce myself to him," she announced. "Come with me."

"No, I'm going inside," I told her. "But if you guys hit it off, you'll have two people to visit in East Lansing."

"Don't go. You have to meet people here eventually, and there's no time like the present, right? For all you know, he might be your next great love."

Doubtful.

"I look like hell, we're basically in a wind tunnel, and I haven't showered today. Surely, fate wouldn't be that cruel again." I turned to walk away, then said over my shoulder, "Have fun."

River had left a few hours ago, and my parents had left the night before. For the first time since I'd gotten to East Lansing, I was truly alone in my apartment and I felt it. A new city and a new life had seemed like a good idea, but once I was alone without any distractions, I wondered if I'd made the right choice. Wondered for the umpteenth time if I was running toward something better or giving up something I loved. Maybe both were true, but either way the outcome was the same. I was all alone in an unfamiliar city and starting school in less than a week. Holy shit.

I wandered into my kitchen to start making dinner—cooking made me feel the most like myself, and I needed to be reminded what it felt like to be Simone—when my doorbell rang.

I didn't know how things worked in the Midwest, but in Oakland the only people that rang your doorbell without having been invited were either trying to sell you something or trying to convert you to the Church of Latter-Day Saints. Back home, I never answered the door unless I was expecting someone, and the same applied here. Except the blinds on the large window in my front living room were raised, and when I turned to look at the door, sunglass-clad eyes stared back at me.

Given our eye-to-sunglasses contact, completely ignoring the door was probably no longer an option, and although I didn't see any religious texts or a set of Cutco knives, I wasn't convinced actually *opening* the door to a stranger was the best course of action. But I couldn't just keep staring through the window and doing nothing.

Thankfully I'd thought to lock my screen door so that when I went to open the front door, there was still a barrier, albeit a somewhat flimsy one, between me and this stranger.

"Can I help you?" I asked in my most faux polite, I'm not in the mood for people tone.

While a storm had all but promised destruction yesterday, now the weather was sunny and the guy was dressed accordingly in shorts, a T-shirt, and a baseball cap.

"Maybe. Are you Simone?" he asked, taking off his sunglasses and baseball cap, releasing the now-flattened brown curls hiding beneath.

"Depends," I said. "Who's asking?"

"Me," he answered. "I met your folks and your girl River yesterday, you know, assuming you're Simone."

Damn. Mom and River were right. He really *was* cute. I took in his whole look, my eyes snagging a couple beats too long on his broad chest. He was wearing a pink Muppets T-shirt, and it was ridiculous, but somehow on him, it made sense. He had a whole scruffy, skater-boy vibe, and though it wasn't usually my thing, on him it was kind of working for me.

"Hey, eyes up here," he said, jerking me out of what I thought was an inconspicuous perusal of his body. Geez, was I that out of practice?

I met his gaze, and he smirked at me. Busted.

"Yes, I'm Simone. Did you need something?" I asked, trying to get my footing back under me.

"This dropped out of one of your bags," he said and reached into his back pocket, producing an unopened pack of gum. I'd been looking for that.

"You came over here to return a pack of gum?" I asked, incredulous.

He shrugged and smiled. "Yeah. It's your gum, right?"

I nodded. Was this the Midwest kindness my dad had mentioned? There's no way most people would have gone out of their way to return a pack of gum.

He seemed harmless, but I still wasn't completely comfortable opening my screen door to retrieve it.

"I appreciate the gesture," I said. "But you can keep it."

He shrugged again, and I watched as he tore open the pack and slipped a piece between his lips.

"Listen, if you're gonna keep ogling me like that, you may want to consider investing in some sunglasses."

I chuffed out a laugh. This guy. We needed to be done with this conversation.

"All right, dude. I'm about to make dinner. I'm starving. Thanks for stopping by, and I'm sure we'll get a chance to talk another time. Enjoy the gum," I told him and closed the door as he backed up, grinning at me. Walking into the kitchen, I realized I was smiling, too.

CHAPTER TWO

"Oh God, what have I gotten myself into?"

About a week later, I walked into the lobby of Michigan State University College of Law for my first official day of classes, and I tried to decide which decision had been more ill-advised: coming to law school on the advice of a Magic 8 Ball or wearing a suit on the first day. Perhaps they were equally regrettable.

I glanced around the lobby. Most of the folks wore jeans and T-shirts, and a scant few people had niced it up with pressed khakis. Then here I was in pinstripes and heels sticking out like a hair in the punchbowl. Perhaps watching *Suits* and *Legally Blonde* hadn't been the best resources to learn about being a lawyer. I didn't know many lawyers back home, and after that stupid toy told me to go, I had limited time to register for the LSAT, take it, and apply to schools. Trying to figure out how law students dressed wasn't particularly high on my must-know list.

I really, truly wanted to turn tail and go back home. Not home to my shitty East Lansing apartment, back home to my significantly less shitty Oakland apartment. But I would settle for my East Lansing apartment if it meant that I could change into more school-appropriate clothes. I checked my phone, and relief spread through me. I had half an hour before class was scheduled to start. If I called a Lyft, I could make it home, change, and get back to campus with time to spare. I rushed back to the door and promptly slammed my head into something hard. I couldn't see through it, and I was still conscious, so I knew it wasn't the glass door I had walked through moments ago. I looked up, irritated at whatever was blocking my way, and locked eyes on someone's T-shirt-clad midsection.

"My fault," a deep male voice said.

"No problem. Excuse me," I said, trying to get around the man. I didn't have time for pleasantries; I needed to call a Lyft and get home.

Leaning down, trying to look at my face, the person said, "Hey, slow down. Are you okay?"

"I'm fine," I mumbled.

Any other day I might have appreciated his concern, but right now, I was annoyed he was slowing me down. This suit had to go, and if I didn't get a Lyft in the next two minutes, I'd be stuck in it all day.

"Simone?" he asked.

Hearing my name, I looked up at the face trying to peer into mine and immediately recognized him as the guy that had shown up at my apartment.

"Oh yeah, hi," I responded, with a quick wave. "Can't talk, I'm in a hurry."

I maneuvered around him as he held up his hands and moved out of my way. Smart move on his part. "All right, don't let me stop you," he said.

He eyed me, amused, as I pushed past him and barreled back through the lobby doors to the outside, furiously pulling up the Lyft app on my phone. I had ridden the bus to campus, which had taken about fifteen minutes, but a Lyft had to be faster than that, didn't it?

No, as it turned out, it did not.

Much to my chagrin, the app said the Lyft would pick me up in fifteen minutes. By the time it picked me up and dropped me off at my apartment, I would likely already be late, and I didn't want to be late on my first day of class.

"Fuck," I said to no one in particular.

"What's the problem, Suit?" I recognized the same deep voice from inside.

"Exactly that. This damn suit," I replied, realizing my clothes and my current situation in them couldn't be changed before class started. "What the hell was I thinking?"

A small smile played around his lips as he took in my appearance, eyeing me head to high-heeled toe. "Yeah, a suit might've been a bad call."

I glared at him. "Dude, way to add insult to injury."

He chuckled. "What? I'm agreeing with you. And if it's any consolation, it looks damn good on you."

I glanced down, smoothing my skirt over my hips. It was a very slight consolation, but I'd take whatever I could get at this point.

I gave him a furtive half smile that grew larger when he held out his elbow for me to take. "Thanks," I said, taking it and feeling, if not better about my choice of clothing, more resigned to it.

"Come on, let's go inside," he said, opening the door.

I followed him reluctantly. At least I looked the part even if I didn't feel it.

• • •

Walking into Contracts, my first class of the semester, I noticed there were name plates on each of the seats.

Hm, welcome back to elementary school.

I settled into my seat and peeked at the girl sitting next to me. She looked as WASPy as they came, despite her creamy brown skin, with her pink headband, blunt haircut, and French-tipped nails. Was there a name for Black WASPs? Carltons maybe? But whatever, who was I to judge? I was the one wearing the full suit. Though, to be fair, she had a briefcase propped against her seat and wore sharp-pointed kitten heels, so perhaps we were tied for most ridiculous. I glanced at her name tag: *Tiffany Alston*. She looked like a Tiffany with her expensive shoes and bag. A tad Trumpy if you asked me. I debated whether or not to introduce myself, but before I made up my mind, Tiffany leaned close enough that I felt her hot breath on my cheek.

"I heard this professor's a real bitch. Supposedly she makes at least one student cry every semester, but that shit's not going to happen to me."

Stunned, I stared at her, trying to process her calling our professor a bitch.

"Ugh, I hate assholes who think just because they have some fancy degree they can be dicks to whoever they want. When I'm a professor, I'll be cool as fuck."

Jesus, how could someone say so many expletives in such a short period of time?

Floored, yet impressed by her filthy mouth, my impression of Tiffany was on its way to a complete 180-degree flip. I was still trying to compose myself to say something back to this foul-mouthed woman when she stuck out her hand.

"Tiffany Alston. What's your name?"

"Simone Alexander. Are you from Michigan?" Was this a

Michigan thing or a Tiffany thing? Either way, I was intrigued.

"L.A. I grew up in Manhattan Beach. What about you?"

"Nice. I'm from the Bay Area. Oakland."

Before we could marvel at the fact that two Californians both ended up in the same school in the same section when most of the other students were from Michigan, the classroom door swung open and our professor walked in.

With her gentle wrinkles, she looked about seventy years old and walked with a cane. Well, walked holding a cane. It never actually touched the ground as she traversed to the front of the room. Like Tiffany, she had a headband around her icy blond hair and wore a long-sleeve flannel plaid dress despite the heat outside. She was dressed like someone's nana, but something about the way she dragged her eyes around the classroom made me think she was anything but a cookie-baking, candy-carrying grandmother.

"I see you've found your seats. The first hurdle is over, and it seems you all aren't incompetent."

Oh. Crap.

Tiffany leaned over and said, "Looks like I was right about the bitchiness."

The professor came from behind the podium where she had left her cane and started pacing in front of the first row.

"I'm Jessica Patton, and I'll be your Contracts I and Contracts II professor. You'll likely hate me this semester and even more so next."

She handed a stack of papers to Tiffany and looked at her over her rimless glasses. Tiffany stared right back at Professor Patton, unflinching. Respect.

"Ms. Alston, please pass those to your neighbor." She continued pacing the front row. "Folks, your syllabus is online, but I like to hand out the paper copy as well so as not to encourage students to browse the internet during class. It has everything you need to know about this class—reading assignments, deadlines, and grading expectations. Most of you will probably do poorly, but this university curves all the 1L grades to a B, so you stand a fighting chance."

My eyes bounced around the classroom to see if anyone else was petrified and was met with varying degrees of stricken faces.

"I will call on you in alphabetic order to brief cases, and I employ the Socratic method. I will also call on students at random as I see fit. Be prepared for class and we won't have any issues."

Panic slammed its way into my body as Professor Patton looked around the room and let her eyes rest on me.

"You in the," she paused and looked me up and down, "pinstripes. What is the Socratic method?"

Oh God, she was calling on me. Why was she calling on me? It was probably the suit. If she thought I knew anything about the law, she was about to be sorely disappointed.

I wracked my brain trying to remember what I knew about the Socratic method. I had heard of it before but didn't know exactly where, and my brain could only register that scene in *The Paper Chase.*

"Are you planning on answering the question or just staring at me?"

Well, damn. This woman was scary, but I had to say something, so I tried my best to explain the Socratic method. "Sorry, Professor. It's the, um, way of asking questions that, uh, leads to a certain answer."

Professor Patton walked, still unassisted by that cane, to my seat. She gazed at my name tag.

"Class, Ms. Alexander has given you an excellent example of

the type of answer that will not be acceptable in my classroom. Tell me, what was wrong with your answer, Ms. Alexander?"

Shouldn't she have known that if I knew what was wrong with my answer, I would have given a different one?

"Professor Patton, with all due respect, if I had a better answer, I would have given it to you."

I cringed internally. I should not have said that out loud.

"I appreciate your candor, Ms. Alexander, but that doesn't take away from your appallingly wrong answer," she said as she looked me up and down. "Don't come to my class unprepared. If you're not ready, don't bother to show up. I won't accept anything less."

She walked away from me, and I sat, both stunned and humiliated.

"Can anyone help Ms. Alexander with her answer?"

A few hands around me were raised, and Professor Patton started to call on someone in the first row, but before she could call on anyone, a voice boomed out from the back of the room.

"It was in the online syllabus you posted. The Socratic method is the method of teaching employed by Socrates to promote critical thinking. It consists of questioning students in order to lead to a greater understanding."

I recognized that baritone voice immediately. Right. Of course River's buddy from my apartment complex was also a first-year law student. And a gunner. I heard somewhere law school was full of people trying to prove they were the smartest in the room, and it looked like this guy didn't disappoint. Wow, and he had seemed so normal, nice even.

Professor Patton nodded her head. "Very good, Mr. Whitman." She fixed her gaze back on me.

"Ms. Alexander, you could learn something from your classmate here."

She then addressed the whole class. "You are all adults here, and I expect you to be prepared for my class. Prepared means being on time, having done the reading, and having briefed the cases. I hope this won't be a problem."

Wow, Tiffany was spot on with her description of Professor Patton. She was indeed a bitch.

The rest of the class continued without incident, but based on this first interaction with Patton, I suspected Contracts would not be my favorite class.

Tiffany and I ambled out of the classroom together, she with her briefcase and me in my suit looking like we were cosplaying lawyers. I stopped to adjust the strap on my shoe as Tiffany made her way to the elevator and out of the corner of my eye saw someone sidle up next to me. I tipped my head up to see who it was.

"Suit," he said. "It looks like we're in the same section."

Lucky me. Any goodwill I'd developed in our earlier interaction was shattered. Professor Patton had knowledge-shamed me, and this character had made it ten times worse. Who bothered to point out that something was in a syllabus besides a professor? He could have just answered the question like a reasonable person. *I* knew I hadn't looked at the syllabus online, but everyone else didn't need to know.

Plus, I couldn't believe someone in a bright yellow T-shirt that read "These Guns Don't Run" and had white arrows pointing at the person's arms insisted on mocking my clothing choices.

"Looks like it," I replied, deadpan.

"Love the enthusiasm. I'm Silas, by the way," the guy said and held out his hand. I paused and shook it begrudgingly. I hadn't really processed his height until he was standing so close to me, but he was impressively tall. I wasn't a short woman by anyone's standards. At nearly five foot eight I was significantly taller than the average woman, and Silas was about four inches short of being a foot taller than me.

And fuck it all, Silas was still cute. Cuter than I'd even thought when he'd stopped by my apartment. He was still scruffy with too much stubble and too much curly hair, but under all that shaggy dark brown hair, he had playful, jade green eyes that I hadn't been able to see well through my screen door. Not my usual type at all, but I could see why someone might be into him. Too bad he had effectively colluded with Patton to embarrass me in class. People like him drove me crazy. Too eager to show off what they knew.

I nodded my acknowledgment and hurried to catch up with Tiffany, but my long legs were no match for Silas's longer ones, and he kept up easily.

"Aren't you going to officially introduce yourself?"

"Simone Alexander," I told him, then said pointedly, "but you can call me 'Ms. Didn't Read the Syllabus.'"

"Ouch," he said. "That was kind of sharp, don't you think?"

"So was that jab you took in class, but that didn't seem to stop *you*, did it?"

"Quick," he retorted. "I like that in a woman."

"Arrogant. Not my favorite trait in a man," I responded.

Tiffany was still waiting at the elevator for me, and I was ready to be done with this guy.

"All right, well, I have to go now. Tiffany's waiting for me. I'll see you around."

I started walking toward her, and he followed.

"Hang on, have you gotten your books for class yet?" He looked down at my bag. It was conspicuously empty except for my laptop.

"I haven't had a chance to make it over to the bookstore yet. Why?"

When my parents had helped me pack up my apartment in Oakland, they had asked if I planned to take my car, and I told them I wouldn't need a car in East Lansing: "I barely use mine here. And besides, it's a college town. Everything should be fairly close and walkable."

My parents did that thing where they silently communicated that I had no idea what I was talking about, but for some reason they didn't say it out loud. They had never not voiced their opinions on a matter, so I took their silence as agreement that my thoughts were correct.

They were not.

The only things near my apartment were other apartments, the Quality Dairy, and train tracks. As a card-carrying West Coaster, when I thought about the Midwest, which was rare if ever, everything about the middle of the country had been kind of petite in my mind except for the food portions and the people (I had heard the men were cornfed and strapping), but I had no idea how spread out things would prove to be. While East Lansing was small, it wasn't small enough to walk everywhere like I had thought it would be, and a car was a necessity.

"I'm heading over to the bookstore right now to pick up a couple things," Silas said. "Do you girls want to ride over with me?"

CHAPTER THREE

Tiffany opted out of letting Silas drive her to the bookstore, but not wanting to take the bus again in my uncomfortably warm suit beat out probable good sense for me. I texted River to let her know where I was going and who I was with, and I figured if he tried anything, I could bust out my Krav Maga moves. I'd only gone to one class, but in an emergency, the important stuff would probably kick in.

River: *Simone, I vetted him for you and he's fine.*
River: *Actually, more than fine from what I remember.* ☺
Simone: *What do you mean you vetted him? How?*
River: *IG. We have a couple mutuals.*

Her IG sleuthing didn't give me a ton of confidence, but all things being equal, I wasn't about to walk or take the bus, so I gratefully accepted his offer.

"Thanks for the ride," I said as we walked out of the building together.

"Not a problem. I was going that way anyway. Plus," he said as he cleared his throat, "I was kind of an ass in class, blurting out the answer like that, and I wanted to make it up to you."

At least he knew he had been a jerk in class. That scored him a couple brownie points.

August in Michigan was ungodly hot, and by the time we

made it to his ride, I felt like I'd been dipped in hot soup. His behemoth gas guzzler in slick silver was the kind of truck we shunned back in Northern California where taking care of the environment was tantamount to taking care of your child but was commonplace from what I had seen in Michigan. But at the moment, I couldn't have cared less as long as it had air conditioning.

"So what's your story?" he asked as he opened the door to let me in and reached out a hand to give me a boost. I guess chivalry wasn't dead. He folded his body into the seat next to mine and closed his door as I gave him the abridged version of my life.

"I'm from Oakland. I have a regular, nuclear family and a dog named Rachel. Uh, I like to surf and be outside as much as I can, and I like to cook. I went to Berkeley for undergrad, and now I'm here."

"We'll get back to the cooking thing later, but you surf? I didn't know Black people surfed."

I rolled my eyes. It drove me crazy when people said ignorant shit like that. Why wouldn't Black people surf?

"Excuse me?" I said, mentally taking away the brownie points he'd just earned. He was now hovering at a solid net zero.

"What?" he asked.

"You can't go around saying shit like that," I retorted.

"Why not? I *didn't* know Black people surfed. No one in my family surfs, and none of my Black friends surf."

I shot him a look.

"Why does it matter if no one in *your* family surfs? That doesn't make it better."

"Damn, Suit. I'm just saying that none of the Black people in my world surf, including my Black family members, of which there are many. It's nothing personal. I'm surprised, that's all."

Aside from the fact that this country boy seemed a little narrow in his thinking, I was equally surprised to hear he might be Black. Yeah, his skin was pretty tan and his hair awfully curly, but I assumed his tanned skin was seasonal and courtesy of the sun from working in cornfields or tipping cows or whatever he did for fun. Was it possible he had some DNA melanin in him?

"Are you actually Black or do you just have a few Black play cousins you feel a kinship with?"

"Woooooooow. I'm not sure how things work in California, but here you don't go around questioning someone else's Blackness. But, color police, yes, I'm Black. Creole to be precise. My grandparents and my mom were born and raised in New Orleans, and the three of them look just like me. Green eyes and all. Is that okay with you?"

"Whatever, it was a fair question. And for the record, I wasn't questioning your Blackness. It was more of a clarification. Plus, I can't have been the first person to ask you that."

"And I thought Bay Area folks were supposed to be liberal and open-minded. Don't you know we come in all shades, girl? I'm just as Black as you."

Appropriately chastened, I rolled down the window to get some fresh air and took in the scenery. Large patches of greenery flew by as we sped through town. I glanced over once to check the speedometer to see if we were speeding, and it read twenty-five miles per hour. Maybe country air made everything feel freer and faster. I even kept my eyes peeled for the cows I thought had to be somewhere with all that grass.

Enjoying the air conditioning and taking in my new surroundings, I almost forgot Silas was in the car next to me.

"I'm so glad you asked, Simone. Of course, I'd love to tell you about myself." The car was so silent, the sound of his voice surprised me, and I jumped in my seat.

"Huh?" My brow furrowed at his question. What was he talking about?

"I asked about your background, but you didn't ask about mine besides insinuating I wasn't Black enough, so I thought I'd give you a little nudge in the right direction."

Smart-ass. But he wasn't wrong.

"Uh, sure. What's your story besides your family being from New Orleans?"

He chuckled.

"I'm glad you asked, Simone. I was born and raised in Pleasant Ridge—that's a suburb outside of Detroit—and went to this fine institution for undergrad. I'm an only child, and half of my parents are lovely."

"What else?" I asked. An answer like that had a story behind it, and I wanted to know more.

"Mom's a photographer. Have you heard of Lauren David?" I nodded, impressed. She was like the Anne Geddes of fashion. If you knew anything about fashion, you knew Lauren David.

"Don't be impressed. She's a helluva photographer but a fairly shitty mom, so it was mostly me and my dad. My parents never divorced or anything, and when she's around, they're together. She just isn't around that much."

He paused, took a deep breath, and continued.

"My dad's an accountant and raised me pretty much alone. I turned out all right, though. It was really important for Pops to be a good father since his dad wasn't around a lot. Thank God for Papa. Next to my dad, he's the best I've got."

"Who's Papa?"

"Keep up, Suit! Papa is my dad's grandfather. My great-grandfather."

"You didn't say that at first, but okay, I'm with you now."

I had a hard time wrapping my head around the fact that Silas was giving me his whole life story in the span of three minutes and was somehow insulted that I couldn't keep up.

"Papa raised my father and helped raise me since Mom wasn't around most times." He paused, and his face tightened a little. "He died a few years ago."

I opened my mouth to offer my condolences, but we had pulled into the parking lot of the bookstore, and he was out of the car before I got the words out. I hopped out, grateful for the reprieve from the Whitman family tree.

Harried students crammed themselves into the aisles of the bookstore clutching cell phones I guessed were settled on websites containing information they would need for the upcoming semester. Most likely books. The youngest students of the bunch basically had neon arrows flashing over their heads that read "freshmen." Their eager eyes paired with tentative smiles and squishy round faces that hadn't quite shaken the chub of youth gave away their teenage status. The older students mostly looked put out at having to navigate the bookstore, period.

"Here. You're gonna need this case book, too," Silas said, coming up behind me and handing me a thick black book with *Civil Procedure* embossed on the front in gold. It weighed a ton, and I needed at least three more of the books I assumed would be of similar weight. There couldn't possibly be that much law, could there? I walked up and down each row picking up books as I found them with Silas pointing out the ones I didn't immediately see. My lack of gym time became apparent as I lifted the last book, and Silas must have noticed. "Need me to carry those for you?"

Silas was only holding a few pens and a planner. He must have ordered his books online or something.

"You don't mind carrying them?" I asked.

"You look like you're about to collapse. It's either carry the books or carry you, and much as I'd like having you in my arms, I'd much prefer it be when you have full use of all your faculties. Hand 'em over."

I dropped the books into his open arms.

"You know, pretty boy, your charm would carry a lot more weight if it wasn't prefaced by an insult."

"Ah, you think I'm pretty," Silas joked, fluttering his eyelashes at me.

"Come on," I said, angling his body toward the checkout line. "Let's get out of here. Do you need anything else?"

I looked around the store to see if anything besides books caught my eye and noticed that the lines were long, extending into the aisles.

"Nope, I got all my books a couple weeks before class started."

Wait, what? A couple *weeks*? I'd barely had my apartment packed a couple weeks ago.

"Next," the cashier said when it was finally our turn. Silas let me go ahead of him, and I deposited my books on the counter. Watching the total cost of the books skyrocket in front of me, my panic joined its ascent.

"All right, your total is $2,173.52."

"Pardon?" It sounded like the cashier had said my books would be almost $2,200.00 but that couldn't be right, could it?

"Your total is $2,173.52," the cashier said a little more slowly this time. Holy shit. I was already broke. I winced as I handed him my credit card and prayed that coming to law school would eventually pay off.

CHAPTER FOUR

I called Rivvy as soon as Silas dropped me off at home. She answered on the first ring.

"How was it?" she asked at the same time I said, "Silas is a law student."

"Yeah, I know," she acknowledged, completely nonplussed at the information.

"Why didn't you tell me?" I screeched.

"I dunno. Thought it was something that would come up organically when you met. Did he not mention it?"

I could almost see her sitting in her desk chair, hair flipped over her shoulder, shrugging at what she would assume was a perfectly reasonable assumption.

I rolled my eyes. "Rivvy, I barely spoke to him when he came to the door. Also, how'd you know we would meet?"

"Oh. Yeah. I may have suggested he find a reason to introduce himself to you. Didn't think he'd stop by your place, though. Hot and bold. Not a bad combo."

I rolled my eyes again and briefly thought about my mom telling me as a teenager that if I rolled my eyes any further back in my head, they'd get stuck there.

"Yeah about that. Would we call him hot? I mean, he's really cute in a Matthew McConaughey barely showered, maybe smokes weed, and plays bongos all day kind of way, but hot? I don't know. Are you sure it's not just because he's so tall?"

She laughed and said, "His height doesn't hurt, but no, he's hot. Plus it turns out he's good friends with Nik."

"Who's Nik?" I asked.

"You remember Nik. My freshman-year roommate."

The only thing that came to mind when I thought about Nik was red hair. I vaguely remembered River's shower being peppered with orange strands the one time I'd gotten a chance to visit her our freshman year.

"Oh yeah. She knows Silas?"

"Yeah. They knew each other from summer camp or something like that. She said he's a good guy."

I shrugged even though she couldn't see me. "I don't know yet. He was kind of a dick in class, but then he offered me a ride to the bookstore and was a little bit charming." I paused. "Did you know he was Black?"

"Of course I did. Didn't you?"

"Not at first. Not until he color-shamed me in the car."

The short "hm" Riv hit me with said it all.

"Anyway, he offered to drive me to class in the morning since I don't have a car, so we'll see."

When I had mentioned to Silas that I didn't have a car, he said he would pick me up at eight a.m. for class the next day and didn't give me a chance to turn him down. Not that I would have. Since we were in the same section, our schedules were more or less the same the rest of the semester. It would be nice not to have to take the bus, and I was a tiny bit curious to learn more about Silas. A tiny bit.

"Let me know what you think after you spend a little time with him. He seemed like a really nice guy, and I'm sure you could use some friends while you're there."

She was right. I probably did need to make some friends, otherwise it was going to be a long three years, so when Silas knocked on my door in the morning, I plastered a toothy grin to my face and opened the door.

"Whoa there, Suit, why the Joker smile? You planning on offing me? You know these wannabe lawyers will be itching to solve my murder."

I couldn't help but laugh. My cheeks did feel extra stretched and my teeth were dry from the energy I was expending to look more approachable. When I laughed for real, my whole face relaxed.

"That's better. You ready to hit it? My ride's downstairs," Silas said, reaching for my backpack.

There were only a few stairs down to the parking lot, but my bag was heavy, and I was glad not to be hauling it. I looked around for his truck, but it was nowhere in sight.

"Uh, did you forget to bring your truck?" I teased. Surely he hadn't forgotten the most crucial piece of a ride to campus... the ride.

"It's nice out. We're taking the bike," he responded.

Oh crap, did he expect to get on the back of his bicycle? All things being equal, I would rather ride the bus since I hadn't ridden on the handlebars of a bike since I was twelve and broke my arm doing it. I looked around again, this time for a Schwinn, and my eyes landed on a Vespa. I looked from Silas to the Vespa, and when I looked back at Silas again, the grin on his face told me that was our ride.

"No way! That's our ride?" I asked, not quite believing that this giant man would ride a scooter but also wondering how he fit onto it. He was tall but not skinny, and his body would take up a lot of space on the scooter. Which also begged the question, how was I supposed to fit on there, too?

"Hell yeah, I do. Don't you know trucks are terrible for the environment, California? I'm all about the Vespa. It's my second favorite ride, especially when I'm just going from home to class."

"Then why did you drive the truck the other day to campus?" I asked.

"So that if I ran into a cute girl who needed a ride to the bookstore, I'd have more than enough space for us and her books," he said with a wink.

"Uh-huh, and what would you have done if Tiffany had decided to join us? There's no cab in that truck."

"She's small, and the bed of the truck is pretty spacious."

"You wouldn't have," I squawked.

"Of course I wouldn't have," he said. "But I was grateful she turned me down since I didn't have a plan B."

I was feeling a little grateful she'd turned him down myself.

"Seriously, though, why the truck?" I asked, now genuinely curious.

"I had to pick something up and I needed it. Getting to drive you was an unexpected bonus," he explained. "Anyway, are you ready to hop on?"

"Yeah," I said. "But where are we supposed to put our stuff?"

Silas strode the few steps across the parking lot to the green Vespa and grabbed one helmet from the handlebars and another from the small top box on the back. He tossed me the one from the top box and climbed onto the scooter, yanking his helmet on when he was settled.

"Hand me your bag," he said, reaching for it. "I keep mine between my feet, but I'll hook yours onto the back."

I climbed behind him, then had no idea what to do with

my hands. Was it awkward to wrap them around his waist? Realizing I had no choice if I didn't want to go flying off the back, I put on my helmet and wrapped my arms around his middle. It was solid muscle where I expected it to be more doughy. Those T-shirts he wore weren't doing his body any favors.

"Hold on tight," he said over his shoulder before taking off.

The Criminal Law classroom looked identical to the one where Contracts had been held the day before, but the vibe in the room was immediately warmer. The professor was standing in the front of the room talking to another student, a woman whose name I hadn't caught from the day before. They were smiling and laughing together, and the student didn't look at all intimidated. I looked down at my phone where I was still keeping my schedule to find out this professor's name: James Mason. Professor Mason, much like Professor Patton, looked like someone's grandparent, but the difference between the two fell beyond just gender. Something about the way he interacted with the student made it clear that he loved his job. Or at least loved his students. His face was open and friendly chatting with the woman. Even though students flooded into the room as it neared time for class to start, Professor Mason never appeared rushed.

I looked up at Silas, and he was watching the interaction between Professor Mason and the student as well. He had a slight smile on his face that I bet mirrored my own.

"I like him already," Silas commented. "I hope his class is good."

There were no name tags at the seats in this classroom, so Silas and I walked to the front of the room to claim seats together. I could already tell this was a class where you wanted to be as close to the front as possible. I looked around and found Tiffany sitting a couple rows behind us. I hadn't seen her when we walked in. When she looked up from her computer, I waved for her to come join us, but she gestured around the area in front of her, which was already occupied by her Bluetooth mouse and keyboard, a cell phone, a bottle of water, and a half-eaten pastry. It would have taken her half the class just to pack up all her crap.

Next to me, Silas thumbed through our Criminal Law book. I nudged him and whispered, "Did we have reading for this class, too?" He seemed to be on top of things.

"Why are you whispering? Class hasn't even started yet." The room was quiet enough, except for the sound of other people whispering and leafing through their casebooks, that Silas's voice reverberated through the room, drawing attention to us both.

"Uh, because everyone else is whispering?" And also, outside voices tended to be more appreciated outside.

Still speaking in his normal tone of voice, Silas said, "Whatever. Yeah, it was all right. Better than the shit we had to read for Contracts."

"Excellent, sir! I'm glad to hear my class's cases look more interesting than those from Contracts." Another voice, even louder than Silas's, sounded from the front of the room. "I never cared much for Contracts, either. What did you all talk about this first class? I'm assuming it was the ever-titillating offer, acceptance, and consideration?"

"Yes, sir. That's mostly what we covered yesterday." Silas appeared to enjoy Professor Mason's attention.

"Good, good. Glad to know I haven't gone completely soft in the head. Just wait until you get to *Hawkins v. McGee*. You all should enjoy that one." He reached out to shake Silas's hand.

"Nice to formally meet you, Mr. Whitman."

Surprise covered Silas's face as he gripped the man's proffered hand. "Nice to meet you too, Professor."

Professor Mason walked back behind the podium.

"Good morning, future lawyers. Are you miserable yet?"

The class chuckled a little. I surmised that, like me, they weren't sure how to take the boisterous professor.

"Ah, sounds like the answer is 'no.' Give it a few weeks. I'm Professor James Mason, and I will be teaching you all about crimes. And I suggest you pay close attention. You may find it helpful if you find yourself on the wrong side of the law. You all do want to avoid jail, I presume?"

The class laughed more audibly this time.

"Great! Let me tell you a little about myself. I grew up here in East Lansing and completed undergrad and law school at the University of Michigan. Go Blue!" Much of the class groaned at his use of our rival school's slogan.

"Of course we have some diehard Spartans in class. I'd be disappointed if we didn't," he said and continued. "I moved back here to East Lansing sometime in the eighties and became an Ingham County public defender. I helped drunks stay out of jail and protected the Constitutional rights of even the baddest of bad guys because class, remember, that's what this is all about: the Constitution. After twenty years of hanging out in prisons and cavorting with the 'always innocent' crowd, I decided to put my skills to use in the classroom. I've been teaching here ever since."

I liked Professor Mason so far, and I suspected I'd like

his class as well.

"Unlike Contracts and Civil Procedure, Criminal Law is sexy. This is where all the good stuff happens."

Professor Mason moved out from behind the podium. Though his voice was imposing, the man himself looked unassuming. He had gray-streaked dark brown hair and soft wrinkles on his face that made him look more wise than old. In fact, the closer he walked to my row, the less he looked like a grandparent. He couldn't have been more than about sixty years old. He also wasn't much taller than me and likely weighed twenty pounds less, but he took up a lot of space in a room.

"Like many of your other classes, we'll be using the Socratic method here, but since you all are adults, I won't be giving you assigned seats. I will, however, be doing random calling. I have notecards with all of your pictures on them, and every class period I will ask someone to shuffle the cards. When we break down the cases, I'll draw from the notecards, so please be prepared. Class participation counts for twenty-five percent of your grade. You don't always have to be right, but I need to see that you tried."

Silas raised his hand.

"Yes, Mr. Whitman?" Professor Mason looked out at the class. "By the way, I've memorized all of your faces and names, so don't think you can hide when we pass each other in the halls."

"What's the craziest case you ever tried while you were a public defender?"

"Good question, Mr. Whitman, and I'll tell you all about it when we start discussing murder."

. . .

"**D**o you have a study group yet?" Tiffany asked when we met up after Crim Law. We had an hour between classes, and she and I decided to grab lunch together. I had invited Silas, too, but he said he had somewhere to be.

"No," I admitted, puzzled at her question. It was only our second day, and I hadn't really talked to anyone other than Tiffany and Silas, so of course I didn't have a study group. Did anyone else?

"You need one. This shit is too dense to try to do by yourself. You'll burn out."

"Do you have a group already?" I asked Tiffany, expecting her to say no.

I was even more perplexed when she said, "Fuck yeah, I do."

Wait, what? How?

"How? We've only been here two days."

"Yeah, but a bunch of us connected a couple of weeks before school started. Didn't you get the email from Dean Hargrove about how we should prep for the first day?"

I'd gotten the email, but I had summarily ignored it. I theorized that I could read everything later once school had started. I hadn't been excited about starting law school, and I was nervous as hell. It wasn't until a week before I was supposed to leave that I had even fully accepted I was going. I had even found a mini keychain Magic 8 Ball at the airport and bought it to ask if I should get on the airplane. It had answered, "Without a doubt."

"Hm, I guess I must have missed it," I told Tiffany, slightly embarrassed at my complacency. People who actually wanted to be lawyers studied hard for the LSAT so they could get into a decent law school. I just wasn't one of those people. Instead, I'd bought a book, studied for an hour a day for three weeks, and then took the test and somehow scored a 159. It wasn't an "oh my God she's an LSAT savant" score, but it was respectable considering I had barely studied and the highest score you could get was a 180.

"Do you want to join my group?" Tiffany offered. "We've only met once so far, and I'm sure they wouldn't mind another person to help with the outlining."

"Outlining?" I asked. It was becoming quite clear I was well behind the curve.

Tiffany looked at me like I'd grown a third eye on my cheek.

"What the fuck, Simone? Didn't you read any of the material they sent out? It's basically the only way to take notes in law school."

I hadn't. Not one single thing. Acknowledging that I was going to law school was one thing. Actively participating in it before it even started was a different story.

"I'll have to go back through my email and see, but yeah, I'll join your group. I promise, I'll get it all together before the next meeting." And I really would. If I was going to do this thing, I might as well try to do it right.

"You better, otherwise the gunners in my group will eat you alive. They're all after the same summer associate positions, and those things are competitive as hell." She had a slight smirk on her face when she said, "I assume you haven't thought about firms you might want to interview with?"

I gave Tiffany a look.

"I didn't think so. You'll see at our next study group what I mean about the gunners. Meanwhile, I'd start seriously thinking about summer associate positions if you want a chance at a job after you graduate. You don't want to be stuck twirling your thumbs after you take the bar."

I really didn't. I had already had one semi-failed career. Now that I was here, I certainly didn't want a second one.

CHAPTER FIVE

It was a full two weeks into school and I'd barely had time to get outside, so I wanted to take a walk and talk to River. She and I had been playing phone tag for days—well, less tag and more chase since she'd called me three times and I hadn't had the breathing room to call her back yet—but it was Saturday, I needed to take a study break, and I really wanted to talk to my best friend. We hadn't talked since that first day of classes, and I missed her. Outside, I pulled up her contact, but after the fifth ring I hung up. I sent her a quick text telling her to call me when she got a chance and walked past my neighbor Suzy's apartment, giving her a mental middle finger, then, after checking to make sure no one else was around, the real thing.

Suzy was driving me crazy. A few days after I'd moved in, she came over to introduce herself. I had heard the light knocking on my door but assumed I was imagining it until I saw a face peek into my window, functionally scaring the daylights out of me. It had been the second time I'd had a face in my window in a week, which seemed excessive. I had cracked open the door to find a tall, lanky brunette attached to the face at the window.

"Hi," I said. "Can I help you?"

"Yes, hello. I'm Suzy. I live next door."

"Oh hi, Suzy! It's nice to meet you. I'm Simone." I had opened the door wider and stepped back, motioning for her to come in, and she stepped into the door, looking around nervously. What did she think, the bogeyman was going to jump out and get her?

She looked around the room disapprovingly and said, "I hope I'm not disturbing you. I just wanted to let you know that I'm getting my master's degree in piano performance, and I practice early in the mornings. Sometimes late at night, too. If it gets too loud, knock on my door, and I'll play more quietly. Thanks, bye." And she then walked away. I hadn't actually seen her since. Not even in passing. But I heard her. A lot. And though I'd knocked on her door a few times to ask if she could keep it down, she never answered. She probably couldn't hear the door over the playing. The morning serenade didn't bother me so much, but at night, I wanted nothing more than to bust into Suzy's apartment and Hulk-smash the shit out of her piano.

"Hey, what did that window ever do to you?" someone yelled. I looked over the railing and saw Silas there sitting on his Vespa.

Caught giving the middle finger to a window.

"The better question is what are you doing outside of my apartment again?" I asked.

Silas climbed off the scooter as I walked down the stairs.

"Hazard of being neighbors," he said as I got closer. "Occasionally you get the honor of seeing me out for a ride on my hog."

Silas and I lived about two minutes away from each other. Like me, he chose to live in university housing rather than having a longer commute or needing to get roommates. He mentioned he had debated living at home with his dad to save a little money but had opted out when he found out that student housing was both cheap and close enough to campus that he could get out of bed half an hour before class and still make it to campus on time.

"Hmm, not sure I'd use the word honor, but I can't say I mind the view," I said. And I didn't. He was wearing another one of his stupid T-shirts but this one, unlike the others, fit him like it had been tailored for his body. It was tight, molded to his biceps, and had it been a size smaller I would have assumed he shopped at Baby Gap, but he wore it well. Paired with his flat stomach and low-slung jeans, Silas was a very welcome sight. "What are you up to?"

"Other than lucking out finding you? Nothing. Thinking about heading over to the Dairy Store. Have you been yet?"

I'd heard about the Dairy Store, but I hadn't ventured over there yet. MSU's Dairy Store made ice cream and cheese that were rumored to bring grown men to their knees, and since my love of ice cream was only eclipsed by my love of cheese, the journey seemed overdue.

"Not yet, but I want to. I heard the Spartan Swirl is life altering," I told him.

"True story, I was seven the first time I tried Sesquicentennial Swirl—that's what it was called back then—and my dad had to bribe me to leave the store. I had eaten both of my two scoops and thrown up, then threw a full-on tantrum because he wouldn't let me have any more. He promised we could come back the next day if we left the store right that second."

I laughed. He sounded like as big an ice cream fiend as me.

"Anyway, I'm down to take your Dairy Store virginity."

I checked my phone to make sure I hadn't missed any calls or texts from River, and I hadn't. "Yeah, let's go."

Silas started toward his Vespa, but I stopped him with a hand on his arm. "Do you mind if we walk? I want to get a little fresh air."

"Not at all," he said. "I wouldn't mind some fresh air myself. I'm not used to being inside so much."

It was nice to be able to enjoy the weather. I loved being outside but didn't get to do so as much as I would have liked. Working in a restaurant was long hours, and when I wasn't working, I was sleeping, but I got at least one full day off most weeks, and I tended to use that time to recharge, taking hikes or bike rides. Just things to move my body and get outside. Here, the only outside time I'd gotten so far involved walking from building to bus or, when Silas drove me, building to scooter or truck.

"How have your first couple weeks been?" I asked.

"Not bad. Not nearly as hard as I expected it to be."

"If this isn't hard, what'd you think it would be like?" I asked Silas as we started to walk.

Hearing that it wasn't hard for him was wild since so far I thought it was damn near impossible. I'd complained to my parents after the first week, and they had gently reminded me that of course it was hard.

My mom, ever the realist, had said, "Well, sweetie, what did you expect?"

I had answered her as honestly as I could, even though I was pretty sure she was asking a rhetorical question. "I expected it to be like undergrad, honestly. I have a few friends that went to other grad programs, and they didn't mention anything like this."

"But none of your friends are in law school," she'd said, her voice full of pride. If I managed to make it through this law school hellscape, I would be the first lawyer in my family and the first person with a doctoral degree. It's not as though my parents were uneducated people themselves. My mother and father had both earned bachelor's degrees, and my mother had a master's degree as well. It was just that to them, and the rest of my family, going to professional school was the pinnacle of success, and I was going to be the first person to do it. Beckett had considered going to grad school, but when he built an app and sold it to Google for an eight-figure sum, he decided he'd rather travel. Said it was his personal learning experience.

"That's true, but still. It's hard."

"You've got this. I don't have any doubt you can do it."

"What can we do to help?" my dad had piped up. He had already sent me several care packages, which felt like a godsend whenever one showed up at my door. I think he'd even sent a couple in August before I officially started because one had shown up two days after my first class, and the rest had trickled in over the next few days.

"You can keep sending me care packages and help me get my car here next year," I told him. My parents laughed, told me they were there if I needed them, and hung up the phone.

"I'm not saying it's not hard, Suit," Silas remarked, bringing me back to our conversation. "I'm just saying it isn't as hard as I thought it would be. My boy Keith made it sound near impossible."

Whoever Keith was, his view of school sounded much more in tune with my own. I considered Silas as we walked. Usually the gunner types like him were insufferable in and out of the classroom, but so far he didn't seem like that at all. In fact, outside of class he was downright pleasant.

"So Suit, how does a California girl end up here?" He held up his right hand and pointed to the middle of his palm, indicating where in Michigan we lived. I knew little about my new state, but I knew that. Everyone here seemed eager to show where they lived in the state using the palm of their hand. As someone light on geographical knowledge, I loved the visual reminder.

"I applied to, like, three law schools, and they were all in states I'd never been to. I lived in the Bay Area my entire life, and I supposed if I was going to disrupt my entire life, I wanted it to be somewhere brand new," I replied.

"Makes sense. That was brave, moving somewhere completely foreign to you," he said.

I didn't know if brave was the word I'd use. Desperate? Maybe. Foolhardy? Probably. But I appreciated the compliment nonetheless.

"It was almost the exact opposite for me," he continued. "We traveled all the time when I was younger. Lauren was in a different state or country every few months, and my dad tried to meet her wherever she happened to be. I suspect she didn't love it, but we could never stay longer than a week or so. I've been to almost every continent, so when it came to college and law school, I wanted to stay local since there aren't that many places I haven't been."

"Did you like traveling like that?" I asked him. I'd traveled a few places out of the country, mostly in Europe and Mexico, but I hadn't been to nearly as many places as I would have liked. I wanted to go to South America one day. Rivvy's folks invited me to go to Brazil with them one year when we were in high school, but I got sick right before the trip and had to miss out.

"Minus the fact that we were meeting my mom there, I loved it," he said. "I met people all the time, and when I traveled for work after college, I was able to visit some of the friends I'd met around the world."

Strolling through campus, for the first time I took in how beautiful it was. The brick buildings and the foliage were unmatched, but the thing I found most striking was how quiet it was. There were no people on campus protesting or proselytizing unlike at Berkeley where any given time of day someone would have a screechy microphone and a sign telling everyone all the things they did or did not believe in. As much as I liked Berkeley's activism, the quiet was awfully nice.

"We're here," Silas said when we reached Anthony Hall. "You're about to have your mind blown."

The long hallway to get to the Dairy Store was dark and dingy and the store itself was small but crowded. The line to get in was drifting toward the exit door. The space itself was nothing to write home about, but as the line moved closer to the dairy displays, I was intrigued. There were all the normal things one would expect from a dairy store like cheese and butter, but there was also something I'd never seen before: chocolate cheese.

I tapped Silas on his shoulder. "Uh, what's chocolate cheese?" I asked.

He looked up from where he was gazing at the ice cream freezer. "Huh?"

"Chocolate cheese," I repeated. "What is it?"

"Hard to explain. It's something you kind of have to try yourself."

I was curious about what it was but not curious enough to try it. There was too much room for flavor error with something called chocolate cheese. Maybe next time.

"We're almost up," Silas said. "Do you know what you want yet?"

There were so many flavors, and most were original to the Dairy Store. There were names like Buckeye Blitz, Izzo's

Malted Madness, and of course, the Spartan Swirl.

"I'm gonna go with Spartan Swirl. Your story clinched it for me."

"Good choice. Get it in a waffle cone, too," he advised. "They're made in-house."

With our cones in hand, his Izzo's Malted Madness and my Spartan Swirl, we opted to eat while we walked back home. I waited until we were outside to take my first lick.

When the bright-green, cake-batter ice cream touched my tongue, my hand shot out on its own accord, and I gripped Silas's forearm.

"Oh. My. God. This might be the best ice cream I've ever tasted," I gushed, closing my eyes. I took another lick. "How is it this good?"

He chuckled. "I know, right? I heard there's something about the fat content in the ice cream that makes it so good. I don't know if that's true or not, but it's my favorite ice cream, bar none. Want to try mine?" he asked, holding out his cone.

I wrapped my hand around his and brought the cone to my mouth. I took a long lick and couldn't stop the moan of pleasure that escaped my mouth. It was truly a gift to the senses.

When I opened them, Silas was right there, staring at me with heavy lids and his lips slightly parted.

"That might be the best thing I've seen all day," he said. "Want another lick?"

It was Friday night, and I was home reading. No matter how hard I tried, I just couldn't stay on top, let alone ahead, of the syllabi for my classes. If I *just* had to read, I was certain I would've been fine since most of the cases were interesting. Plus, I had always been a fast reader and enjoyed reading, but reading in law school gave the entire act a whole new meaning. Many of the cases, especially in Contracts and Civil Procedure, were incredibly old with many dating back to the 1800s, which made reading them that much more difficult. Combine that with having to be doubly prepared for the classes that had random calling, it made reading for class an excruciating experience. So far I had only been called on randomly once—not counting the first day in Patton's class—and thankfully it was for Professor Mason's class and the Crim Law cases were particularly interesting. He had asked me about a case from 1884 called *R v. Dudley and Stephens*. Dudley, Stephens, Parker, and Brooks were castaway at sea for weeks without food or water. The only sustenance they had were some turnips and a turtle. After twenty days at sea, the defendants, Dudley and Stephens, proposed that someone needed to sacrifice himself to save the others. Dudley and Stephens, against Brooks's opinion, decided to sacrifice Parker since he was the sickliest. The two men killed Parker, and all three remaining men feasted on his body. Four days later, they were rescued, and Dudley and Stephens were charged with murder. Professor Mason had been relatively easy on me only asking me to recite the facts of the case before moving on to someone else.

As soon as I opened my Contracts book to read for Monday's class, my phone vibrated, giving me the excuse to take a break I needed. "Hello?" It was a number I didn't recognize or have saved in my phone, but it had a Michigan area code.

"What are you up to tonight?"

I smiled, recognizing Silas's voice.

"Studying. Who'd you have to bribe to get my number?"

"Don't flatter yourself. All the law students are listed in the directory. You didn't get one?"

I guffawed into the phone. "The only people I've really talked to are you and Tiffany, and I see both of you in class every day. Why would I need your number?"

Ignoring my comment about not needing his number, Silas said, "Put away your books and get dressed. We're going out tonight."

"What makes you think I'm not dressed?" He was right, I wasn't. I was wearing my CAL Berkeley sweatpants, a holey tank top with no bra, and fuzzy socks.

"Throw on something respectable. I'll be there in fifteen minutes." Silas hung up without saying goodbye.

He was right, I needed to get out of the house. I walked the ten feet from my living room to my bedroom closet to see if I could find something reasonably attractive to wear. I had mostly been living in jeans and T-shirts since the suit debacle, and at home I primarily wore pajamas when I wasn't studying. I didn't even know where we were going—Silas hadn't given me a chance to ask—but I didn't care since I had been virtually a hermit and was excited to get out of the house.

Digging through my closet, I found a weathered pair of dark denim hip-hugging jeans, a green, low-cut tank-top that showed the ample cleavage of which my mom regularly pondered its origin, a shrunken—a size too small—black blazer, and my very favorite pair of stilettos. The outfit screamed casual sexy. I smacked my lips together, appreciating the chance to wear my favorite Fenty lipstick color, and heard a car pull up out front. I ran out of the bathroom and through the kitchen to look out of my front window. Sitting on the grass in front of my complex was Silas's pickup truck.

I tossed my lipstick into a small clutch purse and ran outside. Silas opened the passenger door from the inside, and I hoisted myself into the seat.

"You're insane. My neighbors are going to hate me. What prompted the showy arrival?"

"It's called door-to-door service, California. Ready to see the big city?" he said.

I giggled and glanced over at him to see he was smiling, too. The dimple in his left cheek got deeper the harder he smiled, and he smiled a lot. Silas's curls were loose, though it looked like he'd gotten a haircut because it was tamer than usual, and he sported his usual day-old stubble.

Silas was attractive by anyone's standards, but I preferred my men clean-cut and well-coifed, not scruffy and driving a pickup truck. Silas was indeed sexy, but he wasn't my type, so it confounded that whenever I was around him my stomach did a little flip-flop.

"Where are we going?"

P ulling into a parking space on Grand River, Silas turned down the radio that, a moment ago, had been playing the Beatles. I looked out of the window and saw we were across the street from Dublin Square Irish Pub. Bodies spilled out onto the front stoop, and inside, people loitered around the host stand waiting to catch the disinterested host's eyes. He ignored them and kept texting whoever had his undivided attention. I shook my head at the spectacle. "Here goes nothing." Silas didn't respond. I looked over at him, and he was staring at me.

"What? Why are you looking at me like that?" He observed me so intently I momentarily wondered if I had toothpaste on the side of my mouth still. I didn't think I did, but I rubbed at the corner of my mouth just to make sure.

Silas shook his head and looked away. "Nothing. Ready?"

"Yeah, who's going to be here?" I asked, a little nervous. It wasn't that I was shy exactly, but I hadn't talked to many people outside of Tiffany and Silas. I hadn't even made it to my first study session yet, though I planned to go to the next one since Tiffany had gotten the okay from the others in the group for me to join.

"It's a beginning-of-the-year 1L party. Didn't you get the email?"

I'd started checking my emails pretty regularly, but I didn't remember seeing anything about a 1L party.

"Nope. So all of the 1Ls will be here, not just our section?"

"Yup, as many as decide to show up."

Despite my nerves, I was excited to formally meet more of my classmates. With Silas's help and one or two drinks, I would be fine. Silas turned off the car and climbed out before I even unbuckled my seatbelt. As I unclasped it, the passenger door opened, and Silas stood there with his hand out to help me down.

I gripped his hand tightly so that I wouldn't trip and fall in my stilettos. When my feet were firmly on the ground, I thought he would let go of my hand, but he didn't. Instead, he interlaced our fingers and flashed that dimpled smile, catching me off guard, and I couldn't help smiling back at him. We walked into the restaurant still holding hands, but not wanting to give anyone the wrong impression, I let his hand go under the guise of pointing out Tiffany.

"Look, Tiffany's over there. Let's go say hi!"

Students took up every inch of space in the small bar. There was hardly enough room to maneuver, and everywhere I turned I recognized people that I'd either seen in class or in the law school lobby. Silas and I threaded our way through several different groups of people as we made our way to Tiffany. Along the way, Silas stopped to say hello, doling out hugs or daps. As he stopped and chatted, I hoped he would introduce me to his friends so I could meet a few more people. Instead, he leaned over and tried to whisper, "I've talked to all these people, but I can't remember anyone's name." Silas was Mr. Popular—everyone loved him—and no one even clocked that he never uttered their names.

We were almost at Tiffany's table when Silas stopped to talk to a guy who looked familiar, though I couldn't quite place him.

Silas greeted him with that half-hug, half–high five thing guys do so their bodies didn't actually touch. "Hey, man! I didn't think you'd make it out tonight."

"Yo, I almost didn't, but I thought, 'Screw it, I can study any time.'" Their interaction was warm, showing a closeness Silas didn't seem to have with the others. The guy wasn't in our section. I knew that for sure; I would've remembered that face. Maybe he was in one of the other sections? Silas's giant body left only the guy's forehead and arm in my view, and I couldn't get close enough to look at his face to figure out how I recognized him. On my tiptoes, I was trying to peer around Silas when the guy stepped to the left directly into my line of vision.

He hooked his thumb at Silas. "I guess his trifling ass isn't going to introduce us. What's up? I'm Keith." Like magic, right before my eyes Silas turned into a tomato. It was strange to see him embarrassed since so far I hadn't seen Silas look anything but completely confident and at ease.

"My bad. Keith, this is Simone. We're in the same section. Simone, this is Keith. We grew up together. He's in the JD/MBA program and finished his 1L year last year," he said, then turned to Keith. "Making you technically a 2L, so I'm not sure you should even be here."

Yup, that was it. I'd noticed him in the halls at the law school. He was awfully hard to miss.

"Nice to meet you, Keith. I thought you looked familiar." Keith and Silas were like night and day, and Keith, unlike Silas, was just my type. Not quite as tall as Silas, he was still a respectable six foot two with smooth, coffee-colored skin, dark-chocolate eyes, and lips that almost rendered me speechless. He reached out to shake my hand, and when our palms touched I could have sworn the lights flickered a little. We stood there gripping hands and smiling for longer than was necessary. I glanced down at our hands, and wow, even they were sexy. Rough but cared for. Silas interrupted breaking the trance we were under, and it was probably a good thing he did.

"Simone, didn't you want to go holler at Tiffany?" I barely remembered we were in a bar with other people, let alone that I wanted to talk to Tiffany. I removed my hand from Keith's and stepped back, giving myself a little more breathing room.

"Oh. Yeah. Sure. Thanks."

I waved at Keith, not wanting to touch him again. "It was really nice to meet you. I'm sure I'll see you around."

He examined me a moment before he said, "I'll try my hardest to make sure we do." Keith looked pointedly at Silas, whose eyebrows had shot to the top of his head before he responded, "Yeah, for sure, for sure. Simone, I'll catch up with you in a minute, all right?"

I waved a quick goodbye and walked the last few feet

across the bar to where Tiffany sat. She wore her usual country club getup, which I had gotten used to seeing but still found amusing. Her hair was held back with a black velvet headband, and she donned a green cardigan, khakis, and shiny black flats to match her headband. She had a martini in her right hand and a vape pen in her left. Up until that moment, I didn't even know she smoked—she never smoked at school—and I was pretty sure you weren't allowed to vape inside of bars even if what came out smelled like cotton candy. It was surprising that no one told her to put it out, then I remembered it was Tiffany and someone probably did and she handily dismissed them. Tiffany was in her element, holding court with four handsome guys, each one directing a wide, toothy grin her way. They were from our section but I couldn't recall their names for the life of me.

"So I see you finally decided to come over and grace me with your presence." She pushed through the group of guys to give me a hug.

"Sorry. I came with Silas, and he had to stop to talk to everyone he's ever met. You having fun?"

Tiffany gestured to the table, where there were two empty martini glasses and a second vape pen I assumed had been emptied. "Enough fun. Why are you so late?"

"I didn't even know about this thing until Silas told me."

Tiffany hooked her arm through mine, pulling me toward the bar.

"Didn't you get the—?" She stopped herself before finishing the question, but I knew how it was going to end.

I frowned at her. At the end of Civ Pro a couple weeks ago, Tiffany had asked me if I got the study guide the professor had suggested, and when I asked her what study guide, she'd told me to get my shit together and start checking my fucking email. Her exact words. I knew she was right, and I really did start checking it. Daily. But apparently this one had been sent before my renewed relationship with my inbox.

She cracked up. "I'm kidding."

"How long have you been here?" I asked.

"Long enough to know I'm ready to drink myself stupid and fuck a couple of these future politicians. Let's get you a drink."

Oh. Okay.

I ordered my usual whiskey on the rocks, then changed my mind before the bartender started to pour and decided to try something new at the last minute: a dirty vodka martini, the same thing Tiffany was having. I took a sip and shuddered at the briny, antiseptic taste. I cautiously took another sip, which went down much smoother. "Not bad. So who were all those guys you were talking to when I got there?"

The four men she had been chatting with all dispersed as soon as Tiffany left the group. I couldn't tell if they were friends with each other or not, but once she was no longer involved in the conversation, they must have lost interest.

"Just a few of the guys from our section. We were all studying late in the library a couple days ago and ended up grabbing late-night pizza together. They're all right, just a little uptight."

"Cute though, no?"

"Yeah. Like I said, you have to fuck a couple of them from time to time to remind yourself you're more than just a case reading, outlining machine."

She had a point.

"Let's get another round and we can talk about how we can get you hooked up with one of them. Not one of mine, of course," she said as she perused the room, "but I'm sure we can find you someone delicious to play with."

I followed her gaze around the room, and my eyes landed, then lingered on Silas, then shifted to Keith. Someone to play with didn't sound bad at all, but I wasn't sure if I wanted Tiffany to help me in that arena based on what I'd seen of her taste in men. Clean cut I liked. JFK Jr. clones? Not so much.

Despite spending most of my time at school with Tiffany, her life outside of school was a bit of a mystery to me. While Silas was an immediate open book, Tiffany was taking a little longer to open up.

"So, Ms. Alston, let me get another drink, then I want to hear your life story in twenty minutes or less. That's just about how long it'll take for the second martini to kick in, and then I'll consider finding a new buddy. Deal?"

She took a long drag of her vape pen.

"Deal," she said as she exhaled, and the cotton candy scent washed over me.

I settled onto the bar stool and got comfortable while Tiffany launched into her family history. I learned she had mostly grown up in Manhattan Beach as she had told me when we first met, but she was actually born on the East Coast where her parents had lived for most of their lives. She said that after her parents had her, then her sister five years later, they decided their daughters needed more sun, less snow, and easy access to the beach, so when she was five years old, they drove cross country where her parents had bought a house on the beach after only having seen it in pictures. She went to a conservative all-girls private school in L.A. where they wore uniforms, and when she graduated high school and went off to college, she realized how much she hated having to choose her clothing every day, so she went back to wearing a uniform. She told me she had only basic colors in her closet and that all of her clothing could be worn in any combination while still looking put-together. I learned that she loved her little sister Cartier as much as I adored my older brother and that the hardest thing about being in Michigan was being so far from her.

I couldn't help the laughter that bubbled up when she said her sister's name. "Wait, wait, wait a second. Your sister's name is Cartier and your name is Tiffany? What were your parents thinking?"

Unamused, Tiffany explained that her mother had grown up blue collar in Queens and always aspired to be wealthy. As such, she earned top grades in high school, college, and law school, then had gone on to become a high-powered intellectual property attorney making partner at her firm after only seven years. It was clear Tiffany was proud of her mother.

"After she made partner, she treated herself to a pair of diamond earrings from Tiffany's. The night she bought the earrings was the same night she discovered she was pregnant with me. When she found out she was pregnant with my sister, she surprised my father with a Cartier watch. So, yeah."

"Wow. Your mom sounds amazing. Is that why you decided to come to law school?"

Tiffany nodded. "Yes, and also I like to argue. It seemed like a good fit for me. What about you? How did you end up here?"

I wanted to tell her my Magic 8 Ball story, then decided against it. She was so hell-bent on being a lawyer, and I had applied on a desperate whim. Telling her the truth felt like an insult to her dreams, so I was relieved when Silas walked up, allowing me to avoid the subject of what had brought me to law school. I hadn't seen him in a while, and it was obvious that like me and Tiffany, he'd had more than a couple drinks since we separated. He looked a little unsteady on his feet and was even more boisterous than usual.

"Ladies, hello." He bowed deeply at the waist and spilled a little bit of his beer on the ground. Tiffany rolled her eyes, and I laughed. At least he wasn't calling us girls anymore.

"It looks like you've been having a good time. I thought I'd lost you," I said.

He shook his head vigorously from side to side. "Nope, you could never lose me in a crowd. I'm six foot four." He had a good point. I never really lost sight of him in the small bar area. From what I saw, he had spent the night schmoozing with our classmates.

"Come meet some people. You can't spend all night talking to just her." He flicked his head in Tiffany's direction.

I saw Tiffany out of the corner of my eye, and I could tell she didn't appreciate Silas's comment.

"And why shouldn't she just hang out with me? It's not like you've been integral in her meeting anyone new." Tiffany looked affronted. I didn't want the only two people I knew getting into an argument, so instead of trying to play referee, I told Silas to find a table with whoever he wanted me to meet and I would join him in a minute. He nodded, shot Tiffany one last irritated look, which she responded to in kind, and headed over to a table full of people that looked like they jumped out of a J. Crew ad.

As soon as he was gone, I turned back to Tiffany. "Do you have some kind of issue with Silas?"

Tiffany took a sip from her third martini. How was she not on the floor?

"He's an asshole in class, and if that motherfucker interrupts me one more time when I'm trying to answer a question—" She shook her head like she'd thought better of finishing the sentence, and I wondered how it would have ended. Knowing

Tiffany, it was going to be some next-level *Ocean's Eleven* sabotage.

But she'd noticed his obnoxious class behavior, too. At least I knew it wasn't just me he bothered in class.

Tiffany downed the rest of her martini in one impressively large gulp and walked toward Silas and the rest of the table. She turned back to me. "Are you coming?"

Silas's table was packed with people, some I recognized from our section and a couple I didn't recognize at all. Keith was also there. Along with Silas, Keith, me, and Tiffany, there were Kevin, Alison, Jack, Courtney, Rafael, and Tyler.

"Then I was like, 'Dude, it's not gonna happen. You've had like nine beers and can't even stand up,' so I called a Lyft and sent his drunk-ass home. I didn't want him passing out on my couch!" Courtney had everyone cracking up about her date from the week before.

"Shit, did he make it home?" Kevin asked.

"I guess. I mean, Lyft didn't charge me extra for a body so..." Courtney tried to sip her wine but looked at everyone's shocked faces and couldn't keep a serious face.

"Kidding, kidding. He texted the next day and said he was sorry for being a drunk fuck and asked if we could try again."

Rafael leaned into the table closer to Courtney and asked, "What did you tell him?"

"I didn't tell him anything! I just sent him a Venmo request for $135. The cost of the ride and the $100 Lyft charged me when he puked in the car!"

Everyone laughed at Courtney's awful date and tried to one up her with their own bad date stories.

At one forty-five a.m., the bartender yelled, "Last call." By then I had had one more dirty martini and half a subpar glass of wine, and I was feeling every single one of those drinks.

Silas was at the bar waiting to close his tab, and Tiffany had left about thirty minutes before last call when one of the guys from her smiling quartet texted her to come over. I'd never seen Tiffany move that fast.

"Hey, should I get a Lyft or do you want to walk?" I had to study in the morning since my earlier study session had been shot to hell and getting some fresh air might help the hangover I sensed was going to make an unwelcome appearance in the morning.

"No, it's all good. Keith can give us a ride home. He didn't really drink tonight."

Well, shit. It wasn't like I was sloppy drunk, but I wasn't sober and certainly not at my best. I didn't want Keith to see me looking like a train wreck.

"Ah, okay. In that case, let me grab a Lyft. I don't want Keith to have to make two stops. Will you wait here with me until my ride comes?"

"Don't be ridiculous, Keith doesn't mind dropping us both off. Hell, he could even drop me off at your place and I can walk from there. It's not a big deal." He motioned to someone, and I stood up and leaned around the bar to see who it was. Keith. He was standing near the exit looking ready to leave. Silas yelled across the bar, "Yo, Keith, you mind giving Simone a ride home, too? She lives right around the corner from me."

Mortified, I tried to duck behind Silas, but he noticed and moved to the right so I was no longer behind him.

Instead of yelling across the bar like a lunatic, Keith walked over to where we were still waiting at the bar for Silas to get his credit card and receipt.

"As long as you don't mind riding between us in the middle seat on the way home, I'm happy to give you a ride." He smiled at me, and I just stood there blinking and nodding my head. *Smooth, Simone.*

The three of us walked to Keith's car with Silas keeping a steady stream of conversation asking Keith about school and what he was getting into for the rest of the weekend. I, on the other hand, had become incapable of forming words, let alone full sentences. Thankfully it was a short walk from the bar to his car. Keith stopped at an old Crown Victoria.

"Why are we stopping?" I asked.

"This is my car," Keith said as he unlocked the doors manually. I hadn't seen someone use a key to unlock a door since I was in second grade. "It was my grandfather's old car."

"I've only seen these vintage cars on old seventies shows." Silas and Keith laughed as I climbed into the passenger side with Silas sliding in after me. Keith's button-down shirt, boat shoes, and khaki pants didn't seem to fit the car. He was so put together and cool, and the car was...neither. Not that it mattered, but it was a funny contrast.

As soon as Keith started the car, Silas slid his arm around the back of the seat. It wasn't exactly around my shoulders since he wasn't touching me, but it felt very intimate, and I saw Keith eyeing us out of the corner of his eye. Silas didn't seem to notice. He just kept chattering away until we arrived at his house.

"Man, why didn't you drop Simone off first?" Silas made no move to get out of the car.

"It was out of the way to drop her off, then double back to drop you off. This way I can drop you off, drop her off, then hop right on the freeway. Trust me, dude, it makes sense."

Silas didn't look like he believed it made sense, but he couldn't argue with Keith when we were already in front of his house. Looking resigned, he undid his seatbelt and reached over to give me a hug.

"Thanks for coming out tonight." He gave me a quick peck on the cheek as he got out of the car. He leaned back into the window, thanked Keith, and told me he would call me tomorrow. Before we pulled off, I slid over onto the seat he had occupied and put on my seatbelt.

"You didn't have to move. It was plenty comfortable having you here." If my skin wasn't a warm cocoa brown, I definitely would have been blushing.

He continued, "So, what's up with you and Silas? You guys together or something?"

I hadn't said more than twenty words to Keith the entire evening, and now he was asking about my dating life?

"We're friends. No biggie."

Plus, I thought to myself, I was pretty sure I wasn't his type. All the women he introduced me to at the bar lacked the melanin my skin had in spades, and he seemed to really enjoy their company. On the other hand, Keith would have known Silas's type already and maybe that's why he asked.

Keith glanced over at me and smiled. "Good to know."

We pulled into the parking lot of my building, and Keith turned off his car.

"What are you doing?" The smile he gave me coupled with him killing the engine hinted at what he wanted—an invite into my apartment. If I wanted to take Tiffany's advice, Keith was the ideal candidate. Sexy oozed out of his pores plus he was really nice. I had never had a one-night stand, and my college roommate didn't understand how it happened.

"We're in college," she'd told me after one of her conquests slunk out of our apartment. "We're supposed to be having all the sex and fun." She'd joked that until she met "the guy," she'd be happy to "fuck and roll" her way through life.

"It's late. I just wanted to walk you to your door. Is that okay?"

Oh. Maybe I'd misread his cues and he wasn't trying to hook up. But did I?

"Oh. Yeah. Thank you." As we got out of the car, Keith walked around to my side of the car to help me out and held my elbow, guiding me to the front door. It was awkward, but it was also sweet that he wanted to make sure I safely got to the door. On the other hand, I also felt a little like a grandma he needed to help across the street.

"It was really nice meeting you tonight. I hope we get the chance to hang out again," he said, steering me toward a front door that wasn't mine. I tugged him back in the direction of my door.

"Thanks for the ride. I hope we see each other again, too."

I reached out to give him a hug when he reached out to shake my hand. His hand ended up grazing the side of my breast, and he yanked it back like it had burned him.

"I'm sorry. I'm so, so sorry."

"No worries. I know it was an accident." I reached out to hug him again, and this time we connected and embraced quickly.

"I'll wait here until you get inside."

I hurried to grab my keys out of my tiny purse and opened my door.

"Good night, Keith."

CHAPTER SIX

"Can you tell us about consideration, Mr. Yu?" Patton walked up the stairs and stood beside Kevin's seat.

Kevin sat next to Silas in the back row. Even though he was several rows away from me, I saw the panic in his eyes. It wasn't his turn to brief a case, but as promised in the first class, Patton was taking the opportunity to cold call on someone, and today was poor Kevin's day.

He started to speak, his voice quiet and shaking slightly. "Consideration is the—"

"Mr. Yu, you're an adult person in law school. I'm going to need you to project your voice. Now please, start again," Patton said.

Kevin turned bright red, and I couldn't blame him. Patton's specialty was making her students feel two inches tall.

He started again. "Consideration is the bargained-for exchange of goods or services between parties."

Patton nodded and made her way back down the stairs to the front of the room. Caneless. Again. Class was over, but Patton continued to talk, and no one made a move out of their seats. The level of respect she commanded was impressive.

"Class, I know it's early in your legal careers, but now is the time you want to start thinking about where you'll work this summer."

Hm, Tiffany was right.

"For those of you interested in transactional law, this class is going to be your lifeline, but you will need to have stellar grades in all of your classes to get a coveted summer associate position."

Tiffany had mentioned summer associate positions, and when I'd googled them, more information than I needed came up along with several law firms, many of whose names I'd seen on buildings in downtown San Francisco.

"Each firm hires a class of students for the summer to work in either litigation or transactional law. The vast majority of the summer associates work in litigation, and at the end of the summer, those who have done an exemplary job and proven themselves competent may be offered an associate position once they graduate," Patton explained.

"Summer associates are paid on par with first-year associates, so for those of you looking to offset your student loans or have some income over the summer, this might be a viable option."

Now a summer associate position at a law firm sounded like something I could sink my teeth into.

Patton continued, talking about her experience as a summer associate, but I had tuned her out. Working as a summer associate seemed like a dream option. I would get paid and be virtually guaranteed a job when I graduated. I had lingering questions that I still needed to figure out the answers to, like what was the exact difference between transactional law and litigation, but those could come later. I wondered if I could get a summer position doing something with employment law.

Patton was explaining some of the requirements needed

when I tuned back in.

"In order to be competitive, students need to maintain at least a 3.6 grade point average. In law school, that is no small feat, and in my class, receiving an A is a luxury saved for only the most outstanding students."

Even with the mounds of work, I was confident in my ability to perform well on tests. I had always been a good student, and with the addition of a group to help, I imagined studying would be even easier.

"Chang, Lowe & Sanders has a litigation position that I encourage all of my top students to pursue, even if you're interested primarily in transactional work. It offers ample experience to work for an elite firm where any of you would be privileged to learn. They work primarily in hospitality, but their reach is broad. They have offices all over the country."

Chang, Lowe & Sanders sounded like a good start, and I wanted to apply for the position. Even though my work in hospitality was behind me, with my background in the restaurant industry and my—hopefully, fingers crossed—decent grades, I might be able to land this summer position.

"All right, Elle, are you ready for your first study group?" Tiffany asked after Patton's class. They had to reconfigure how the group divided work once I joined since I'd missed the first couple sessions.

Tiffany had taken to calling me Elle, after Elle Woods from *Legally Blonde*. She wasn't wrong exactly, but to my credit, at least I hadn't chased a man to school.

"So the group is Kevin, Courtney, Rafael, Silas, me, and

you?" I asked.

"And Pierce. He asked if he could join. He's an annoying-as-fuck gunner, kinda like Silas, you know, but his outlining skills are stellar."

I cringed at her description of Silas as a gunner. He was nothing like Pierce generally, except that in class, he sort of was. That first day wasn't the first or last time Silas had attempted to trample everyone with his intellect. Thankfully, he hadn't done it to me again.

We met in one of the empty classrooms on the third floor, and when we walked in, Silas was already there waiting for the rest of us. He was engrossed in his laptop and didn't seem to hear us come in.

"Silas?" I said, not wanting to startle him.

"Hey, what's up, Simone?" He stood up and gave me a quick hug. He also took my heavy wheelie laptop bag and placed it on the desk. As an afterthought, he said, "Hi, Tiffany."

"As always, lovely to see you, Silas," Tiffany said, her voice dripping with sarcasm.

The two of them were like oil and water. Both smart, both driven, but Tiffany detested how Silas acted in class and refused to acknowledge he was different at all other times. Silas despised the fact that Tiffany despised him and treated her accordingly.

Before they could antagonize each other any further, Rafael and Kevin came through the door.

I sat down and motioned for Tiffany to join me, but she was preoccupied talking to Rafael and her neck was getting an intense workout from the sheer amount she flipped her hair.

I didn't have time to fully analyze the situation before Silas asked, "Are you applying to any summer associate positions?"

"Yeah, I think so. The one at Chang, Lowe & Sanders seems cool."

"I'm in the same boat. Long term I want to be a public defender, but working in the private sector will get me some serious litigation experience, and I could be like the sexy Johnnie Cochran."

I laughed. "I could see you now, charming all the jurors."

He put his arm around my chair and moved me closer to him. "I was worried you hadn't noticed."

"Oh, stop," I said, nudging him with my shoulder. "Don't let it go to your head."

"Too late, California."

I shook my head at him and couldn't help but smile.

"Moving right along, you heard what Patton said about the grades? You think you'll do all right in her class?"

"Yeah, and you will, too. We've got this crew, and you and I can do a separate thing from time to time if you want."

I appreciated his offer. The reading for Contracts alone was kicking my ass, and we were just getting started.

Sneaking up behind us, Kevin moved Silas's arm from behind my chair. "Break it up, lovebirds. This is a study session, not a date."

Kevin pulled out his laptop and connected it to the screen at the front of the room. When he did, his outline popped onto the screen.

Damn, they weren't messing around. I thought it would be a more casual discussion about our outlines, not a full-on class presentation, complete with projectors.

"We're going to go over the outline for Criminal L—" Kevin started to say before Silas interrupted him.

"Contracts first. We did Crim first last week but Contracts is harder this week."

"My apologies, Whitman," Kevin said, sounding peeved at the correction. "We're going to go over our outlines for

Contracts first," he said pointedly. "Then we'll do Civ Pro, and if there's time, we can start on Con Law."

I should have brought a snack. I thought the group would meet for an hour, maybe two, but from the sound of things, we would be here all night.

I nudged Silas. "How long do these sessions usually last?"

He shrugged and said, "A few hours depending on how much reading we had and how complicated it was."

I must have looked dejected because he asked, "Why? What's the matter?"

"Nothing. I just wish I'd had time to grab a snack."

Without hesitating, Silas reached into his bag and pulled out a bag of Cheetos.

"Do you want 'em?"

I didn't want to take his snack, but I was starving.

"You don't mind?"

"Not at all, they're yours," he said and handed me his bag of Cheetos.

Grateful, I tore into them hungrily before stopping to offer Silas some, but he pulled out his own bag.

These sessions must be crazy long if Silas had to bring two bags of chips to make it through.

"Hey, before we really get started, are any of you guys planning to apply for that summer associate thing Patton mentioned?" Rafael asked.

"The one at CL&S? It sounds like good experience," Courtney responded. "I might apply. We'll see. My dad wants me to join his firm after I graduate, so I don't know if it makes sense for me to try to get a summer position or just work with my dad."

I listened to my study group discuss the pros and cons of the position. I needed to kick some serious grade ass if I was going to be a competitive candidate.

CHAPTER SEVEN

"Y ou have any plans this weekend?" Silas asked after our civil procedure class.

The only plans I wanted to have involved sleeping. Studying and Netflix would be involved at some point, too, but sleeping was the most critical. I was exhausted. Every night this week, I had had at least three hours of reading. Shit was dense. Dense and boring.

"Nothing, really. Probably hanging around the house." It sounded lame even to my own ears. "You?" I asked.

"Hadn't thought about it. I might head to Lansing and hit up the grocery store."

My ears perked up at hearing that. After commuting to campus for a month, I came to the conclusion that not bringing my car was a bad idea. A really bad idea, actually. Getting to campus was annoying but easy enough. The bus ran every fifteen minutes, and even if I missed the first one, it wouldn't take long to catch the next one. Plus, on days when he wasn't at the library early in the morning, Silas drove me. It was everything else that was hard. I never knew a simple task like grocery shopping could be such a chore. At home, I went to several farmer's markets a week and grocery shopped daily. I didn't love it, but it was a habit I'd picked up working for Jordan. He insisted on the freshest meat and produce. It was one of the few things I appreciated about working in his restaurant. Here, the good grocery store was several miles away in Lansing, and the bus to get there didn't run that often, which left me doing my food shopping at the shit local grocery store close to my apartment. For staples like rice, bread, and pasta, the local grocery store was fine. It was more than fine for cheese and milk since the university had its own dairy here on campus and the grocery store kept the dairy section well-stocked with campus-produced dairy products. The problem was with the produce. I was a pescatarian, and at home, eating healthy was just a part of life. I didn't have to think twice about finding good-quality fruits and veggies because they were everywhere. In mid-Michigan, eating healthy was a luxury. The produce at the local spot was always over-ripe or so under-ripe that it was inedible for a couple weeks.

"Want some company on your grocery trip?" I ventured. To sweeten the pot, I added, "I'll cook you dinner if I can tag along."

"Hell yeah," he said. "I hate grocery shopping, and I don't cook. We can go tomorrow afternoon."

"Sounds good," I said, relieved that he was willing to let me join him. "What do you like to eat?"

"Whatever you want to cook me, girl! Beggars can't be choosers."

I wanted to see where Silas lived. "Do you care if I cook at your apartment?"

"We can cook wherever you want. I'll even make sure to clean my place tonight. Don't want you tripping over my boxers in the kitchen."

I laughed, something I'd found myself doing more and more of whenever I was with Silas. "All right, dude. I'll see you tomorrow." I waved to him and walked away. It wasn't until I was at the bus stop waiting for the bus that I wondered why Silas would have boxers on his kitchen floor.

S ilas said that he would pick me up at four p.m. and was right on time, his truck pulled up in front of my house.

"Thanks for the ride," I said, depositing a quick kiss on his cheek, then yanking myself back. Was it weird to greet him with a kiss? I never had before, but it didn't feel weird.

"No problem, California. Anytime."

I wasn't sure exactly when Silas started calling me California instead of Suit, but I was glad he did. I wanted to put that whole business behind me.

"Do you have a preference in grocery stores? I planned to hit up the big one in Lansing, but I'll go anywhere as long as it's not that shitty one next to us."

"Do you guys have any health food–type stores around here?"

"You're in the country now. What do you think we know about health food stores, California?"

I wasn't sure if he was joking or not. I glanced over to see if he was smiling, and I could see the corners of his lips turned up slightly.

"Shush," I said, smacking him lightly on his arm. "I can shop anywhere as long as it has good produce."

"Cool, that narrows it down to two places. We can either hit Fresh Thyme Market or the big chain store."

"Never been to Fresh Thyme. Let's check that one out."

Fifteen minutes later, we pulled into the parking garage

of a quaint grocery store with bin after bin of fruits and vegetables lining the entrance.

"Be still, my heart," I said, overjoyed at seeing all the produce.

"Looks like we picked well. C'mon, let's go in."

Even though I loved to cook and I loved to eat good food, I never enjoyed going to grocery stores. It wasn't the actual act of shopping that bothered me the most. What really irked me were the lines. It seemed like people were always ill-prepared to shop, like they'd never been to a grocery store before. Then there was always that one person that insisted on paying in cash with a $100 bill that took forever for the cashier to verify was real and then make change for it. I mean really, who didn't have a debit card at this point?

"Are you a shopping cart or handbasket type of girl?" Silas asked.

"Buggy all the way. Handbaskets are a fool's game. They never carry as much as you think they will."

We headed over to where the buggies were lined up, and Silas pulled one out for me and one for himself.

"Before we get too far, I need to ask you a question," Silas said, though I missed the glint in his eye that would have warned me that he was about to say something crazy.

Surprised at my body's reaction, I found myself slightly nervous when I answered, "Yes?"

"Did you really just call a shopping cart a buggy?!"

I barked out a laugh that matched his own deep chortle. "Obviously. Nobody calls it a shopping cart!"

"Wrong! Nobody calls it a buggy. Well, nobody north of the Mason-Dixon line. You a secret Southerner? Is this sexy California girl thing all a ruse?"

"Bless your heart," I said in a fake Southern accent. "You've discovered my secret." Then in my normal voice, I added, "Do you want to divide and conquer? It'll move this process along."

"What's the point in grocery shopping with someone if you do it separately?" Silas reasoned. "No. You're stuck with me. What do you want to hit first?"

An hour later, our respective buggies were full of food and my cheeks hurt from laughing so much. Silas was silly with a capital *S*. In the short time we were at the store, we had played a rhyming game with the rice, written dirty limericks about fruit, and he had created a whole new persona for himself asking folks who worked there about cereal. By the time we got in line, I wasn't even sure if I had bought everything I needed to make dinner for him.

I put my haul onto the conveyor belt, and Silas piled his on behind mine. I handed him the thing to divide our groceries, and he put it down, separating our purchases. There was one person ahead of us who was about to be rung up.

"Hey, can you do me a quick favor? It'd be nice to have some wine with dinner, but I don't know anything about picking out wine. Can you grab a bottle?" Silas asked out of nowhere.

"It's about to be my turn. Just go grab something white that isn't chardonnay. I'm not that picky."

"You're cooking me dinner. We should have a nice bottle of wine to go with it. I can pay for mine first."

I sighed audibly, pretending to be irritated at the request, but I was surprised and secretly glad he wanted to have some good wine with dinner. The chef in me hated the idea of a bad pairing. "Fine, I'll be right back."

The store wasn't crowded, so I was able to get to the wine section, pick a halfway decent wine that I recognized, and get back to the register in under three minutes, but by the time

I got there, the clerk had already rung up my groceries and was halfway through Silas's.

"Shit," I said, putting the wine with the rest of the groceries. "We can tally up the total for mine in the car or back at your place. I'll Venmo you." I shouldn't have left the line. Dealing with money stuff with friends was awkward, especially new friends, when you didn't know how they dealt with that sort of thing.

"It doesn't matter," Silas said easily as he shrugged. "We'll get it worked out."

In the little time I'd known Silas, nothing seemed to faze him. Everything about Patton's class caused heart palpitations for me, but when I had asked him about it, all he said was that she didn't seem so bad. When we discussed our homework and the sheer volume of readings we were trying to get used to, his only response was that we were both smart and it shouldn't be a problem. I didn't know if it was confidence or idiocy that guided his life, but I suspected it was well-earned confidence. There was something about this Michigan boy that screamed, "I'm the shit and I don't give a shit whether you agree," and I liked it.

Backseat full of bags, we drove to Silas's apartment listening to Michael Jackson's greatest hits, car-dancing and singing along. Silas's falsetto game was strong. When "PYT" ended and we had sufficiently caught our breaths from laughing so hard at each other's awful singing voices, I asked Silas, "Do you ever feel guilty listening to Michael Jackson with everything he was accused of doing?"

He looked thoughtful before saying, "Guilt isn't the word I would use. Suppose I let myself feel guilty for listening to Michael Jackson. In that case, I'd have to feel guilty for listening to the Jackson 5, Janet Jackson, Justin Timberlake, and all of the artists that were so heavily influenced by his music, and I don't want that hanging over my head. He's too much a part of Black music history, music history in general really, to let myself feel guilty every single time I hear his music."

I nodded at him, impressed. "I see we've been listening to Wesley and Jenna." He chuckled and nodded, thankfully knowing the hosts of my favorite podcast, *Still Processing*. "Nonetheless, well said, Mr. Whitman, and I fully agree."

"And hey, at least we can still worship Prince, right?" he said.

"Yup, and nothing makes me happier than listening to 'Sign O' the Times' on a rainy night," I said, feeling a little homesick.

"Swap 'Sign O' The Times' for 'Purple Rain' and we've got ourselves a perfect night."

Smiling, he lifted a hand to give me a high five, which I returned with fervor. After our palms met, he gripped my hand and wrapped his fingers around it, immediately bringing back to mind the night I met Keith. Though touching Keith had ignited a spark, now, sitting with Silas alone in his truck, hands connected, a full-on flame threatened to appear. Silas and I had spent ample time alone, but today felt different. At least it did according to my body, which was overheating from our casual high five. Maybe it was the Prince discussion. His music had a habit of turning people on, but it was usually the music itself, not a passing comment about him.

I grasped at straws trying to analyze my reaction to Silas and kept landing at the same place: I liked him.

CHAPTER EIGHT

Silas's apartment didn't look much different than my own. He had the same one-bedroom layout that I was still getting used to in my own apartment. His, however, did not sport the university chic furniture that mine did. In fact, his furniture looked downright comfy. He had a worn big brown sofa that took up most of the small space in his living room, a large flat-screen television, and a smattering of photos that decorated his walls. I took it upon myself to look around, checking out the kitchen to see if he had the proper cooking utensils and peeking into his bedroom to be nosy. I wasn't surprised to see that he had a king-size bed shoved into the small bedroom. Silas's body was too long for him to fit comfortably into anything other than a king.

"Does my place pass the test?" he asked, coming up behind me.

"Don't sneak up on me like that," I shrieked, startled at being caught ogling his bedroom.

"Simone, the place is like six hundred square feet, and I weigh over two hundred pounds. I don't know how you didn't hear me walk up behind you."

I knew how. Looking into his bedroom had me imagining Silas in there getting ready for bed, and I zoned out wondering how his chest looked under those T-shirts he insisted on wearing. After riding with him on the Vespa and feeling his hard abs, I was pretty sure I would like what I saw.

I moved away from him back into the kitchen and started opening cabinets in a bid to shake the image of a bare-chested Silas from my mind.

They were virtually empty. Not even a pack of cheap ramen noodles.

"Uh, don't you eat here? Why is there nothing in your cabinets?"

Silas had bought himself so little at the grocery store—mostly snacks and drinks—I expected his kitchen to be well-stocked. It wasn't.

"I have food," he said and showed me a cabinet full of junk food.

"That's not food. Those are snacks, and bad ones at that."

"Cheetos are not bad snacks, thank you. It doesn't matter, though, because I have you here cooking for me. I assume we'll have leftovers?"

I appreciated his gall.

"Go sit on the couch so I can cook."

I wanted to show off a little for Silas. He knew I liked to cook, but I hadn't yet mentioned that I'd worked as a professional chef. While we were shopping, I had bought a collection of things but hadn't told Silas what I was making. Ipsa's was a California farm-to-table fine-dining restaurant, but my favorite dishes to cook were soul food. Our menu for the evening was macaroni and cheese, collards, candied yams, and fried red snapper. My grandmother always fried catfish, but I couldn't stand the stuff.

"Yooo, are you making what I think you're making?"

I jumped at hearing Silas's voice so close behind me.

"You scared me. And if you think I'm making macaroni and cheese, then yes, it's what you think," I said as I nudged him out of the way with my hip. Unprepared for getting hip-checked, Silas stumbled a little and grabbed me around the waist to keep his balance. He righted himself quickly but eased his arm fully around my waist, pulling my back close to his front.

Whoa. Being this close to Silas was doing weird things to me. I tingled in all the right places, and the butterflies in my stomach paired with the overwhelming desire to turn around and press myself against him just to feel his chest against mine were unexpected.

His arm still around my waist, Silas leaned his head down so we were almost cheek to cheek. Just a tiny little turn to the left and my lips would graze his.

"Mmmmm, smells delicious," he murmured.

"Me or the food?" I asked, baiting him.

"No contest, California," Silas said as he tilted his head into my neck.

Oh.

"You smell fantastic. That's a scent I wouldn't mind smelling every day," he said and dragged his nose down the side of my neck.

"You smell like cake."

"Thanks," I said, trying to sound natural. It wasn't coming easy since the main thoughts running through my brain had everything to do with Silas and zero to do with food.

"Keep smelling like that and I might have to see how you taste." I bit my lip and shivered involuntarily at the thought of the five o'clock shadow rasping against my face and wherever else he wanted to explore on my body.

I turned around in his arm. "You know what they say about your mouth writing checks," I dared him.

"Oh, this is one I'd be more than happy to cash," he said.

Caught up in the tempting images, I briefly forgot what I was doing until Silas blurted, "California, watch out. The pot's boiling over!"

I jumped out of his arms to see the milk and butter concoction boiling over the edge of the pot about to spill onto the floor. It brought me to my senses and the task at hand. Cooking.

I cleaned up the mess on the stove and turned my back to Silas again, trying to concentrate.

"I'm gonna put the mac and cheese in the fridge while I get these greens and yams going. How hungry are you?" I asked. Soul food took time to make.

"I'm not in any hurry. Especially now I see what you're making. I can't remember the last time someone cooked a good soul food dinner for me," he said.

"Happy to oblige," I said, then had a thought. "Do you know how to make candied yams?"

"No. They aren't part of my limited repertoire."

"Do you want to learn how? It's not that hard."

He looked like I'd asked him if he wanted to dumpster dive, freegan style.

"What?" I asked. "You don't believe in cooking?"

"Of course I believe in cooking as long as it's someone else doing it." He paused, then said, "Anyway, the kitchen isn't really where I do my best work."

I barked out a laugh. "You may as well have pointed to the bedroom and said, 'This is where the magic happens.' Cheesy."

He grinned down at me and said, "I know, but I wanted to see you laugh, so mission accomplished. And yes, I want to learn to make candied yams. I'll probably burn them, but I'm down to try."

"**D**o you have a peeler so we can start these potatoes?" Silas stared blankly around his kitchen, seeming to wait for the potato peeler to jump out at him.

"It's, uh…" His confused face was adorable. "It's in the drawer?"

I opened every drawer in the kitchen, and while there were screwdrivers, screws, a sock for some reason, and a variety of other things that didn't belong in a kitchen, there was no potato peeler.

"That's okay, we can use a knife." Shockingly, he had an expensive butcher block full of knives sitting on top of his counter. "Can you hand me the paring knife?"

He stared at the butcher block, reaching then pulling his empty hand back a couple times before I shook my head and reached around him to pull the proper knife out of the block.

Was it possible he really never cooked? Based on his lack of kitchen resources and knowledge, I'd believe it.

"Have you seriously never cooked in here?" I asked. How could he not cook? He was an adult that lived on his own, and eating out or having prepared meals got repetitive. At least it did for me. Plus, I couldn't imagine not cooking when for so long it had been my entire life. It was hard for me to imagine that everyone didn't love cooking or at least know how to do it. The spices, the smells, the creativity, and of course the finished product.

"I've never cooked anything that didn't come out of some kind of package. Why? Does that bother you?" he said and frowned.

"No, why would it bother me? I think it's weird, but it doesn't bother me," I said. "Okay, here's the paring knife. Have you ever taken the skin off of an apple in one go around?"

I crossed my fingers that he had because peeling a potato with a knife was risky, especially if you didn't want to end up with a trip to the ER.

"Oh yeah, my pop and I did that when I was a kid."

"Okay, it's the same basic idea," I told him, handing him the knife and the potato. "You just have to be a little more careful with potatoes because they're—"

"Shit!" he spit out. "How the hell do you do this without cutting yourself?"

A trickle of blood dripped down one hand, and he was trying to cover it with his other hand. Only the tiniest piece of skin was off the potato. How had he managed that? He'd barely even gotten started.

I handed him a paper towel. "Are you okay?" I asked.

"I'm cool. It's just a little cut."

I eyed him as he clutched his hand with the paper towel.

"Come here and let me rinse it off so we can see how deep it is." It didn't look like there was a lot of blood, but I'd found out the hard way sometimes deep cuts take a minute to really get bleeding.

He dragged his feet the few steps it took to get to the sink where I stood waiting with the water running.

"Put it under the sink so we can see if it's deep."

I waited by the sink, but he wouldn't let go of the towel.

"Silas?" I asked, hearing the concern in my voice. He was starting to look a little green. "Can you let go of the paper towel so I can see it?"

"I'm cool," he repeated. "I don't need to see it, but hey, do you mind if I sit down for a second? I'm feeling a little lightheaded." He was also breathing a little heavier than usual.

Lightheaded? Aside from that first trickle, it didn't seem to be bleeding all that much.

Silas stumbled, looking a little wobbly, as he made his way to the couch, and as soon as he sat down, he bent over putting his head between his knees. What was going on with him?

"Uh, Silas?" I sat next to him and put my hand on his back.

"I'm cool," he repeated for the third time even though it was clear he wasn't. His head was still between his knees, though his breathing had slowed. I couldn't believe it. Tall, manly man Silas was afraid of a little blood.

"Shit, Silas. Do you have hemophobia?"

"No. What's that?" he asked, starting to lift his head to talk to me.

"Hemophobia. Fear of blood. Because it seems like you might."

He turned and looked at me, embarrassment all over his face. "I wouldn't say it's a phobia, but I can't stand blood. Especially my own." He started to laugh a little. "I shouldn't even tell you this, but when I was in college, my roommate and I watched a horror movie. I think it was one of the *Saw* movies. Anyway, there was this scene where Jigsaw—" I stopped him.

"No need to describe the scene. I hate gory movies."

"Yeah, me too. Anyway, there was a ton of blood in the scene, and next thing I knew, my roommate was shaking me awake. The last thing I remember before fainting was getting up to go to the bathroom. Apparently, I got up and fell straight forward, barely missing the coffee table. He said it looked like a redwood going down." He shook his head like he couldn't believe himself. "The next thing I remember is him waking me up."

I felt terrible for him but also wanted to laugh and wasn't hiding it very well.

"It's all right, California. Go ahead and laugh. You know you want to."

I burst out laughing. "That's a terrible story, and I'm so glad you didn't hurt yourself, but it's hilarious."

"I know, I know. My roommate never let me live it down."

"I bet he didn't. I wouldn't have, either." I reached out for his hand. "Can I see the cut? I don't think it's bleeding anymore, but look away while I check it out."

Silas looked up at the ceiling while I peeled the paper towel off his hand. It wasn't a particularly deep cut, but it probably could use some Neosporin and a bandage.

"Do you have any Band-Aids?" I asked, covering it back up and walking to his bathroom. I looked under his sink but couldn't see any.

"Check the medicine cabinet. I think there are a couple in there."

I found the Band-Aids, but he didn't have any Neosporin, so I used a clean paper towel to wipe off the cut.

"You're good at this," he commented. "Were you a doctor or something in your before life?"

I didn't bother looking up when I said, "I used to be a cook. There were a lot of cuts in my previous line of work."

· · ·

"Ms. Alexander, I can't believe I've known you for over a month, and I didn't know you could throw down in the kitchen like that," Silas said, sprawled on his couch looking full and satisfied.

"There's a lot you don't know about me, Mr. Whitman. I'm full of surprises," I said.

"I don't doubt it," he said, sitting up and moving closer to me on the couch.

"Can I pour you some more wine?" I asked, comfortably full and wine happy.

Silas and I had already finished the first bottle of wine with dinner and started on a second one he had in the apartment. Miracle of miracles, it wasn't bad at all. I had assumed since he had so little food in his apartment and had asked me to pick out the wine in the grocery store that his alcohol selection would be questionable, but I was surprised to find he had more than a few decent bottles.

"Yeah, let's do it. It's Saturday night. We've earned a little fun."

I got up and poured him a glass of wine, then topped myself off and sat back down next to him.

"So I know you went here for undergrad, but how'd you end up in law school?" The more I spent time with Silas, the more I wanted to spend time with him and learn what made him tick.

"Ah, that's kind of a long, involved story," he said and took a sip of his wine. "Kind of a woe-is-me sob story if I'm being honest. Do you really want to hear it?"

"I do. We've got wine, and I've got time to spare tonight."

He took another sip of wine and set his glass down on the coffee table. "I was a business major in college, but I minored in creative writing and met my buddy Oliver in one of our poetry classes. I'd watched a little too much *Love Jones* and had some misplaced thoughts that maybe Darius Lovehall might be my kindred spirit."

I tried to imagine Silas in college on stage doing spoken word, and it kept flashing *does not compute.*

"I was terrible, but Oliver, he was impressive. Writing was his passion, and he lived and breathed it. But like a lot of artists, he went to some dark places when he worked and started drinking to combat his demons." He paused and took a deep breath.

"Anyway, we stayed friends after college, and one night after work, he and I went to get drinks and he drank a little more than he should have. I tried to take his keys but—" Silas shook his head at the memory. "He tried to drive home and ended up hitting another car. He didn't have any injuries, but the person he hit ended up paralyzed from the waist down. Oliver had a public defender, but the guy was too busy and couldn't really give his case the time it needed. Oliver ended up going to jail for several months, and he was never quite the same. Still hasn't really gotten his life back on track."

Silas looked heartbroken but determined. Wanting to offer some sort of comfort, I grasped his warm hand in mine, pulling it into my lap, and waited for him to finish.

"Anyway, even though he altered someone else's life course, his life was changed as well in no small part due to the fact that he didn't have adequate legal representation. Oliver was completely in the wrong—no question about it—but he also deserved his due process. After hearing what happened to him, I knew I wanted to be a better part of the justice system and help make change, so I came to law school."

I didn't know what to say, so I said nothing and instead leaned over and hugged him. He wrapped his arms around me, pulling me close, and we stayed that way for a long time. When I finally pulled back, he left his hand on the curve of my waist, absently rubbing up and down my side.

"I'm sorry that happened to your friend, but I'm glad people like you are here."

"Thanks," he said. "Sorry to be such a downer but—"

"Nothing to apologize for. I'm happy you shared with me."

Much like earlier in the kitchen, Silas's hand heated my body from top to bottom. He was barely touching me, but his light touch felt like a full-body caress, and I could barely stand it. On the one hand, I tried to remind myself that this was Silas for goodness' sake. He rarely shaved, had a T-shirt for every occasion, and his hair was about two inches past needing a haircut, even after he got haircuts. But god, he smelled good. Not cologne or body wash good. He smelled better. It was eau de Silas, and it was intoxicating. I swayed into him without thinking and breathed in his heady scent. I looked up at him and found him watching me, his gaze lazy but singularly focused on me. I couldn't help but stare back except when he lifted his hand and stroked my cheek, my eyes drifted closed as I sank into his hand. When I opened them again, he was right there, inches from my face.

"Simone?" he said, seeming to ask if this was okay, and it was more than okay. My brain might have shorted out because my thoughts were alternating between Silas's mouth and Silas's kiss on a loop.

I nodded, leaning in eager to close the inches between our lips, when a phone rang. I jerked back, not knowing if it was my phone or his, but feeling mostly annoyed at the interruption. Silas and I were about to kiss, and I wanted it to happen.

"Shit," he said. "I'm sorry, I need to take this. It's my mother, and she never calls. I need to make sure my dad's okay."

I nodded again and tried to shake myself out of my Silas haze.

"You go ahead and take it. I need to get home anyway. It's getting late and—"

His phone continued to ring, but he said, "Don't go. It should be quick, whatever she wants. Stay and I'll walk you home. Please?"

It was the "please" that almost did me in, but I needed to get out of there to think. Much as I wanted Silas, a part of me, a part that was increasing the more distance I had from our almost kiss, thought it was a bad idea. That dating him would be too disruptive.

"It's fine. Take your call and I'll talk to you tomorrow," I said as I headed to the door. "Thanks for the ride to the grocery store."

He stood there, phone in his hands, indecision etched all over his face. To make it easier on him, I waved goodbye and left before he could stop me.

CHAPTER NINE

"What's the deal with this weather?" I asked Tiffany as we left Criminal Law with Kevin and Silas. I knew she would be the only other person that understood fifty degrees was cold and anything colder than that was freezing.

"Ugh, I know," Tiffany commiserated.

"What do you mean?" Kevin said. "This is that good crisp fall weather everyone dreams about."

"Nightmare more like it," I muttered under my breath.

"You're always cold," Silas piped in. "What are you gonna do when it actually gets cold?"

"It's actually cold now. I don't even want to think about when it gets colder than this," I said, shuddering.

Kevin and Silas both laughed.

"But on the upside, we're about to get into cuffing season," Kevin said, giving a hasty wave to a blond girl I hadn't seen before.

I had learned a lot of new mid-western lingo like calling soda "pop" and saying "highway" rather than "freeway," but "cuffing season" was a new one for me.

"What's cuffing season?" I asked.

"It's what Kevin is right in the middle of working on with Sasha," Silas answered, nodding toward the girl Kevin had waved to. Neither of the boys bothered to explain any further, just chuckled amongst themselves.

Still out of the loop, I glanced over at Tiffany to see if she knew what he was talking about. She was paying no attention to the conversation because Rafael had walked up and she was in deep flirt mode with him, lip licking and all. She was pulling out the big guns and wasn't going to be any help. She'd mentioned a couple of weeks before that she thought he was cute, but I hadn't heard anything else about it. In fact, a couple of days ago she had mentioned that she was still doing the dirty with one of the future politicians. That definitely wasn't Rafael with his nose ring, man bun, and save-the-world rhetoric. I made a mental note to remind myself to ask her about that later.

"All right, I give. What's cuffing season?"

Silas slipped his arm around my shoulders before answering. "Cuffing season is the time between October and March when people start to pair off to make sure they have someone to keep them warm and keep them company during the winter months."

"Shut up, that's not a real thing," I said, swinging around to face Silas. My abrupt movement knocked his arm from around my shoulder.

"It is!" Kevin said, jumping in. "That's why I haven't had as much time to hang out with you guys. I've only got a couple more weeks before cuffing season is in full swing, and I need to snap someone up."

Kevin was out of his mind.

Rafael had wandered off, and Tiffany had gotten back into the conversation.

"Girl, I can't believe you haven't heard of cuffing season," she exclaimed. "I'm from California, too, and I've heard of it." She then lowered her voice to a whisper and said, "I'm in the middle of trying to lock someone down for winter."

"Who, Pierce?" I asked.

"Oh no, I can't stand Pierce. He's just scratching an itch for the time being. Whoever I decide to lock down for cuffing season has to be someone I actually like. I can't talk to Pierce for longer than five minutes without wanting to punch him in his fucking face."

Guess that answered my question.

I didn't know what invisible force dragged the question out of me, but before I could stop myself, I asked Silas, "What about you? Do you have someone locked down?"

I held my breath, waiting.

It had been a few days since our almost-kiss, and he hadn't said anything about it or tried to replicate the situation. When I got home that night, I'd received a text from him thanking me for dinner and mentioning wanting to finish what we started.

He trained his eyes on me. "I've got someone in mind, but I'm taking it slow. I want her for more than just cuffing season, you know?"

Out of the corner of my eye, I saw Kevin and Tiffany elbowing each other and laughing. What were they, twelve?

"So then what happens after cuffing season?" I asked in an attempt to, well, not change the subject exactly, but at least get on some stable footing.

"Nothing, unless you really like your cuffing partner."

"So, you just break up with them?" I asked, bewildered at the idea of spending five months getting close to someone and then just dumping them because the weather was better.

"I mean, you don't have to. You can keep dating your cuffing partner if you want, but if you don't really like them all that much, you can just break up, no harm no foul," Kevin explained like he couldn't believe I was so naive.

"So do you have anyone in mind for cuffing season?" Tiffany asked me, smirking.

I definitely had someone in mind. If I was being honest with myself, I wanted Silas and for much more than cuffing season, but since we hadn't talked about anything, I was hesitant to admit to it. Especially in front of this chatty crew.

"I will be deep in cuffing season with my Contracts book. His red cover and taupe pages will keep me good and toasty this winter," I said, side-stepping her question.

Tiffany put her arm around me and said, "Oh, we can do better than that. There's some cuties in our class, don't you think?"

"And that's my cue to leave," Kevin said, peeling off from the group to head toward the library. Silas followed him, throwing a wave over his shoulder to me and Tiffany.

"When finals are over, we're going to Detroit, and we'll have a real girls' night. Leave these lame-ass dudes at home to twiddle their fucking thumbs. All right?"

"I'm down. I just need to get through midterms. Have you started studying yet?" I asked, nervous to hear Tiffany's answer. Tiffany was the kind of person that bought Christmas wrapping paper in July. She always had a notebook full of lists that she checked off every day and was so on top of things, I was sure she had started studying already. I, on the other hand, always ended up with the $0.99 paper from Walgreens that always ripped when you tried to cut it.

"Nothing too crazy. I've just been reviewing the outlines for a couple classes. I haven't started studying for real just yet," Tiffany answered as we walked toward our Legal Writing class. Legal Writing was the one class that we didn't have with everyone in our section, so me and Tiffany were in one class, but Silas and the others were split between the other two classes.

We rounded the corner to get to the section of the building by the smaller classrooms. Usually, the only people that used the rooms were 1Ls for their Legal Writing class or to study when they didn't want to go to the library. Tiffany and I weren't quite late, three more minutes and we would have been, but the hallways had started to empty out, giving us an almost completely clear path to our classroom. We hustled our way through the few folks still milling around the hallway, and right before I made it into class, I felt my wheelie bag hit something. I looked down, and in my haste to get my ass into a seat before class started, I had slammed into someone's ankle.

Silas teased me mercilessly about my wheelie bag. The first time he'd seen it, he had asked, concerned, if I had back problems. When I told him no, he took that as carte blanche to begin open warfare about the bag. Anytime we were in an elevator together, he would clear the way, making sure no one got run over by the wheels. He preferred to take the stairs, he said it helped him stay fit, but knowing I hated carrying the wheelie bag, he always took the elevator with me. If by some chance we got stuck taking the stairs, he would scoop the bag out of my hands, like he did that first day he picked me up, and spin the wheels while we walked up the stairs. He also regularly asked if I was really twenty-six because only people over the age of fifty pulled their bags instead of carrying them. "It's possible," he joked, "that you could actually be fifty-five and we'd never know. You know Black don't crack." At his comment about my age, I tapped his leg gently with the bag, and he'd squealed like I'd poked him with a sharp stick.

"Dammit, California, that shit hurts. Better be glad you tried it on me first. Watch out you don't roll over some stranger's foot. You know that's a lawsuit waiting to happen."

With Silas's voice in my head warning of an imaginary lawsuit, I gently panicked and immediately started apologizing. "Oh shit, I'm so sorry. Are you okay?" I looked down at the person's ankles I had hit, trying to make sure there wasn't any blood. My wheelie bag had been known to cause serious damage, though mostly to myself. The person's ankles were bare from pants that were a hair too short. The look was almost too trendy. Seeing no blood, I looked up, wondering whose ankles I'd nearly mangled, and came face-to-neck with Keith. I was about to say hi to him when Tiffany whispered loudly in my ear, "Cuffing season," before darting into class. Ugh, I could kill that girl.

"What did she say?" Keith asked, watching Tiffany as she left.

"Nothing. She's just being silly. It's good to see you."

"It's good to see you, too. I was hoping I would run into you."

He was?

"You were?" I said.

"Yeah. I didn't get a chance to ask you for your number after the bar, and when I asked Silas for it, he hemmed and hawed about it saying he wasn't sure you would appreciate him giving out your number."

Silas was right there. I loathed when people shared my phone number without asking me about it first. Except, in Keith's case, before the other night with Silas at least, I might not have minded so much.

"So, can I get your number?" he asked.

Any other time, I would have given Keith my number without a second thought, but I wanted to see if anything came from the other night with Silas. It seemed like there might be something there. Then again, he had had all weekend to say something about it and he hadn't. Maybe I had read the situation wrong and he was looking for a friends-with-benefits kind of thing, but when he had shared the story about Oliver, it felt like he was opening up to me in a more-than-friendly way.

Ugh, why was this confusing?

"Why don't you give me your phone number instead?" I asked, feeling extremely proud of my workaround. This way, I could decide if or when I wanted to talk to Keith.

"Yeah, all right, that works," Keith said and rattled off the digits. "Call me, pretty girl. I'd like to take you out sometime."

He moved a step closer and put out his arms to give me a hug. I was about to walk into them when I heard someone say, "What's up, Keith? What are you doing in the law school building? Aren't you supposed to be in the business school on Tuesdays?"

Recognizing that voice was becoming second nature. I stepped back, away from Keith, and turned to see Silas loping down the hall.

"Nothing, man, just coming to grab a book and I ran into Simone."

"Well, where's the book?" Silas asked, irritation evident in his voice.

"I ran into Simone first, and I haven't had a chance to grab it yet," Keith replied, looking at Silas like he was out of his mind. "What's your problem, man?"

"Nothing. Let me walk with you to grab it," Silas said. "Simone's about to be late for class."

I looked down at my phone, and he was right.

"Shoot, thanks, Silas. I gotta run. I'll talk to you guys later," I said and hurried down the hall, happy for any reason to get out of that situation.

As I walked to class, I glanced back to see Silas moving down the hall with Keith. He looked back one time and held my gaze before I turned and opened the door to the classroom.

"Whoa, were you sitting on top of your phone?" I said when Silas answered his phone after one ring.

He chuckled. "Kind of. I tried to call you yesterday after I ran into you and Keith, but you didn't pick up. I wanted to talk to you. Are you busy right now?"

"Not really, I'm just sitting here trying to read for Contracts tomorrow. That's why I called you. Have you read *Hadley* yet?"

"Not yet, but it's on my list. I'll read it later unless you want to get together to read and discuss it? We could grab a bite when we're finished working. There's a chill little Italian spot in Lansing I want to try. You want to check it out with me?"

"What? Like a date?" I said, feeling emboldened.

"Yeah, like a date. I'll pay for it and everything."

"You don't have to pay for me. I'm perfectly capable of paying for myself."

I wasn't. I was broke as hell, but he didn't need to know that.

"I know I don't *have to*, but I want to," Silas said. "Let me treat you. We'll study this afternoon and then go out to dinner. It'll be fun."

Studying didn't sound amazing, but dinner with Silas did.

"That all sounds phenomenal, except for the studying part," I told him honestly. "Where do you want to study? And please don't say the library. You know I can't study there. It's too quiet."

"Why yes, Simone, it's very quiet because. It's. A. Library!"

I sighed into the phone. "Thank you, Silas, I'm aware that's the point of the library. I just can't study in complete silence like that. Why don't you come over here?"

"Yeah, all right. That works. I'll see you in about an hour."

I looked down at my clothes, debating whether to change into something nicer. On the one hand, we were studying, and I didn't want to look like I was trying too hard. On the other, it was Silas, and I wanted to look good for him. Fighting hard against my base desire to impress him, I opted to leave on the purple short shorts and CAL Berkeley sweatshirt I had been wearing all morning. I groomed a little, though. I didn't want him to think I was completely disgusting.

I ran a hand and some shea butter through my curls and was in the middle of brushing my teeth when Silas knocked on my door an hour and a half later. I answered and was stopped in my tracks by his appearance. He looked good. Really good.

"What took you so long and why are you dressed like that? Aren't we studying here?"

He looked down at his clothes, then back at me. "Dressed like what?"

"Like that!" I sputtered as I waved my hand up and down his broad-shouldered figure taking up most of the space in my doorway.

Silas looked more put together than he ever did in class or anywhere else, for that matter, and I liked what I saw. He wore a gray sweater that complemented his green eyes and jeans that didn't look like they were on their fifth week of wear, and his usually floppy mop of hair was tamed with gel or something. Dammit, I knew I should have changed into something nicer.

"I didn't know if I would have time to change before dinner, so I just put on what I planned to wear out later. Stop being weird and let's go study. I brought snacks." I kept staring at him and had the distinct feeling my mouth was hanging open. He really did look sexy. Seeming unnerved at my assessment, Silas pushed past me into my apartment and sat down on the couch. It was weird having him in my apartment. I mean, it was bizarre having anyone in my apartment because I hadn't had time to invite anyone over, but it was especially bizarre having him here. Back at home I had people over to my place regularly. I loved hosting dinner parties and game nights, and my family came over once a month for Sunday dinner. Not having that close interaction here felt strange, but I liked having Silas in my space.

"Why are you staring at me like that?" he asked. I hadn't realized I was still staring at Silas until he pointed it out.

"You just—you clean up so well. Usually you look like you just climbed out of bed and came to class."

He rolled his eyes and propped his feet on the coffee table. "Whatever. Get your book so we can study."

For the next four hours, we trudged through our readings for Contracts and Criminal Law, then methodically briefed each of the six cases assigned to us for the classes. Having Silas there to discuss *Hadley* helped tremendously with understanding the case. When we finally took a break at four, I had a handle on the particulars of each of the cases for Contracts and wasn't too worried about having to brief it the next day as long as I could do one last review before class. Finally, the facts made sense, and I understood the main issue and rule of law. I put my Contracts book on the floor next to me and rested my head on the back of the couch, happy to get a break. After working with Silas for the past four hours, I saw how he did his readings so quickly. He didn't believe in taking breaks until absolutely necessary and he read extremely fast. In the time it took me to read one case, he was finished reading and had already started briefing the case.

"I'm tired and hungry," I announced. The snacks Silas brought over had disappeared hours ago. The Cool Ranch Doritos, Rock n' Rye Faygo, and Oreos were fattening and delicious. I hadn't eaten a Cool Ranch Dorito since I was in elementary school, and I had forgotten how addictive they were.

Silas looked over at me and smirked. "I knew you'd be hungry. Get dressed and let's go. We have a seven thirty reservation."

CHAPTER TEN

"**W**hy did we need to leave so early for a seven thirty reservation?" I asked when we got in the car. Silas had insisted we leave at five thirty when Lansing was only like a ten-minute drive from our apartment complex.

"I wanted to show you something real quick before dinner," Silas said. "You seem a little stressed, and this place always calms me down."

I couldn't imagine Silas being stressed about anything. He was always so relaxed, even when he was annoying as hell in class. He never seemed to be fussed about the normal shit that had everyone else, me included, on edge.

"That's why I come here when I need to mellow out. I don't usually tell folks about my spot, but there's someone I wanted to introduce to you."

Who would Silas want to introduce me to? Clearly it was too early to meet his family. Maybe his friends from college? More childhood friends? I didn't know if I was ready to meet them, either. One almost kiss definitely didn't qualify for friend-meeting status. Not yet, at least. The last time I'd met a boyfriend's friends, they were the ultimate assholes and were part of the reason we broke up. Well, that and the fact that he was thirty and lived in his mother's basement, but it was definitely a combination of those two things.

"Who do you want me to meet?" I asked, suddenly nervous.

"Do you trust me?" Silas asked with a smirk on his face.

I trusted Silas, but the smirk taking up his face made me wonder if I maybe shouldn't.

I hesitated, then said, "Yeah, I guess. Should I?"

He flashed a smile and winked at me.

About ten minutes later, Silas slowed down and turned onto a narrow dirt road, then put his truck into park.

"You ready?" he asked.

If walking around in dirt was involved, then no, I wasn't ready. Especially not when I was wearing my cutest stilettos.

"Nope, not at all. What are we doing here?" I looked around and saw a giant barn down the road. "Are we at a farm?"

The barn was weathered, making the wood look gray and discolored, but instead of it seeming run down, it was charming. The sort of place someone who wanted a boho chic wedding would pay thousands to rent in Sonoma.

"I wouldn't call it a farm, city girl, but there are a few animals here," he said as he rested his hand on the small of my back and nudged me forward. "You can't walk out here in those shoes, though. There should be a few pairs of boots in the barn. What size do you wear?"

"An eight and a half."

He swung out of the car, and I admired him walking down the dirt road, appreciating how sturdy and solid he looked. When he ducked into the barn, I looked away to take in more of my surroundings. Tucked off to the side of the barn stood a light blue farmhouse. Like the barn, the house looked weathered, but unlike the barn, the house was rundown. Not offensively so, but a good power wash and coat of paint would have done wonders to the little structure.

"Here," Silas said, returning to the truck and handing me a hideous pair of black rubber boots through my window. "Put these on." He pulled a pair of thick socks out of his back pocket and stuck those out as well. "These too."

I obliged, mostly out of curiosity.

"Does the person I'm meeting live in that house?" I asked him. I changed out of the stilettos and pulled on the socks, then the boots he'd handed me. They were a hair too big.

"Nope. The house is empty. Has been for years."

"Whose house is it?" I asked as I swung my legs out of the door and met Silas in front of the truck. Since the boots were a little too big for me, I had trouble keeping up with his brisk gait. As I half jogged next to him as we neared the barn, it finally clicked.

"Uh, Silas, does the person I'm meeting have fur?"

He grinned at me and grabbed my arm, pulling me into the barn. "I wouldn't call it a person and I wouldn't say it had fur. Hair is a better description for Jackson."

Silas stopped at the barn and shoved the heavy door aside. On either side of the barn were large stalls holding several horses.

"Holy shit, Silas. They're beautiful," I said, then sneezed.

"I know," he said and grabbed my hand. "Come on, I want you to meet Jackson."

We walked to the back of the barn, and in the very last stall was a chestnut brown horse sticking his head out waiting for us.

"Hey, buddy, I missed you," Silas said, approaching the horse with his hand out.

The horse whinnied and nudged at Silas's outstretched hand. Silas dug around his pocket for a second before producing a carrot I didn't know he was hiding. The horse nabbed it from his hand as Silas stroked his nose.

"Jackson, there's someone I want you to meet," he said, pulling me closer to the horse.

"Wow, can I pet him?" I asked.

Silas nodded, and I reached out to rub Jackson's nose. He was so soft and didn't seem to mind me petting him at all.

"Whose horse is he?" I asked, then sneezed again.

Silas looked at me curiously and said, "Mine. Why else would we be here?"

"Yours?'" I said, rubbing my eyes. "I didn't know you rode horses. You never mentioned it."

"Yeah, I've been riding since I was little," he explained. "Before Papa moved up here to help Dad raise me, he lived on a little sugarcane farm in Louisiana. They had a couple horses, some pigs, and a few goats. Nothing big, but the horses were always my favorite. Papa swore I was born in a saddle."

I smiled at the sweet story, then blanched when I realized what he'd said. Did he expect me to ride Jackson?

"So," I said, absently petting Jackson's nose, "you come out here to ride."

"Yeah. I try to come out a couple times a week. I wish I could come more, but I can barely find time to sleep most days."

I knew the feeling well. River and I still hadn't connected since our schedules never seemed to align. I hadn't even had a chance to fill her in on what almost happened with Silas.

"And you brought me out here because...?"

"We're gonna ride, California. You ever been on a horse?"

I had been on a horse a total of once. And I wasn't even sure you could technically call it a horse or really even riding since I was two at the time and it had been a pony for Beckett's birthday.

"Depends on how you define horse," I said, knowing full

well I was stalling.

Silas waved his arm around the barn. "If they looked like these guys, then you've been horseback riding. Anything else doesn't count."

I sneezed and rubbed my eyes again. Something in the barn had my allergies going hard.

"Well, then, I've never ridden a horse and it doesn't look like I'll be starting today." I scratched my increasingly itchy nose and gestured down my body. "I'm wearing a dress."

"Haven't you ever heard of riding sidesaddle?" Silas said, looking completely serious.

I gaped at him, trying to decipher if he was joking or not.

His face broke into a grin, and he laughed. "I'm fucking with you, Simone. If you want to ride, I can grab you some clothes from inside. If you don't, no big deal."

I wanted to impress Silas, but horses were big. And fidgety.

Silas stopped petting Jackson and wrapped his arm around my shoulders, giving me a squeeze.

"Take a chance. You might like it." I got the distinct impression he was talking about more than horseback riding.

He was right. I needed to be brave.

"Get me the clothes," I told him before I changed my mind. I figured I could put them on over my dress.

He grinned. "I'll be right back."

I wondered whose house this was that he felt comfortable enough to go in with such ease.

"Jackson," I said, stroking the horse, "whose barn do you live in?"

He whinnied in response. Too bad I didn't speak horse.

"Here's some sweats and a sweater," he announced, walking toward me. Stopping in front of me, he asked, "Do you want to change in the car?"

"I'm good. I'll throw them on over my dress."

"You sure?" he asked.

I pulled the sweater over my head and shoved my arms through the holes, then shimmied the sweats over the boots and up my legs, hiking my dress up along the way. In no way did I think it was sexy, but when I looked up at Silas, his heavy-lidded gaze was fixed on my legs.

"What?" I asked.

"Nothing. Just enjoying the view," he admitted.

I blushed, suddenly nervous. "Yeah, right. Let's get this over with." I tried to walk out of the barn, but Silas grabbed my arm and pulled me back to him.

"We don't have to do this if you don't want to. We can give her another carrot and go to dinner." He paused, then continued, "But I wanted to share this with you. I don't bring too many people out here, but I wanted you to meet my girl."

"Wait, what? Jackson's a girl?" I asked, stunned. "Why's her name Jackson?"

"Because that's what I named her."

"Thank you, smart-ass," I said, and he chuckled. "Why'd you name your girl horse Jackson?"

Silas pulled out his phone and typed in a few words. A second later, Outkast blared from the speakers.

"Outkast was my favorite group for a long time, and when Dad and Papa took me to pick her up, the song 'Ms. Jackson' was playing on the radio," Silas explained without any guile. "It seemed to fit her, so it stuck."

Everything about the story screamed Silas.

"Well, all right, Ms. Jackson," I said, addressing his horse. "I'm ready."

Silas opened the stall door and slipped a lead over Jackson's neck, then led her out of the stall and looped her lead to the side of the barn to get her saddled. When her saddle was properly fitted, he led out a stunning white horse with black spots, like the horse version of a Dalmatian.

Pushing a bale of hay over to where Jackson stood, Silas said, "You're going to step on this, put one foot in the stirrup, then swing your other leg over the saddle. She's gentle. She'll stand still for you."

I was dubious. Jackson was a whole lot bigger than that pony I remembered, and even though Silas swore she was gentle, there was no doubt if she decided to buck me off of her, I would be a goner. I stood next to her, rubbing her side and trying to psych myself up for riding. Aside from the fact that I was scared, I couldn't stop sneezing. Every time I stepped near Jackson, my eyes watered, my nose ran, and the sneezing started again. Was I allergic to horses and didn't know it?

"And you're going to ride right next to me?" I asked.

He nodded. "I promise, I'll be right next to you on Suzette. Scout's honor," he said, holding up the Scout's salute.

"Were you a Boy Scout?"

"Do I seem like the Boy Scout type?"

He absolutely did not.

"So the Scout's honor means nothing is what you're telling me?"

Silas laughed. "It doesn't mean shit to me, but the Silas honor does, so get on Jackson and I promise I'll be right next to you, all right?"

I nodded. Silas's honor I trusted.

I scooted a little closer to Jackson and stuck my foot in the stirrup, but when I swung my leg over her back, I misjudged how much power I needed and the next thing I knew I was lying ass-first in the pile of hay next to Jackson.

"Shit, Simone, are you okay?" Silas ran around in front of

Jackson to her other side to check on me.

"Nothing's hurt but my pride. Good thing hay is so soft," I said, sneezing three times in a row and trying to pick hay out of my hair.

Confident I was fine, Silas started to laugh. "Girl, you went over that horse like a sack of potatoes."

He looked at me a little closer and, laughing still, rubbed at his nose. "You've got a little something there."

I touched my nose and to my horror it was completely wet with snot. Gross.

Silas reached into his pocket and handed me some paper towel. "It's clean," he said.

I wiped my nose and hands and tried to shake off the embarrassment.

I was still sitting in the hay, figuring out how to make myself disappear, when Silas offered me his hand to help me up. "You sure you're okay?"

"I'm good, physically. My pride's just emotionally wounded. No big deal. Let me try it again," I said, starting to walk behind Jackson.

"Whoa, whoa, whoa," he said, stopping me with a hand on my waist. "Never walk behind a horse. Even one as gentle as Jackson. Something could spook her, and you don't want to be on the business end of a kick."

Keeping his arm around my waist, Silas guided me in front of Jackson and back to her side.

"All right, this time I'll give you a boost when you put your foot in the stirrup. Ready?"

I wasn't, but I put my foot in the stirrup anyway. When I did, I felt Silas's hands cup my ass and push upward until I was fully seated in the saddle.

"Now hold onto the reins while I hop on Suzette."

I pet Jackson's neck while we waited for Silas to join us. Being on horseback wasn't too bad at all, and Silas was right, Jackson was very sweet.

I was rubbing my eyes when Silas and his horse sidled up next to me and said, "You've been rubbing your eyes and sneezing kind of a lot. Are you allergic to horses?"

"I don't know, maybe. It's too late now, though, so let's go. What do I do to make her go?"

"Right, I forgot you don't do this," he said.

I guess my being ankles over ass didn't jog his memory about my lack of horse-riding skills.

"Hold the reins firmly but loosely in your hands, and when you want her to walk, give a gentle squeeze with your legs. That will get her going, but if all else fails, she'll follow Suzette since I'm riding her."

I banked on the second half of his statement being true because the first half meant almost nothing to me.

"I'm ready. Stop gawking at me and lead the way," I told Silas.

He rolled his eyes and gave Suzette a squeeze with his legs, quickly releasing them. When she started walking, I did the same with Jackson, and she followed behind them.

"Hey, I did it!" I said, excited about my newest feat. "I'm riding a horse!"

Silas chuckled. "We'll do a quick loop around the property, then we can head to dinner. It should only take about half an hour or so."

· · ·

"This isn't nearly as bad as I thought it would be," I told Silas after we'd been riding for a while. "It's peaceful."

"You think I'd take you to do something you'd hate? Give me a little credit here," Silas shot back.

"Fair point," I responded, taking in the scenery around me. The grounds were stunning. Everything was meticulously manicured, and I now saw why Silas said it wasn't a farm. The only evidence of farming was the myriad animals popping up every few feet. So far I'd seen several goats, a few cows, something that appeared to be a llama but that Silas said was an alpaca, and one cat that had taken to following the horses.

"By the way, who lives here, Silas? You never did tell me whose place we were at."

When Silas didn't answer immediately, I glanced over to see if he'd heard me. Since he was looking directly at me, I figured he had. But he still didn't say anything.

"Uh, Silas?"

"Yeah, yeah, sorry, California. It's, uh, it's actually Papa's place. Or it used to be at least."

I must have looked shocked because Silas said, "What?"

"This place was your great-grandfather's house? It's amazing. Who lives here now?" I asked.

"No one, really. It's been more or less empty since he died. There's a staff that takes care of the animals, and I do when I'm here, but the house itself stays empty."

"I can't believe you have this beautiful place and choose to live in our shitty apartments. What were you thinking?"

"I'm thinking it would be awfully lonely to live out here in my dead great-grandfather's house. But I don't want to talk about this anymore. Tell me something about you. How come you never mentioned that you were a chef until the other night?"

Of course he'd want to know about my past.

"I was a chef, it didn't work out, and now I'm in law school. It's a tale as old as time," I quipped, really wanting to avoid the topic.

"It's really not. How did you go from chef to future lawyer? That's not the most typical transition."

I knew it wasn't, but I hadn't talked much about what happened with anyone, so I didn't say anything, hoping he would forget he even asked the question.

He didn't. Instead, he said, "C'mon, California, I'm just trying to get to know you. That's all. No judgment, just curiosity about the woman I've been spending time with, okay?"

I sighed and nodded. I still didn't want to get into the whole embarrassing story, but I gave him the truncated version. "Basically, I was working at a high-end restaurant and accidentally did something to piss off my boss. He lit into me, and I quit."

When I explained it that way, it sounded flighty, but it was close enough to the truth.

"Just like that, you quit?" he asked, disbelief evident in his voice.

"More or less. And when I realized I didn't want to go back to cooking, law school seemed like a good idea and now we're here."

The horses stopped at a small grassy patch and snacked on a few dandelions.

"Sounds rough. You think you made the right decision?"

"I don't know," I told him honestly. "It was a spur-of-the-moment decision, and I didn't have a lot of time to process it before I needed to start applying. Once the machine started, it took on a life of its own. I'm not sure I've even fully processed it yet, but ask me again next semester."

Silas nodded and pulled his phone out of his pocket. "We should probably get going to make sure we're on time for our reservation."

CHAPTER ELEVEN

I was grateful when we pulled up to the restaurant and Silas stopped at the valet stand instead of hunting for a parking spot. My shoes were perfectly walkable, but I was tired from riding and starving. I didn't want to wait any longer to eat than I had to.

Judging by the way the other patrons looked as they stepped out of their cars, and the way Silas had shown up at my door dressed, I was glad I decided to dress up a little. Somehow Silas had managed to keep his clothes impeccable while we rode. I was just happy I'd been able to cover my dress since it would have been destroyed when I took that dive into the hay. I wanted to look good going out with Silas. It was our first real date, and I wanted to show off. I wore my favorite long-sleeve purple dress that dipped low in the back and hit mid-thigh and a pair of silver shoes I had splurged on when I got my first check at Ipsa's. Even though the outfit was a little over the top, I felt good in it.

Before the valet could help me out of the giant truck, Silas jumped out and high-tailed it to my side to open the door. The young, ginger-haired valet looked a little put out, but I loved being the recipient of Silas's gallant deed.

"You ready to see what all the hype is about?" Silas tucked

my arm into his, and we strode arm in arm into the restaurant.

Silas's description of the restaurant was mostly inaccurate. While the decor and name hinted at the fact that the restaurant was Italian and it was indeed small, there was nothing that appeared chill about it. It was very classy.

"Good evening. Do you have a reservation?" the host asked.

Silas looked a little nervous in a way he hadn't at the farm and was fidgeting slightly as he said, "Yes, we have a seven thirty reservation under Whitman."

The host scanned her list on the computer.

"Yes, Mr. Whitman. We have your table by the window ready." She grabbed two menus. "Please, follow me."

She led us through the dimly lit main dining area. Each of the twenty tables we passed held a vase of fresh lilies and lit tea candles atop the white tablecloth, along with couples of various ages holding hands across the tables or feeding each other small bites of food.

"Here we are, Mr. Whitman. No flowers as you requested." The host had led us through the main restaurant into a smaller back room with even fewer tables. Our table was by a window that faced the garden outside. Like the other tables in the restaurant, it held the tea candles, but instead of lilies, our table was free of flowers.

"Thank you." Silas looked from the host over to me. "That day Tiffany got those flowers for her birthday, I noticed you couldn't stop sneezing, and I didn't want you snotting your way through dinner." He paused. "But I wish I'd known you were allergic to horses."

"Um, first I wouldn't have been snotting my way through dinner. I'd be sneezing like a lady and daintily wiping my nose with a hankie," I said. "Second, thank you. I appreciate the sweet gesture."

Silas cracked up and seemed to relax a little. "There was absolutely nothing ladylike about those big horse sneezes at the barn. A couple times I thought it was Jackson," he joked.

The host pulled out my chair and when I was seated placed my napkin in my lap and the menu in front of me. She did the same for Silas.

"Your waiter will be here shortly. Have a good evening, Mr. Whitman."

Silas nodded a quick thank-you at the host before she walked away.

"This place is fancy. Reminds me a little of Ipsa's. How did you find it?"

Silas shrugged and looked away from me. "I passed it a couple times on my way to the mall and thought it looked good."

Other than the line of cars, the restaurant was nondescript from the outside. There was nothing really to indicate the restaurant would be particularly good or elegant on the inside, so I was surprised Silas even noticed it let alone drove by and wanted to try it. It was probably the line of cars that had piqued his curiosity.

I perused the menu, noting both the items and the prices. "It *does* look delicious, but it's so expensive. Are you sure this is where you want to eat tonight? I really, really can't afford anywhere this nice."

"Simone, I told you, tonight is on me. It's a date. I said I wanted to take you out, so let me take you out."

"All right, fine, I'll shut up about it."

"Thank you. Let's relax a little and enjoy dinner. We'll be back on the grind tomorrow, so we might as well relax tonight," he said and settled back into his chair. "You feel like you're ready for your grilling?"

"I do, thanks in part to you. Discussing the case one-on-one outside of our study group helped a lot."

"Good," he said and handed me the wine menu the waiter had left on the table. "Do you want some wine? I checked out the menu on my phone while you were getting dressed and some of the reds look really nice. Are you good with a red?"

I nodded yes to the wine and gaped at Silas until the waiter came to take our drink order.

"We'll do a bottle of the Cabernet Franc," Silas told the waiter with no hesitation. I was dumbfounded at Silas taking control like that. He was so nonchalant about most things, but this in-charge Silas was dead sexy. But it was perplexing how he suddenly knew about wines. Cabernet Franc was not the most common wine out there, and yet he asked for it specifically.

The waiter asked if we were ready to order.

"We're not quite ready yet," Silas told her. "Can you give us a few?"

"Certainly, sir. I'll be back shortly with your wine."

Silas had ordered us a very spendy bottle of wine.

"All right, dude, what gives?"

Silas furrowed his eyebrows and asked, "What are you talking about?"

"We're broke law students but somehow we're at this pricey restaurant and you ordered that expensive bottle of wine. Are you secretly Magic-Miking on the side? Oh God, is that why you were worried about your boxers being in the kitchen? I know you don't have a regular job, so what's with the heavy spend?"

"The wine's not that expensive, and I told you already, I've been wanting to try the food here. What's your issue?"

"Yes, but how can you *afford* it here? Student loans

definitely don't give us enough for this, so how are you paying? Is this a trick? Are we going to dine and dash?"

Silas frowned and crossed his arms over his chest. "Thanks for the vote of confidence. Are you always this neurotic on dates?"

I could tell Silas was getting irritated, but my curiosity was getting the better of me and I couldn't help myself. The average entrée on the menu was not cheap, and while I went to these kinds of restaurants when I had a full-time job, usually as part of my job, I sure as hell couldn't afford La Pergola or anywhere like it right now.

"Yes, actually, but that's not the point."

Silas sighed, exasperated. "Why would I take you out somewhere I couldn't afford? Simone, I told you the other night I had a grown-ass man job before I started law school. I'm thirty-two years old. You're a broke law student. I'm not. I'm doing just fine. Paying for school out of my own pocket and everything. Do you have any more questions?"

Welp. I officially felt an inch tall.

"I'm sorry," I said. "I'm just nervous, but that's no excuse." I had forgotten that he'd had a job before law school, but it must have paid a ton more than my cooking job did because I had exactly no dollars in the way of savings and relied almost completely on student loans. River, and everyone else who knew me, told me when I climbed the ladder of inference I scaled the whole thing, and this conversation proved their point much as I hated to admit it.

Silas's face softened at my admission, and he stretched across the table to grasp one of my hands in his. It was rare that I felt small, but his big hand dwarfed mine. The nerves he seemed to be feeling when we got here had vanished or else they had transferred over to me. He stroked his thumb up and down the back of my hand, and my tension began to ease. This was Silas. There was no reason to be nervous with him. The wine arrived before I could say or do anything else offensive, and Silas was right: the wine was perfection. After a few sips of the rich, peppery liquid, I calmed down enough to have a real conversation.

"So tell me more about this grown-ass man job you had before you came to law school?"

"Like I said the other night, I worked in management consulting for seven years."

I felt silly having asked him all those questions about how he could afford the restaurant when I had completely forgotten he'd had a full-on, well-paying job before he came here.

"Did you like it?"

"I didn't hate it. I made a shit-ton of money and was able to do all of the things I needed to do and most everything I wanted when I had time," he responded, then proceed to tell me about the ins and outs of management consulting, which would have been boring coming from anyone but Silas. He managed to make it sound intriguing.

After two glasses of wine and way too many courses of food, I was not only relaxed, I was near catatonic. I yawned when the waiter brought the bill to our table. Without fanfare or much acknowledgment, Silas grabbed the bill and slipped a card into the leather holder.

"Can I get the tip?"

Silas shook his head. "No, stop it. I said I was taking you to dinner, so I'm taking you to dinner. That means tip and all, and if you let me, I'd like to do it again."

I blushed knowing I would love for Silas to take me out again.

• • •

S ilas got his card back from the waiter, and we walked to
the valet stand to wait for his truck to be brought around.
It seemed like the valet was taking forever, and I was freezing.
I shivered against the wind and mentally prayed for the valet to
hurry. I hadn't brought a jacket and felt awkward asking Silas
if I could borrow his. Instead, I moved a little closer to him in
the hopes that I would absorb some of his heat. He grew up in
this absurd weather and it didn't seem to be affecting him at
all. It could also be that he had the good sense to wear a coat
and I had clearly left my good sense back in Oakland. Silas
must have felt my body shaking because he edged closer to me.

"You cold?" he asked.

"Freezing."

Instead of removing his jacket and putting it around me
like I thought he would, he pulled me to him and wrapped
both of his arms around me, tucking me into his jacket.

"Better?"

It was better. Much, much better. His arms were a steel
band around my waist, and I felt his biceps flexing as he
tightened his grip around me. I leaned my head into his chest
and sighed.

"You feel great."

I felt his soft laughter more than heard it. "Oh, yeah?"

I nodded against his chest. "I'm thinking about taking up
permanent residency here. Do you mind?"

The valet pulled up with his truck before Silas had a
chance to respond. The valet opened my door, and I quickly
climbed inside before Silas had a chance to come around and
help me. It was probably better that he not touch me at this
precise moment. I didn't want to accidentally haul off and

jump into his lap in the front seat of his truck. Well, I wanted to, but not necessarily in such a public space.

When we pulled up to my apartment, Silas parked the truck in an actual spot this time. The moment my feet touched the ground, Silas slipped his arm around my waist and walked me toward my apartment door.

"I had fun tonight, California. Thanks for letting me take you out."

"La Pergola might be my new favorite restaurant," I said. "Everything was delicious. I hope we can go again one day."

"I'll take you there again anytime you want."

At my door, Silas dropped his arm from around my waist and stood watching me as I fumbled in my purse for my house keys.

"Found 'em!" I started to turn toward the door to put the key into the lock when I felt Silas's large hand grip my waist. I looked up at his intense, sage-green eyes watching me. He bit his bottom lip and hesitated before bending down and grazing his lips against my cheek. I closed my eyes at the gentle pressure and swayed into his hard body before he pulled away. I looked up at him, disappointed that he had pulled away so fast. He was still gazing down at me, a question in his eyes that I thought I had answered already. I took a step closer to him, closing the slight gap between us, and laced my arm around his neck. That was all the encouragement he needed. Silas's mouth came down over mine with a swiftness that erased any lingering questions. His lips pressed firmly against mine. They were softer than I expected and tasted of the peppery wine from dinner. Wine and Silas were a lethal combination that had me wanting more, so I was grateful when his tongue edged its way between my lips as his hips pressed me against my front door. He ran his hands up the side of my body, and each touch lit up my skin. He ran them back down and they came to rest at my hips, gripping them so tightly I wondered if I would have a bruise the next morning. Not that I'd complain. Lost in Silas, I forgot I was outside of my apartment in clear view until headlights flashed on us, and I yanked my face away from his.

Silas could kiss.

"Wow," he said. "So that finally happened. I've been wanting to do that for a while now."

I smacked his arm and said, "What took you so long?"

He rubbed his arm and laughed. "I wasn't sure if you saw me like that. Then I thought maybe you were into Keith after I saw you in the hallway, but I had to try. It's not in my nature not to try."

I went up on my tiptoes and pulled his head down to mine. "I'm not into Keith, and I'm where I want to be right now, but we have class tomorrow, and I still need to study more," I said. I gave him a kiss, intending for it to be quick, but he wrapped me up and deepened it, leaving me breathless. I felt myself falling again, and I had to wiggle out of his arms to catch myself. I took a step away from him, peeling his hands off my body, and said, "Good night, Silas."

CHAPTER TWELVE

I called River when I got home. I really wanted to tell her about my date with Silas, but she didn't answer. I hoped she wasn't angry at me. She'd called me the week before, but I hadn't been able to talk long enough for it to even count as catching up. I'd texted her back trying to schedule some time to talk, but we hadn't been able to make our schedules align.

Resigned to not being able to talk to Rivvy, I took my books out to study. Silas and I had covered a lot of ground, but there was more I wanted to review to make sure it was solid in my brain. I needed to study a little more after our date, but thoughts of Silas kept rolling around in my head and I couldn't focus. Promising myself I'd study in the morning, I called it a night and went to sleep, but morning came fast. Groggy and still unmotivated to study, I dragged myself out of bed and went to the kitchen to make coffee and breakfast. Even though abject poverty was my constant state, the one thing I consistently splurged on was good coffee beans. There was something about homemade coffee that always made me happy, so every week I hopped on the bus to my favorite coffee shop, Biggby's. As the kitchen started to fill with the nutty aroma of my Colombian roast, I grabbed my Contracts book and laptop and hunkered down on the couch to make sure I knew *Hadley* as well as I possibly could. Unfortunately, *Hadley*'s facts weren't quite as stimulating as the case I had briefed for Criminal Law. I realized just how boring they were when I woke up with my cheek plastered in drool to my casebook. I shook off the sleep and reached for my phone to check the time. It was eight thirty. I had to be in class by nine, and I wasn't even dressed.

Desperate not to be late, I tossed on jeans slung across my chair, thanked all the holy things that I had decided to keep my hair short enough so all I had to do was shake it out to look decent, and pulled on a worn pair of Vans slip-on sneakers. I didn't even have time to brush my teeth, though I did the obligatory breath-in-hand sniff test. It wasn't great, but it didn't smell like a trash can, so I went with it. When I got to the bus stop, the bus was leaving but the driver knew me from riding with him some mornings and waited patiently for me to board.

"Morning, Simone. Running late?"

Out of breath, I huffed out, "Unbelievably late! If you could skip some of those stops, I would be eternally grateful."

"You know I can't do that, but I'll go as fast as I can."

"Thanks, Raul!"

That's why Raul was my favorite. He made my rough mornings, of which there were a lot, softer.

True to his word, Raul drove faster than I had ever seen him drive, and I got to campus with two minutes to spare. I ran up the stairs, which were unusually busy, and into Professor Patton's class just as she started to speak. I slunk into my seat, careful not to bump into anyone, and shot a small smile at Tiffany, who looked relieved that I had made it to class. Patton abhorred tardiness. I checked my watch: 9:01 a.m. Late, but barely.

Apparently, my entrance wasn't as inconspicuous as I hoped, because Professor Patton picked up her cane and walked across the front of the room, stopping directly in front of me. She pointed her cane as she spoke.

"How nice of you to join us, Ms. Alexander. When you weren't here promptly at 8:55, I assumed that you were trying to get out of briefing *Hadley*. I planned to start with Mr. Aarons today, but since you've decided to grace us with your presence, I'll begin with you. Please, whenever you're ready."

"I apologize for being late, Professor Patton. Let me just get my laptop out of my bag and I'll get started."

"Ms. Alexander, had you been here on time, you would have been able to get your laptop out of your bag and get yourself situated. Unfortunately, you weren't on time, so now please, begin with *Hadley*."

I sat in my seat stunned. I had typed up all of my notes on *Hadley* and would have been able to brief it well with my notes, but without them, I worried I was a bit screwed. I looked over at Tiffany, who looked equally stunned. Thinking on her feet like any good lawyer, she slid her laptop over to me.

"Ms. Alston, I don't believe Ms. Alexander needs your help. Kindly slide your laptop back in front of you. Ms. Alexander, we're all waiting."

Shaking, I turned to face my classmates. My eyes landed immediately on Silas, who smiled encouragingly and mouthed, "You got this."

"Well, *Hadley v. Baxendale* is a Contracts case from 1854. It set the precedent for determining consequential damages from a breach of contract." As I spoke, I got more and more confident with my recitation of the facts and issues of law.

"The rule of law from this case determined that a non-breaching party is entitled to damages from those arising naturally from the breach."

For the next ten minutes, I spoke confidently about the case. I had retained more than I thought, and pulling from my memory wasn't as difficult as I had worried it'd be. I answered all of the questions Patton threw at me and wrapped up the case. Satisfied, I bent to get my laptop out of its bag, but before my hand reached it, Professor Patton cleared her throat.

"Ms. Alexander. Since you so ably gave us the information we needed for *Hadley*, I'm sure you wouldn't mind going ahead and briefing *Carlill v. Carbolic Smoke Ball Co.* for us as well. When you've finished with that, we'll go ahead and discuss both cases together."

Like always, I had read all of the cases for Contracts, but because I was briefing for the class, I had overprepared my case to the slight detriment of adequately preparing for the other cases. That combined with my nerves and I remembered almost nothing about *Carbolic Smoke Ball Co.*

"Umm, sure. Okay. From what I remember, *Carbolic Smoke Ball* was about an ad that claimed its company had a product that would prevent colds if used the right way. A woman bought the carbolic smoke ball and still contracted a cold. The issue at hand is whether the defendant's language was puffery or if the defendant actually owed the plaintiff." I knew I'd done a poor job of discussing the case when it only took me about forty-five seconds to discuss it, if that. I turned back to Professor Patton, and she stood at the front, shaking her head.

Professor Patton didn't have a chance to bless me out before I heard Silas's voice ring out from the back.

"She missed a few things, but I can finish up for the class."

What in the actual hell?

Silas discussed *Carbolic Smoke Ball Co.,* and I slid further and further into my chair. Of course he did an amazing job.

He always did an amazing job. And I was pissed. How could Silas do this to me a second time? It was one thing on the first day of school when we didn't know each other, but now, especially after the other night, it was plain uncalled for.

"Thank you, Mr. Whitman," Professor Patton said. Then she turned her attention back to me.

"That was abysmal, Ms. Alexander. The answer seems obvious, so I feel silly asking, but did you even read the case?"

"Yes, I read it. It's just that without my—"

Professor Patton interrupted me, putting her hand up as she moved across the room to stand directly in front of me again. "Do I look interested in your excuses?"

She really didn't.

"In case you are confused, let me be clear: I am not the least bit interested in whatever excuse you have. Your retelling of the facts was elementary at best and your flimsy grip of the rule of law was embarrassing."

Professor Patton walked away from me shaking her head. Too humiliated to look in either direction, I sat in my seat staring straight ahead and didn't move until I felt Tiffany's hand on my arm.

My entire body flushed and the tears welled up, threatening to run down my cheeks. Professor Patton was mean, flat out. I'd seen her eviscerate other people in class, but having it directed right at me was worse than I expected. I always assumed that at some point I would be on the receiving end of her nasty attitude, but having it actually happen was significantly more awful than I imagined. Not only did it embarrass me, it also left me demoralized. Especially knowing that I read the cases and would have been able to brief it just fine with my laptop. Crying in class wasn't an option and neither was leaving, so I sat in my seat barely holding in tears. Tiffany rubbed my back, but I still couldn't look at her. I didn't want to see the pity I knew I would find in her eyes. I just wanted to go home.

"You killed it with *Hadley*," she whispered. "Patton's just a bitter old beast who makes it her job to make us feel bad because she couldn't cut it as a real lawyer."

I appreciated Tiffany's attempt at trying to make me feel better, but the only thing I needed was to get out of that room and far away from Patton.

As soon as class finished, I gathered my belongings and bolted to the door. I had Criminal Law right after Contracts, but I needed to get out of the law school for a while. I didn't even wait for the bus; instead I walked the almost three miles to my apartment. I was never much of a crier, but as I walked home thinking about Patton, the tears flowed down my face. No one had ever gone out of their way to make me feel like crap before. People had been mean, sure, but mean for the sake of being mean? Never. I was grateful I had managed to make it out of class before the buckets started pouring out of my eyes. Tears would have given Patton the very satisfaction it seemed she wanted. I barely remembered the walk home from campus when I opened my front door and slammed it behind me. I sat on my couch to turn on the TV, but I needed a better distraction. *Judge Judy* and *Divorce Court* weren't going to help my mood. I needed a distraction, and I needed to be around people. I wanted to call Tiffany, but she was in class like I should have been, and I was angry at Silas. The rest of my study group friends would be in class with Tiffany. The only other person whose phone number I had that wasn't in my study group was Keith. Crossing my fingers that he didn't have class and would want to hang out, I dialed his number.

Keith answered on the first ring. That was a good sign. "Hello?"

"Hey, Keith, it's Simone...Silas's friend Simone?"

He chuckled and said, "Yeah, I know who you are. I wondered if you'd call. How are things?"

"All right. You know how it goes."

"I'm glad you called. I wasn't sure if you would."

I really wasn't up for small talk right now. I wanted to get out of my house and not think about school or Silas for a while.

"Are you busy right now?" I asked, not wanting to beat around the bush. "I've had a shit morning, and I need to blow off some steam."

"You know it's Monday morning, right?" He sounded slightly amused.

"I know, but that doesn't change the fact that I had a crap morning. Do you have class or are you down to hang out?"

"Both. I can skip a class. What did you have in mind?"

"I don't know, just something to take my mind off everything. Meet me at my place and we can figure it out. You remember where I live?"

"I do. I'll see you in about half an hour."

I had just enough time to shower, brush my teeth, put on a little makeup, and change into a new outfit before Keith came over. I'd left for class grimy, and I didn't want to be tear-stained with stank breath when he got to my house.

Exactly thirty minutes after I had gotten off the phone with Keith, my doorbell rang.

"Damn, you're prompt," I commented and gave him a quick hug. I opened the door wider to let him in.

"When a beautiful woman says she wants to hang out with me, I'd be an idiot to dawdle. You look amazing, by the way. Is this how you usually look going to class?"

One of the best lessons I ever learned from my roommate in college was that when you looked good, you felt good, and

I wanted to feel good or at least better. I rarely wore makeup but I had put on a little face powder and blush, a couple layers of mascara, and my go-to red lipstick.

"Rarely. I just had a bad morning and dressing up makes me feel better."

Just as Silas had done, Keith walked straight over to the couch and made himself at home as he said, "In that case, you must be feeling fantastic."

I was glad I called Keith.

"So Ms. Alexander, how are we going to help you salvage your day?"

I paced behind my couch for a second, thinking.

What would make me feel better? Going home to Oakland, getting in my bed at my parents' house, and not coming out until the memory of this day, and law school in general, faded. I couldn't say that out loud, though. I didn't know Keith like that. Instead I said, "Pancakes and mimosas are a good start, and we can figure the rest out from there."

We hopped into Keith's car and headed straight downtown to find somewhere that served pancakes and mimosas on a Monday morning. We discovered fairly quickly that finding a restaurant that served mimosas on a Monday was a more difficult feat than either of us imagined. Pancakes were easy, but I wasn't eating somewhere that didn't also have mimosas. Outside the fourth restaurant we'd tried, Keith suggested we just cook and make our own mimosas.

"It'll be cheaper and we can drink and eat as much as we want. Let's stop by the grocery store and get a bottle of champagne, some juice, and all the fixings for loaded pancakes. You don't know this about me yet, but I'm an *amazing* chef, and I love to cook for people."

"Well, all right, Marcus Samuelsson, let's give Red Rooster

a run for its money!"

I pulled my phone out of my purse to check the time and saw that I had six missed calls, four voicemails, and sixteen text messages. Four of the calls, two of the voicemails, and all of the texts were from Silas, and the rest were from Tiffany. All were variations of, "Where are you?" "Are you okay?" and "Call me."

"Shit, do you mind if I make a couple quick calls before we go into the grocery store? Tiffany is worried after I left class so abruptly."

I didn't even want to say Silas's name out loud.

"No problem. In fact, why don't you make your calls while I go into the store? That way we can get to the pancakes and mimosas faster, and you can tell me why your morning was tough. Cool?"

"Perfect. Thank you!"

"No sweat. I'll be back in a few."

Keith closed the car door, and I called Tiffany, who answered before the phone finished ringing.

"Where the hell are you? Are you okay? You weren't in Crim Law."

The concern in her voice was clear, and I felt bad for worrying her.

"I'm fine. I just needed some space after this morning with Patton. That shook me up and I wouldn't have been able to concentrate in Crim Law after that, anyway."

"Yeah, she was a dick. You killed it with *Hadley*, though I can't believe she pulled that shit about not letting you get your laptop."

I didn't want to talk about it anymore.

"It's all good; I'm feeling better."

"Are you sure? Where are you, anyway? Did you go home

or what?"

I was about to tell her I was with Keith when Silas called again. Seeing Keith walking toward the car, I hedged my bets and decided to answer Silas's call.

"Tiff, let me call you back. This is Silas on the other line, and he's called a bunch of times. Let me answer his call."

She sounded uncertain when she said okay. "Yeah, he's been pretty worried, too. I'll call and check on you later."

I switched over to Silas's call.

"Hello?" I answered, with no enthusiasm.

"Simone," Silas bellowed into the phone. "Where are you? You ran off after Patton's class."

Yeah, no shit.

"I needed to take a breather," I told him nonchalantly.

Keith opened the backseat door and started loading bags onto the seat.

"All right, we're in business," he said. "I got chocolate chips, strawberries, bananas, sprinkles, and blueberries for the pancakes, and pineapple juice, orange juice, pomegranate juice, and grapefruit juice for the mimosas. I didn't know what you liked, so I got it all."

His deep voice sounded throughout the car, and there was no way Silas hadn't heard him talking.

Keith settled into the seat next to me and rested his hand on my knee. "You ready?"

"Simone?" Silas said slowly, like he was speaking to a child. "Where are you and who is that in the background?"

He paused a beat, waiting to hear my answer.

Before I could formulate a response he asked, "Is that Keith?"

"Yeah. We're at the grocery store getting food for breakfast."

Keith glanced over at me and mouthed, "Silas?" I nodded yes.

I turned toward the window, and I felt Keith's eyes on me waiting to hear what I was going to say next.

"I called him when I got out of class. I couldn't be at school anymore." My tone was clipped, but I couldn't hide my irritation at Silas.

Silas sighed, his voice softer now. "You know I would have left with you if you'd asked. You should have told me, and you and I could have gone to breakfast."

I didn't want to get into it with Silas, so I said, "I gotta go. I'll call you later or something."

He sighed again. "Fine. You need anything?"

"Nope, I'll be all right," I said.

I hung up and turned back to Keith with a bright smile that I was sure didn't quite reach my eyes.

"Thanks for getting everything. You ready?" I said, sounding too perky even to my own ears.

Keith didn't turn on the car. Instead, he twisted sideways in his seat so he could face me.

"Everything all right with Silas? He sounded mad."

"Oh yeah, everything's all good. He was just worried after I left class so abruptly and didn't call him back. No big deal."

"It didn't sound like no big deal, but I'll mind my own business," he said and started the car.

Keith's apartment wasn't in East Lansing like I thought. "Where are we?"

"Okemos. Not too far from East Lansing. It's a little bit easier to rent a spot here because most students want to stay as close to campus as possible."

Okemos. I wouldn't have minded a little distance from campus. Between Suzy's piano playing and the undergrads stomping around in their apartment upstairs, I barely got a break to hear myself breathe.

"I wish I'd known about this building before I moved here. My neighbor Suzy is driving me insane."

Keith's face went blank for a minute, then it cleared up and he laughed. "It can't be that bad. Come on. Let's make breakfast and you can tell me what had you running scared this morning."

Keith's apartment wasn't a typical student apartment. It looked nothing like Silas's, the only other person's apartment I'd been to besides my own, though I imagined Tiffany's was probably similarly swanky. It was clear that unlike my furniture, which was standard-issue dorm furniture, Keith had painstakingly chosen his. Everything matched and nothing had holes or tears in it. His gray leather couch was plush, and when I lowered myself onto it, I didn't so much sit as sink into it. I leaned my head back, starting to relax for the first time since my run-in.

I heard cabinets opening and closing and pans clanging together every couple of minutes.

"Do you need help with anything?"

"No, I'm good. If you want to do something you can come in here, fix both of us a mimosa, and tell me about your morning."

The plush red rug he had on his floor bled into the most well-stocked kitchen I'd seen outside of professional ones. It was a chef's dream. On the sprawling counter was a KitchenAid mixer, a blender, a food processor, and an espresso machine. If those were displayed on his counter, who knew what lived in his cabinets? My fingers were itching to find out.

"Your kitchen is amazing! When you said you liked to cook,

I'm not sure what I expected, but it wasn't this."

"Yeah, I've loved to cook my whole life. I wanted to be a chef growing up, but when I realized they don't make enough money to fund the lifestyle I wanted, I focused my sights on my second passion: the law."

"Same here...kinda. I thought I wanted to be the next Ayesha Curry," I explained, downplaying my background. I didn't want to get into the nitty gritty with Keith at the moment.

He nodded in understanding. "Chef versus law student. How do they compare?"

I bent down to grab the champagne and grapefruit juice out of the refrigerator.

"Where do you keep your champagne glasses?"

A man with such an impressive kitchen set-up definitely had champagne glasses.

"In the cabinet above the sink. Are you avoiding my question?"

Yes.

"No, of course not. I just want to get the mimosas going before the pancakes are ready. By the way, how are they coming along?" I found the glasses easily and poured myself a hefty glass of champagne with a splash of grapefruit juice for color. Faint color.

"They're coming along. I'm making the pancakes plain, and we can add toppings on our own when they're ready."

Leaning around Keith's back to smell the pancakes, I got a whiff of his cologne mixed with the pancakes, and it was unexpectedly pleasant. Silas never smelled like cologne. Not that he smelled bad. He smelled great, like fresh laundry or soap or the mountains, kind of like a deodorant commercial. He smelled clean, though it was dumb to compare Silas and

Keith. Keith was attractive by all accounts, but Silas was Silas.

"Hey." I held up my glass in the air. "You want one of these?"

"Of course. Let me get one with pomegranate juice."

While I made his drink and he took his first sips, I told him about what happened in Patton's class.

"She purposely embarrassed me, and I was only two minutes late. And Silas made it even worse, jumping in to answer like that. Patton barely had a chance to tell me I'd done a crap job before Silas basically cosigned for her."

He looked thoughtful as he put a pancake on a plate and handed it to me. I made myself another mimosa, the alcohol dulling my rage ever so slightly.

"Oh yeah, I had Patton my first year, too. She's tough, but she'll make you a better law student and probably a better lawyer one day. After having her, all my other classes were cake. Trust, by your second year you'll be glad she challenged you."

I doubted that was true, but with my second mimosa starting to kick in, arguing with Keith wasn't high on my list of priorities. Especially if the argument was about Patton.

"If you say so."

"And Silas—" he started to say.

"I don't want to talk about Silas," I told him before he could finish.

"Okay," he said. "But—and hear me out—is there a chance you're being too hard on him?"

A hot, angry flush spread over me. Of course he'd side with his friend. "You have no idea what you're talking about, so stay out of it."

"Fine," he said, putting his hands up. "But you might want to think about why you're so pissed at him. He's a gunner in class, always has been, but it's not really about you."

He ladled another pancake onto the griddle and joined me where I was perched against the counter. He stopped about eight inches away from me and crouched to look directly into my eyes. He wasn't quite as tall as Silas but held his own.

"Trust me, law school gets better. If the worst thing that's happened so far is that you were embarrassed in a first-year class, you're in pretty good shape." He straightened then and stepped an inch closer, forcing me to look up at him. "Do you believe me?"

I nodded. I didn't have the energy to be angry at Silas *and* Keith, and in the whole scheme of things, Keith was great, but his opinion was secondary for me.

"Thanks for keeping me distracted this morning."

Keith smiled. "Anytime, pretty girl. Now come on," he said. "Let's get these pancakes off the griddle and eat. We've barely started your blow-off-steam day, and we have a lot more day to get through."

I grabbed the bottle of champagne from the counter behind me and said, "You get the pancakes, and I'll do the mimosa refills?"

"Bet."

We sat in comfortable silence while we ate. Sitting with my thoughts, I felt Keith's eyes on me, and when I looked up, he was watching me with interest.

"What?" I asked.

"Nothing. You looked engrossed in your thoughts, and I was curious what had you in such a daze. Still thinking about class?"

Due to the alcohol and Keith's friendly company, I wasn't, and I finally felt like there was a chance I would recover from the humiliation. I was, however, thinking about Silas. I wasn't the only one who thought he was a jerk in class, but besides Tiffany, no one else seemed to hold it against him. But, as far as I knew, no one else was exchanging saliva with him so it was different.

"Not really. Being here helped a lot, so thank you."

Keith nodded. "All right, we've put a pretty good hurt on these pancakes. Are you done?"

"Yup!" I said.

"Cool, let's go do something else to keep your mind occupied," Keith said.

"What did you have in mind?" I was as close to relaxed as I could get considering the circumstances and ready to move on to the next activity.

"It's a surprise, but you'll like it."

I snatched my purse from its place on the couch and headed toward the front door. I was up for anything at this point. He could have told me we were going to run naked across campus and through the law school, and there was a good chance I would have agreed.

"Well, come on then, I'm ready to go."

Keith laughed. "Let me grab my keys and we can take off."

Keith went back to the kitchen, and I stood by the door waiting for him. Five minutes later and I was still waiting. He was talking in the back, and it sounded like he was on the phone with someone unless he was having a very heated conversation with himself.

I was about to ask him if everything was okay when the doorbell chimed.

"Hey, do you want me to get that?" I yelled across the apartment.

When he didn't answer, I swung the door open.

"You feeling better?"

Silas's shoulders, as usual, took up much of the doorframe. He looked more tense than I had ever seen him look despite the smile, which didn't reach his eyes. And maybe calling it a smile wasn't right. His lips were stretched and I could see teeth, but smile might have been an overstatement.

"What are you doing here?" I asked, annoyed at the intrusion. My shoulders had finally found their way down from my ears where they had taken up residence, and I was feeling fairly relaxed.

"I thought you could use another friend."

Silas was the last person I wanted to see.

"I wish you hadn't come here."

Silas's face went slack and there was confusion written all over it.

"Why?" he asked simply.

"I don't want to have this conversation with you right now. Keith and I are having a lovely morning, and I don't want you ruining it."

Silas looked like I had slapped him across the face physically instead of just the verbal assault I intended.

"Simone, what's wrong with you? What did I do?"

"I told you, I don't want to talk about it." I tried to close the door on him, but he wedged his big shoulders into the doorway and wouldn't budge.

"We need to talk about this. Right now."

Keith took that moment to come out of wherever he had been hiding in the back.

"You ready to go? I've got everything packed and—" Keith looked taken aback seeing Silas in the doorway. "Oh. Hey, my dude. What are you doing here?"

"I came to check on Simone. She was upset, and I wanted to make sure she was okay."

"That's stand up of you. I think she's cool, though," Keith said, scrutinizing my face.

"Good, but she and I need to talk."

Keith looked from me to Silas and back to me again.

"We're good, Keith. There isn't anything I need to say to Silas. We can go whenever you're ready." I moved closer to the door hoping Silas would get out of my way, but of course he didn't.

"Don't be like that, Simone. After last nigh—" he started, but I didn't let him finish his sentence.

"Fine," I relented. "We can talk, but clearly we can't do it here."

I turned to Keith. "I'm so sorry, but I need to handle this. Can we take a rain check on the rest of the day?" I asked.

Keith shrugged, seeming unperturbed. "No problem. We can rain check whenever you want."

I gave him a quick hug, but when I went to let go, he pulled me in tighter. He spoke so low I had to strain to hear him. "Talk to Silas. Give him a chance to tell you what's going on. It's probably not what you think."

I jerked my head back at his words, and he nodded once at me before turning to go back into his bedroom. I marched out of his front door, shoving past Silas. I didn't have to glance back to see if Silas was following; I heard his heavy footsteps behind me. I started down the empty hallway toward the elevator.

"Do you even know where you're going?" he asked, catching up to me.

"If you don't start talking soon, I'll be going to catch a Lyft back to my apartment."

He rubbed his temples and closed his eyes.

"My car is parked on the street. We'll go to PJ's. It should be empty, and we can have an actual conversation so you can tell me what has you all up in arms."

S ilas and I drove downtown in veritable silence. Silas had tried to broach the subject a couple of times, but the one-word answers I gave him didn't lend themselves to further conversation. I needed to collect my thoughts and figure out what I wanted to say to him.

At PJ's, we had our pick of tables since it was almost completely empty save for the wait staff, a bartender, and some guy in the corner with four empty beer mugs in front of him. He was nursing a fifth. There were plenty of seating options, and typically I preferred a booth, but given the circumstances, the coziness a booth offered wasn't warranted.

On weekend nights, PJ's was popular among undergrads. The drinks were cheap and the bartenders poured with heavy hands. No one left there sober. The bar lived in the basement of a strip mall, and not a single window existed in the place. At night the dark basement with its red leather booths and velvet curtains partitioning off the bar from the rest of the restaurant seemed mysterious and a little naughty. During the day it was straight-up depressing. The booth seats and chairs were torn and faded, and cigarette burns and who knew what else marred the once-pristine velvet curtains. The top of our table was clean, but when I put my purse on the floor, I thought better of it, gum punctuating every surface underneath. I found it hard to believe people ate here on purpose.

"Why did we come here?" I asked. The displeasure dripped from my voice, and I had no interest in hiding it.

"I told you, I want to know why you're so mad at me," he said.

"But why *here*? This place is disgusting."

"What, you wanted to go to a five-star restaurant to tell me why you're mad?"

He had a point.

"So what gives?" he continued. "Patton was a little harsh in class, but obviously you're mad at me and I don't know why."

Apparently, he didn't remember the first day of class where he had done almost the exact same thing, except then he had the wherewithal to apologize for it. This time he didn't even seem to think he had done anything wrong.

"Do you remember the first day of Patton's class?" I asked Silas. I hoped that he would get there himself so I wouldn't have to explain it, but his expression stayed perplexed. I rolled my eyes. "The first day of class Patton asked me about the Socratic method and you said—"

Silas lifted his hand to stop me before I could finish. "Right. I remember now." He furrowed his brow and squinted at me. "But what does that have to do with today?" he asked. He was really still in the dark.

"Silas. You embarrassed me." I watched his eyebrows jump to the top of his forehead. He was genuinely surprised, but that didn't stop me. "Patton already hates me and thinks I'm a complete idiot. She adores you and you demonstrate your competence every. Single. Class period. You have nothing to prove, but you went out of your way to volunteer and make me look dumb when you could have just done nothing. Or hell, even have waited for Patton to call on you but you had to jump in to show how smart you are. We get it. Everyone here is smart, but not everyone feels the need to be so audacious about it."

"California, come on. I was just answering the question."

"She hadn't finished asking the fucking question before you launched yourself in there head first as always."

Silas's face was a mix of emotions, but at least confusion wasn't one of them anymore, and he seemed to finally get it. He took a deep breath and tried to reach for my hand across the table, but I pulled it back. The last thing I needed was for Silas to touch me and try to break down my righteous indignation.

"I didn't mean to embarrass you," he began. "And I'm sorry. You know that wasn't my intent, but no one else was raising their hands, so I figured if I could answer the question, I should."

The look I gave him must have expressed how ludicrous I thought his explanation was, because for the first time since I'd met him, Silas looked uncomfortable. He squirmed in his seat and didn't quite meet my eyes. But he kept talking.

"I understand that you're upset, and I'm truly sorry I was the one who upset you, but to be honest," he said, then looked up at me, "you had to know law school was going to be hard. We have to fight for every grade, every internship, and once we graduate, every job. Being meek in class isn't going to cut it. Didn't you know what you were walking into?"

Hearing him say that shook loose something inside of me, and I exploded.

"No!" I shouted, not caring that we were in a public place. Silas jerked his back, looking shocked at my outburst. "That's just it. I had absolutely no idea what I was walking into. None. I worked as a chef for years and never anticipated that I would want to do anything else. Except as it turned out, even if you're talented and even if you work harder than anyone else around you, even if you sacrifice having a life, not everyone can or wants to live the life of a top chef. It's a punishing lifestyle, and I didn't want that for myself anymore, but when you hang all your plans on one path, pivoting isn't always so easy and it's scary. But I did it, and now I'm here, in the middle of Michigan at a law school I barely knew existed before I applied here, and I'm floundering, Silas. Full-on floundering. I have no idea what the hell I'm doing most days. Before I got here, I knew nothing about study groups or outlining or briefing cases. And the worst part is that I had no idea I was *supposed* to know any of that. I didn't even check my emails because I didn't really think I had to. So no, I didn't know what I was walking into. And it didn't occur to me that my friends, that you, would be my competition." I paused to take a breath. "But I know now."

Silas tried to jump in, but I wouldn't let him. I needed to get this out, and I needed him to hear me.

"I don't know if coming to law school was the right choice, but I'm here and I want to make the most of it, and that means doing well so I can get a summer associate position so I can get a job." I was starting to tear up, and I hated, *hated*, crying. "If I don't have a job, I can't pay off the mounds of debt to my parents and my brother for the years they supported my cooking dreams on top of having to pay off all these law school loans. I didn't have some cushy career that's funding my education. No one but me is paying for this, Silas, and if I fail, I don't want to go crawling back home."

The silence stretched between us, and I looked everywhere except at Silas, but I felt his eyes on me. When I refused to meet them, he gripped my chin and turned my head so I was forced to face him. I swatted at his hand but didn't turn away.

"Why didn't you tell me all this before?" His voice held a note of sympathy, but it mostly sounded hurt.

"Why do you think?" I snapped. "You and everyone else seemed to know the ins and outs of law school already, and I hadn't even known we were supposed to be checking our email over the summer. How do you think that would have made me look?"

"Like someone brave if not a little impetuous and smart enough to know when to move on from something damaging. You know our friends. You know me. I wouldn't have judged you, but I would have understood more. Helped you fill in the blanks."

My anger was subsiding, and when Silas reached for my hand again, this time I let him take it. I was exhausted from the morning and my outburst, and I wanted the comfort his warm hands provided.

"I'm not your competition, Simone, not like that, and I never meant to make you feel like I was. All I want is to support you and for us to get through this together, but you have to show up in class. Be that spitfire I first met. The one who had no issue calling me out on my shit."

I closed my eyes and steeled myself for what I was about to say.

"I heard everything you said, and you're right. I need to figure out how to make all this work for me, and this," I said, motioning between us with my free hand, "is too much. Too distracting. I like you, Silas, but the one and only night I decide to go out on a date with you, with anyone, I screw up in the class I most need to do well in, and I can't have that happen again." There. I said it.

"So what are you saying?" he asked, his voice flat.

I slipped my hand out of his and placed it in my lap. "I'm saying we need to slow this train down. I need some space to study and try to get my bearings straight before I can even consider thinking about dating anyone."

"Even me?" Silas asked.

"Especially you."

"So that makes us...what?"

"Friends," I said, hoping my resolve was as strong as my conviction.

CHAPTER THIRTEEN

"What the fuck is wrong with you?" Tiffany asked after Criminal Law.

For the past week, I'd been licking my wounds and doing some serious navel-gazing so by default, I hadn't been very social. Usually after class, our crew would grab lunch or take a walk to get ice cream at the dairy store, but I'd been giving myself some space from Silas, and avoiding him meant avoiding everyone. No one mentioned anything the first few days, but Tiffany couldn't help the pointed question that escaped her mouth, and I couldn't blame her. None of our friends knew anything about Silas and me, so to them, I was just being antisocial.

"Nothing as far as I know. Why?"

"Are you going straight home again?"

"I'd planned to. Did you need me for something?"

Tiffany furrowed her brows at me, looking exasperated. "No, but it's Thursday, and we have study group tonight. Were you planning to come, or were you just going to tell us all to fuck off?"

"Of course not," I said. "What makes you think I'd blow you guys off?"

Courtney jogged up then, catching the last bit of our conversation.

"The fact that you've been acting weird the last couple days and we've barely seen you. What's going on with you? Are you okay?"

At least Courtney was slightly more delicate in her words than Tiffany.

"Yes. I'm fine. Just still reeling a little after Patton demolished me in class."

Tiffany and Courtney looked at each other, then back at me.

"Girl, you need to get over yourself," Tiffany announced.

My head snapped up at the sharpness of her words.

I glanced over at Courtney to see she was nodding.

"What do you mean?" I asked. Did she think I was being too sensitive? *Was* I being too sensitive?

"You're taking Patton's shit way too personally. You've been in her class for half a semester now. You know how she is," Tiffany said. "She's an asshole. Fine. It's not like she's an asshole *just* to you. She's made like four people in our section cry...during class."

"Yeah, but—"

I wasn't sure how to finish that thought. If I said, "Yeah, but my feelings are more valid than everyone else's," I'd sound like a textbook narcissist. Plus, they weren't. But while it was true Patton was tough on everyone, it did seem like she went out of her way to pick on me from the very first day.

"Yeah, but she made fun of me on the first day," I said, sounding childish and whiny even to my own ears.

"No, she didn't," Tiffany piped up. "She called you out."

Ouch.

"Look," Courtney said. "I'm the last person to defend Patton, but Tiffany has a point. She's kind of like that with everyone. And she didn't make fun of your suit, she commented on your answer which, to be honest, wasn't great."

Tiffany slung her arm around my shoulders. "We love you, girl. We just want you to get all the way in the game."

I laughed, grateful to these two women for their realness.

"It was a good suit, too, if that helps," Courtney added. "Let's go downstairs and get some lunch. I'm hungry."

I was still chuckling to myself when Silas rounded the corner with Rafael and Kevin. The boys must have stayed after class to talk to Professor Mason. I had been trying to hightail it out of there before anyone noticed I was missing so I didn't see they had stayed behind.

"Ladies," Rafael said, kissing each of us on our cheeks. "Good class?"

No one had a chance to greet Raf before Tiffany launched into a whole rant about how she thought it was unconstitutional that vaping inside was a crime when non-smokers could just leave the room. I didn't know what prompted the rant since we'd been talking about larceny in class, but whatever. I tuned her out and turned my attention to Silas instead. He was talking and laughing with Courtney, and I found myself watching him. We hadn't talked in days, and I missed him, once my anger fully subsided. He must have felt my eyes on him, because he looked up at me and gave me a closed-lip smile. Nothing like his usual stunners.

I waited for a natural break in their conversation before I made my way over to them.

"All right, I gotta go," Courtney announced as soon as I walked up.

"She's in a hurry," I commented, watching her rush down the hall.

"Yeah, she said she had to look up a case or something. I don't know," he said, watching her maneuver through the crowd. Then he turned to me.

Gripping the crook of my elbow, he pulled me away from Raf and Tiffany, who were still arguing about vaping. Kevin was there, too, but he was staring off into space, likely trying to ignore their bickering.

"So, uh, you doing all right after the other day?"

He tried to text me a couple times after PJ's, but I hadn't been ready to talk to him yet. I had needed time to digest our conversation. It was freeing to finally tell someone how panicked I was, even though it led to the realization that I needed to hunker down on my studies without a six foot four distraction in the way.

"I'm all right," I admitted. And mostly, I was. Sure, I was panicked about finals and reading and Professor Patton hating me, but that was baseline for me these days. It was the middle of the semester, and like Tiffany said, I needed to get my shit together and stop feeling sorry for myself.

"Are *you* good?" I asked.

Our drive back from PJ's had been quiet, and when Silas walked me to my front door, he looked so forlorn I briefly considered taking it all back. Instead, I gathered those balls he thought I forgot about, gave him a kiss on the cheek, and told him we'd talk later.

He shrugged. "Good enough."

"Good," I replied and took a step to rejoin our friends, but before I knew what was happening, he'd backed me against a wall and put his arm above my head, effectively pinning me there. I could have moved any time, but I just couldn't seem to make my feet go. No parts of our bodies were touching, but I could feel him everywhere when he whispered, "But I'll be better when you figure out just friends is never going to be enough for us."

I inhaled sharply, and he chuckled at my reaction before releasing me and rejoining our friends.

I stood there reeling. I didn't know what made me think my attraction to him was going to disappear because I'd unilaterally decided we were just friends. Silas wasn't any less sexy than he was a week ago, and my pronouncement did nothing to change that.

Gaining my composure, I walked back over to join Tiffany, Raf, Kevin, and Silas.

"We were talking about where we're going to do study group," Tiffany informed me. "Everyone's tired of our usual places."

"Why don't we do it at my apartment?" I suggested. Our meetings had mostly been at school, and we'd had a couple at Courtney's house, but outside of Silas, my friends had never been over to my place. If I had time, I might even cook for them.

"Is this your mea culpa to the group for ignoring us?" Tiffany joked, but I could tell she was half serious.

"Something like that. Come over. I'll grab some snacks and when we're done we can have a little pre-weekend wine. Seven?"

Everyone nodded their approval.

"Cool, I'll see you guys tonight."

Cleaning up my apartment before my friends came over reminded me of Sunday mornings back at home, power cleaning before my family came over. I wasn't messy exactly, but cleaning wasn't my top priority, especially when I was busy trying to claw my way up the restaurant food chain. Here, cleaning wasn't my priority because who had time to clean? Plus, up until this moment, Silas was the only person who had been over to my place, and I never had time to clean before he came over.

I decided against cooking a big meal since a) I didn't really have the time and b) I definitely didn't have the money to feed all those people the kind of meal I'd want to cook for them. Instead, I took the bus to the grocery store and bought fixings for a charcuterie board. Salami (for the carnivores), a few good cheeses, some honey, fruit, and nuts, and I was ready for guests. I also bought a two-liter bottle of Faygo Rockin' Rye for the soda drinkers.

I was setting the charcuterie plate on the coffee table when someone knocked on the front door. It was unlocked, but in case it wasn't one of my friends, I didn't yell for them to come in. When I opened the door, Tiffany was standing there.

"Bitch, I can't believe this is the first time I've been to your apartment. What the fuck are you hiding in here?" Tiffany exclaimed as she pushed past me into my apartment. She looked around and peeked her head into my bedroom before plopping down on the couch.

"It's cute. I don't know why you're trying to hide this place from everyone."

"I'm not trying to hide anything from anyone. Silas has been here a few times."

Tiffany rolled her eyes. "Of course he has, but I haven't and the rest of us haven't. What gives?"

Before I could answer, someone, thankfully, knocked on the door, then walked in. It was Courtney and Rafael.

"Damn, Silas was right," Rafael said and handed Courtney a dollar, then looked over at me. "Silas said your front door would be unlocked. I said there was no way a girl from Oakland would leave her front door unlocked any time, but Courtney said Silas knows you better than anyone else."

Did my friends know more about me and Silas than I thought or were we that obvious?

"It was only unlocked because I knew you guys were coming over. I don't usually leave it unlocked, thank you." I put my hand out to Courtney. "So you may as well give Rafael his dollar back."

Courtney hit my hand. "No chance, girlfriend. I won this one fair and square."

I shook my head, laughing at my friends. I should have had them over to my place sooner.

"Kevin said he's going to be a little late. Something with his YouTube channel, I think, and Silas is on his way."

"All right, there's Rockin' Rye in the fridge and food out here, but help yourself to whatever I have. I'm not sure there's much else in there, but you're free to snack on whatever you find."

I was pulling some paper plates out of the cabinet when the door opened. I didn't turn around to see who it was, assuming it was Kevin.

"Hey, Kev, come on in. Make yourself at home."

I felt a warm body behind me and didn't have to turn around to know it wasn't Kevin. I would recognize his smell anywhere.

"Glad you made it, *friend*," I said, emphasizing the word. But when Silas ran his hands up my arms, then back down again, squeezing my hands, and dropped a lingering kiss on the top of my head, I felt anything but friendly.

"You know you're not playing fair, right?" I groaned, leaning into him. "I've got an agenda and you're trying to blow it up."

"I never agreed to play fair," Silas murmured into my hair. "And I'm not trying to blow anything up. I told you I'd support you however you wanted."

I turned around and ran a finger down the middle of his chest. His breath quickened at the contact, and I took a step closer.

"You know how you can support me?" I asked.

He shook his head but didn't say anything.

"Take these," I said, taking a step back and handing him the paper plates I'd abandoned on the counter when he walked in. "And give them to our friends so we can start this study group."

"You've got a little mean streak in you, California," he joked, taking the plates.

I glanced up and everyone in the living room was watching us, trying to pretend like they weren't. Unfortunately, in a six-hundred-square-foot apartment, stealth wasn't exactly possible.

I had forgotten how much I enjoyed entertaining, and it felt really good to have the crew over to my place.

We had finished studying a couple hours before, and now we were just hanging out drinking wine and eating pizza. We'd ordered a couple of pies when Courtney complained that a charcuterie plate wasn't real food. I had a couple bottles my parents had sent me from Napa that I was more than happy to share, and when Kevin volunteered to grab the pizza, Tiffany yelled for him to pick up more wine as well.

"Okay, guys," Tiffany said, about three glasses of wine in. "Fuck, marry, kill, the professor edition."

There was a collective groan from the group. Who wanted to think about their professors that way?

"Okay, fine. I'll go first," she announced. "Courtney, pick three professors."

Courtney rolled her eyes, but the glint in them told me she loved the game. "Fuuuuuuck, okay. Let's see," she said, squinting. "Shah, Mason, and White?"

"Okay. Kill White, marry Mason, and fuck Shah. Simone, it's your house, so you have to go next."

You learned so much about your friends in a game of fuck, marry, kill. Like, who knew Tiffany wouldn't have killed Shah? She detested her, but apparently hotness overshadowed hatred, which, to be fair, would explain Pierce.

"Spill it, Alexander," Tiffany said when I didn't immediately answer.

I took a sip of my wine. "Let's see. I'd marry Mason because obviously he's amazing, plus he would have stories to tell for days. I'd fuck White because I'm into his little bolero ties, and I'd kill Shah because she's the only one left."

"All right, all right," Rafael said. "Let's change it up. How about Nguyen, Bryant, and Patton?"

Rafael looked around the room, and his eyes landed on Kevin.

"Kev, you're up. Call it."

Kevin didn't even hesitate. "Easy. Fuck Nguyen, marry Bryant, and kill Patton."

The game went on for a while, progressing from professors to actors to singers, but eventually having to fake kill so many people took its toll on us, and we switched the game to fuck, marry, avoid forever. It didn't have the same punch, but we kept our karma intact. Several bottles of wine and rounds of the game later, I checked my phone and saw that it was past

164   *YOU'VE BEEN SERVED*

midnight. Much as I hated to do it, we still had class in the morning, and I had to kick everyone out.

"All right, crew, it's getting late," I announced, standing up and stretching. I'd been sitting on the floor for hours, and my body was protesting. "You don't have to go home, but—you guys know the rest."

Everyone stood up, packed their respective bags, and said their goodbyes. They walked out one by one, giving me hugs as they left, and I was struck by how much I loved these folks. Silas was the last person left in my apartment, and he was making no moves to vacate his spot on the couch.

"Cookie, did you forget where the door is?" I joked and plopped down on the couch next to him.

Despite my angsty last few days, I'd had fun with my friends tonight and gotten out of my head. It was cathartic to take a break from constant internal turmoil and let myself enjoy good company.

"Naw, I just wanted to get you alone for a minute," he said, bumping his knee against mine. "I've been thinking about our conversation, and I do owe you an apology."

I shook my head. "I'm over it, so we don't—" But he stopped me with a hand on my knee.

"No, let me finish. I'm not sorry for speaking up in class, but I could have done it a bit more delicately."

Well, that was true.

"Remember that night you cooked me dinner and my mom called?"

Of course I remember, I wanted to scream, but instead I simply nodded.

"She basically called to berate me for going back to school. She thinks I made a huge mistake leaving my other job, and she's been crazy intent on letting me know it every chance she gets. And I guess—" He paused. "I guess I've been on a mission to prove to myself that I could do it and that she was wrong."

Huh. Silas and I were having the same internal struggle, both terrified we'd made a wrong choice.

"Anyway, I thought you should at least know the whole story so you didn't think I was being an asshole for the sake of being an asshole." His lips quirked to the side, showing off his dimples. "I hope it helps to know I was an asshole with a purpose."

When Silas left my apartment, I went to my closet and dug through a couple of boxes I never got around to unpacking. At the very bottom of one of the boxes was my Magic 8 Ball. I'd felt silly bringing it, but since it was the Magic 8 Ball that had gotten me here, I thought it deserved to go on the full journey with me.

"Magic 8 Ball," I said, shaking the glass orb around, "are Silas and I supposed to be more than friends?"

I waited as the hazy triangle cleared.

Twenty answers this thing had. Twenty. And all it had for me was, "Ask again later."

CHAPTER FOURTEEN

"Open the testing app on your laptop and you may begin," the test proctor said as I sat in my usual seat for our Contracts final. For finals we didn't have assigned seating, but I thought that if I sat in the same place I had been sitting throughout the semester, it might jog my memory if I got stuck on an issue. Too much was at stake for me to screw up on this final, especially after midterms. If I didn't get that summer associate job with CL&S, I didn't know what I was going to do for the summer, let alone the rest of my life. I'd been researching other firms and summer associate positions, and nothing else had piqued my interest as much as I'd hoped. I didn't want to apply to just any position for the sake of applying, but I needed something for the summer.

I opened the final exam on my computer. At four pages, Patton's fact pattern was longer than the others I'd had throughout the week on my other finals. I skimmed through it to get the basic gist, read the questions, then reread the fact pattern so that I could start formulating an answer. I looked around the room, trying to catch a glimpse of Silas.

He hadn't sat in his usual seat. Instead, he sat two rows behind me close to the door so when I looked back I saw that he was engrossed in his work, typing furiously.

Okay, Simone, focus. You told Silas you couldn't date him because you needed to do well on this test, so do well on it.

The mini pep talk to myself served to get me started.

The fact pattern was dense, but we had three hours to dissect it, and I needed every one of the 180 minutes allotted for the test. I took notes in my spiral notebook since the test-taking app effectively locked my computer, and outlined my answer. So far, so good.

Three hours later, the proctor said, "Save your exams and close your laptops. Your Contracts final is over."

I walked out of the room shell shocked and feeling like I had been repeatedly beaten over the head. It was awful.

"That was a real bitch," Silas said when he moseyed up next to me.

"Did you finish early?" I asked him. I had looked back to try to see him a second time, and his chair had been empty.

"Yeah, but not much. I left about fifteen minutes before time was up."

How he had done that I had no idea. I barely finished in the three hours and would have been eternally grateful for at least another fifteen minutes.

There were two more days of finals, but it was the last day of finals for 1Ls. The lobby and halls were packed with bodies but eerily quiet. I took in the faces of many of my fellow 1Ls and imagined my face mirrored theirs: gobsmacked. I had expected celebrating, happy faces at being finished with our first semester but most faces held exhaustion and the slight tinge of fear. But at least it was over.

"When are you going back home?" Silas asked as he used his broad shoulders to push through the throng of bodies to the elevator.

"I leave Friday. Are you staying here over break or going

to your parents'?"

"I'm staying here until Christmas Eve, then I'll head to Pleasant Ridge for a few nights. I think my mom is supposed to make an appearance, so my stay will likely be short-lived. We'll see." He put his hand on the small of my back, causing me to shiver a little, and guided me into the elevator. When we were inside the elevator, he moved his hand, and the loss of his warm hand was almost palpable. We rode the elevator down in silence. There were too many people packed in there to have a real conversation, but as soon as the elevator emptied and we stepped out into the lobby, Silas put his hand back on the small of my back and steered me toward the front doors of the building. My stomach did a little happy dance at having his hands on me again.

"The truck's over there," he informed me. I loved that he didn't bother to ask if I wanted a ride home anymore. "Are you still planning on a girls' night with Tiffany and Court?"

I nodded, climbing into the truck and angling his heater vents toward me.

The three of us were going to Detroit to end the semester right.

I rubbed my hands together, waiting for his car to warm up. Silas noticed and pulled one of my hands between his two and rubbed them to help warm me up. Then he repeated the motion with my other hand until the truck warmed up more and he had to pull his hands away to drive. It snowed the first day of finals (I refused to acknowledge it as a sign), and the cold had kicked it up a notch. Silas had called me laughing after I texted him asking why the hail looked so weird.

"You've never seen snow falling?" he had asked, cracking up into the phone. I hadn't. I'd skied a bunch as a kid in Lake Tahoe, but we mainly went in late spring when all the snow that was going to fall had fallen and I could usually ski in a T-shirt and snow pants. I could never bring myself to go the Jersey Jerry route and ski in jeans.

"I was thinking about hitting up a cider mill tomorrow afternoon. You want to come?" Silas asked when he pulled up and parked in front of my apartment. He turned in his seat to face me.

"Maybe. What is it?" I asked.

"Must be a Midwest thing. They make cider there, but you can pick apples, eat donuts, go on hayrides," Silas explained.

"Sounds cozy."

"Oh, trust me, it is. I'll bring a blanket and we can have a little cuddle party."

It did sound nice, and I couldn't think of a good reason not to go other than my own weak self-control, which seemed like a valid reason not to go, but was I being stupid giving up a day of hanging out with Silas before I wouldn't see him for almost a whole month? Probably, but it was for the best even though everyone else was deep into cuffing season. Kevin had started seeing the girl from the hallway, and Tiffany seemed to have locked someone down, though she wouldn't tell me who. I didn't know what Raf or Courtney had going on, but I doubted either of them would have trouble finding someone if they wanted to. Which left only me and Silas, and from what I'd seen, Silas wouldn't be single long if he didn't want to be. He attracted women everywhere he went, seemingly without any effort. Hell, he was wearing the world's ugliest shirt when we met, and the main thing I remembered was his biceps. Whenever he and I weren't together, he was surrounded by a flock of women trying their hardest to catch his attention. I had seen them rubbing his arm, giggling, and flipping their hair so hard it looked like their heads would swing right off their necks, and somehow he stayed oblivious to it all. Of course, he was his usual friendly self, doling out easy smiles and jokes, but none of them ever seemed to hold his attention long. Either way, if and when he decided he wanted to cuff someone, there was no doubt he would be able to do it, but I sincerely hoped he wouldn't. It was selfish of me, but I didn't want Silas to be with anyone else.

"Come on, California. Throw me a bone. Don't you want to spend some time together before you leave for a whole month?"

Of course I did, but my strong resolve was getting weaker by the second, and cuddling with Silas under a blanket might very well destroy the whole thing.

"Hey, isn't that your neighbor over there?" Silas said out of nowhere.

I was grateful for the intrusion, because if he asked me again, I wouldn't be able to say no, but I wondered why noisy Suzy being outside was newsworthy? She lived in my building. Then I saw what had caught his attention. It wasn't that it was Suzy hanging out outside. It was weird-ass Suzy outside wrapped around some guy, and it looked intense. It was strange enough to see Suzy doing anything other than playing piano and lurking in my window (okay, I'd never actually *seen* her playing piano and the lurking thing had happened once but once was enough), but there was something familiar about the guy she was kissing. I couldn't quite put my finger on it until Silas started honking the horn and yelling out of the window, "Get a room, dumbass!" Startled, the couple jumped apart. The guy turned around and opened his mouth to yell when a look of recognition crossed his face. A beat later, I gasped as recognition dawned on me, too. How in the Twilight Zone did Keith and Suzy know each other? Looking sheepish, Keith leaned into Suzy, whispering something in her ear, then sauntered over to Silas's side of the car while she stood there waiting.

"Thanks for the interruption, asshole," he said to Silas. Then he smiled when he noticed me in the car. "What's up, Simone?"

I gave him a quick wave and tried to hide the giggle bubbling up inside me. Keith and Suzy? It had never even crossed my mind that Keith was dating someone. He never mentioned it. And Suzy? I wondered why he hadn't said something when he dropped me off at home.

Silas smirked at Keith, not even bothering to try to hide his amusement, and said, "I'm taking Simone home, trying to get her to hang out with me tomorrow."

"Looks like you two made up," Keith said. He then raised his fist to Silas's for a fist bump and winked at me. "Glad to see it."

"Uh, so you and Suzy are a thing?" I asked Keith.

He fidgeted a little, then shrugged. "Oh, yeah. Me and Suzy kick it from time to time. No big deal." Beside me in the truck, Silas coughed in a poor attempt to hide the laughter that shook his shoulders. Fair enough. Seeing Silas laugh, I couldn't stop myself from joining in. The whole situation really was funny.

"Shut up, man. You know how it is with her," Keith said, admonishing Silas's laughter.

"Naw, dude, you're on your own here."

Keith shook his head at Silas. "Forget you," he said, then directed his attention at me. "Simone, it was good to see you. I'm sure I'll see you around soon?"

I nodded and waved goodbye as he walked off to join Suzy again.

"What was that about?" I asked Silas once he had rolled

up the windows.

Silas smirked. "Keith's my boy, but I've known him for a long time. He has commitment issues, we'll say."

"So it wasn't my imagination he was hitting on me that first night we met?"

"Oh, he definitely was," he replied. "But there was no way I was going to let him get a chance with you."

That was news.

"He and I had a little talk about you, and he agreed to back off when I told him how I felt about you."

My insides did a little flip flop. How he felt about me?

"We've been friends a long time, and he's a good guy, just not good in relationships."

"So," I ventured, done talking about Keith's relationship foibles, "how exactly did you tell him you felt about me?"

"Good try," he said. "How about this? You first."

"No deal," I said. "Come on. Show me yours and I'll show you mine."

His eyebrows quirked, and without skipping a beat, he said, "With pleasure."

"We're officially motherfucking done," Tiffany yelled while we danced to some nineties hip-hop song about getting around.

Tiffany had driven us to Detroit, and as congratulations for finishing the semester, her mom had offered to rent us a hotel room so we didn't have to worry about how we would get back to East Lansing. We got to the city, dropped off our bags, and went immediately to the nearest bar to pregame before venturing into a club in mid-town. It was a very different crowd than in East Lansing, but I liked it. It was my first time in Detroit, and I could finally see why people loved it. The architecture was stunning, the drinks were cheap, and the club was all kinds of wild. They played a mishmash of nineties hip-hop, top forty, and occasionally threw in some alternative rock for fun. The crowd was ready to party and we were right there with them.

I was having a blast with Courtney and Tiffany, but I couldn't stop thinking about Silas. He was probably out with Kevin and Rafael somewhere doing the same thing we were. At least I hoped he was.

"I need some water and a smoke," announced Tiffany. "Simone, come outside with me." When did she start caring about smoking inside? I'd seen Tiffany take a hit of her vape during our one and only study group in the library when she thought no one was watching, and she had the nerve to get pissed when Rafael asked her to quit it.

"We can't leave Courtney," I said.

Tiffany gave me a look and pointed to a dark corner. I squinted to see what she was pointing at and saw Courtney making out with some girl.

Good for her. She had made it known that she hadn't hooked up with anyone in over a year, since before law school, and her gift to herself for finishing her semester was to get laid. It looked like she was well on her way.

Tiffany grabbed my hand and dragged me with her to the patio. She was staring at me with this glint in her eye that I had come to know meant a question I wouldn't want to answer was about to follow.

"Tell me the truth, bitch. How did you end up in law school? You're not like the rest of us neurotics who were born to do this, so what's your deal?"

I had managed to avoid answering this question from her for an entire semester. I hadn't even fully divulged my secret to Silas. Tonight wasn't the first time Tiffany had asked, but it was the first time I had ever entertained giving her a straight answer. When she had asked before, I had given her the run around saying that it was dumb luck that brought me to law school.

I took a long swig of martini, finishing the half-full glass in one gulp. Tiffany had taught me well.

"Magic 8 Ball," I mumbled.

"What?" Tiffany said, like she hadn't heard me.

I leaned in close to her and said more clearly, "It was a Magic 8 Ball."

Tiffany looked at me like I had grown a third ear in the middle of my forehead.

"What the actual fuck? You didn't come to law school because a Magic 8 Ball told you to. That's ridiculous."

Ridiculous though it might be, it was exactly what had happened. Then I told her the whole story.

Tiffany looked gobsmacked, and she had every right to be.

"You've got to be shitting me. Are you some kind of secret genius?" I was mildly insulted that she insinuated my genius would have to be a secret, but I let it go.

"No, but I'm smart, and I take tests well. It worked out for me."

Tiffany looped her arm around my shoulders and gave me a squeeze. "You really are my own personal Elle Woods. Come on, let's go do a shot and make sure Courtney isn't banging some girl in the bathroom."

CHAPTER FIFTEEN

Tiffany called me crying a few days before Christmas.

"Oh my god, Tiff, what's the matter?" I shrieked into the phone, panicked at hearing her hiccupping sobs.

"It's—it's—it's—" She couldn't seem to finish her sentence.

"What is it? Is your family okay?" I asked.

"They're—they're fine." She started again. "It's—it's—" It sounded like she was struggling to breathe.

"Tiffany, I know you hate to hear this, but you need to calm down and tell me what happened. Take a few deep breaths and try again," I told her patiently.

She breathed deeply on the other end of the line before she spoke, still sounding halted but much more clear. "Grades came back and," she inhaled and exhaled deeply, "I got a B- in Contracts."

I knew I couldn't have heard correctly because there's no way a sane person would be hysterical over getting a B- in a class. Upset, maybe, but hysterical? Then again, was Tiffany considered sane? After our first midterm when she had gotten a B on our Constitutional Law exam, she had stormed Professor Shah's office demanding that she explain her grading process as well as the curve. She also tried to force her to review every single question she got wrong on the exam, which Professor

Shah heartily refused. She had gotten even more pissed off when she found out that Silas had gotten an A.

She went on, "How the fuck did I get a B-, Simone? I didn't get anything lower than an A- in any of my other classes, including Criminal Law, which I can't stand. I think that bitch is out to get me. I participate in her stupid class, I do all the reading...twice. I'm always prepared." Tiffany kept talking, but I stopped listening because it occurred to me that if Tiffany got a B-, there was no way I did any better. Despite my best efforts to prove to Patton that I was a good student, Contracts hadn't gotten any better for me. I had eked by with a low C on the midterm, and that was pretty much a miracle. Tiffany had gotten a B-. Shit.

"Simone, are you listening?" Tiffany asked.

"Of course I'm listening," I lied. Technically it wasn't a complete lie because I heard the words she was saying, just wasn't really comprehending them. Her ranting length was impressive, and my genuine dread at checking my grades was causing a strange sort of ringing in my ears.

"So, did you do okay this semester?" she asked, taking a pause on the hysterics. In high school and sometimes college, I felt like whenever people had asked about grades, what they really wanted to know was if you had done better than them, but with Tiffany her question seemed more curious than competitive. As crazy as Tiffany was about her own grades, she wasn't concerned about how other people did, as long as she did well. Like Silas, she went out of her way to make sure that I got all of the notes and didn't miss anything. So had I known my grades, I would have told her. But I didn't know them. I didn't want to know them until I absolutely had to. Why ruin my break early? I figured I could check them when I got back to school.

"I haven't checked," I told Tiffany.

"What?" she screamed into the phone. "How haven't you checked your grades? Don't you want to know how you did?"

"Whatever, I'll check when I get back to school. What's the big deal?"

I was trying to play it off to Tiffany like I didn't care about checking, but the truth was I was petrified to find out how I had done. Especially in Contracts. Patton's final was hard, and there was a good chance I hadn't done as well as I needed to. After midterms, I was doing fine enough in my other classes, but the thought of seeing my Contracts grade had me shook.

"Are you serious? Don't you recall what the dean said the first day of orientation?"

Of course I did, which was half the reason I hadn't checked my grades. Dean Hargrove had walked to the front of the large lecture hall and waited a good thirty seconds before talking. "Look to your left, look to your right. Come next semester at least one of you will not be here." The room had fallen silent as Dean Hargrove addressed the new class of 1Ls. I hadn't known if the dean was serious or just trying to scare us. Now I knew he was completely serious, and I didn't want to be a statistic.

"How did you do in your other classes?" I asked. I hoped she'd done well. Tiffany worked super hard all the time and had some of the loftiest goals of the group. She wanted to make partner at Emery Perkins before she was thirty-five. In addition to the position at CL&S, she was also applying to EP's summer program.

"That's not the point," she screeched. I touched my ear, shocked at the high-pitched noise coming out of my phone. "A B- on my transcript won't look good."

She wasn't wrong, but my guess was that it was the only

B on her transcript. Probably the only thing lower than an A- if I knew my friend, and I was confident she would get a job anywhere she wanted to go.

"Listen, you're right. I need to go check my grades," I told Tiffany. "You'll be fine. I'll call you tomorrow and we can talk about it more." I hung up the phone and hauled ass up the stairs to my parents' office where I had stored my school laptop and hadn't picked it up since the day I got home. I went immediately to the law school website. My palms were slick with sweat as I typed in my password. I hoped I would have to go through a couple screens before getting to my grades, but nope. I guessed the law school knew what people wanted to see. As soon as I was logged into my page on the portal, grades popped right up. My heart was racing, and I absently checked my pulse to make sure I wasn't actually having a heart attack. I read through my grades one by one, and my heartbeat slowed. Civil Procedure, B+. Criminal Law, B. Constitutional Law, B-. Legal Research and Writing, A. Not bad. The last grade on the page was Contracts, and my heart dropped when I saw my grade: D.

My skin started to get clammy, and the room was spinning. Was I about to faint? I sat down in the office chair and focused on breathing. Was this a panic attack? The longer I sat there, the more I spiraled.

What was I doing in law school, anyway? Obviously I'd made a huge mistake, and with a crappy grade in Contracts lowering my GPA, there was no way I would ever get a job, and if I couldn't get a job, I would have to move back home and live with my parents forever. Beckett would never let me live it down. My eyes welled up and hot tears started streaming down my face.

While I was drowning in tears and my own self-pity,

someone knocked on my parents' office door.

"Come in," I mumbled.

I looked up, and as soon as my mom saw the tears streaming down my face, she closed the distance and wrapped her arms around me.

"What happened, baby? What's the matter?" she asked, concern etched on her face.

I shook my head. My family were the last people I wanted to talk to about this. They and River had worked so hard to get me to school at the last minute, and here I was wondering if I was qualified to go back.

"You don't cry for nothing, Simone, so what happened?" she pushed.

I didn't want to tell my mom about my Contracts grade. I had quit the career I swore was my life's dream and then on a whim moved across the country. It wasn't a particularly good look in your mid-twenties to complain to your mom that you made a huge mistake and that you would probably need someone to help you move back home where you still had no money, no job, and no prospects.

I started to cry again, ugly crying, and I couldn't keep it in.

"I got a D in Contracts," I sobbed.

My mom stroked my hair like she had done when I was a kid and continued to hug me until I stopped shaking and eventually stopped crying. Then she pulled back and took a step away from me.

"And?" my mother asked.

"And by law school standards, I basically failed."

"How? Did you get Ds in all your classes?"

My mother, ever the voice of reason.

"No. But it's not like I aced them all, either. Maybe I was too hasty leaving Ipsa's. Maybe I'm just not cut out for law school."

Hearing myself talk, I wondered if Patton had given me a D because she somehow knew I'd bring the drama. Maybe she thought I'd rock my D like Hester Prynne and her red A.

"Honey, you should have left Ipsa's long before you did. That man was a textbook horrible boss on his best days. It was obviously taking a toll on you, and you hadn't seemed to love it for a long time."

She was right. Jordan's asshole behavior was the final nail in my proverbial coffin, but my distaste for working in professional kitchens had been building for longer than I cared to admit.

"Look, I can't tell you what to do with your life, you're a grown woman, but I want you to really think about whatever you do next. Make sure if you run, you're running toward something you want, not away from something you're afraid of."

"I'm not running away. I'm being chased out. What am I supposed to do then?"

"By who?" she asked, crossing her arms and perching on the edge of the desk she and my father shared. "Last I heard, you had a bad run-in with one professor. Are you planning on letting one person and one bad grade dictate your life and your abilities? Because if so, me and your father need to talk about where we went wrong. If you want to be a lawyer, be a lawyer. Don't fall back on the easy thing just because you're scared of the hard one."

Her last comment felt like a gentle way of saying, "Get your shit together," but she didn't graduate from the Tiffany Alston school of tough love.

My mom gave me a quick kiss on the cheek before announcing that she and my dad were headed to dinner.

I wanted to talk to someone else. Someone who would

understand the gravity of the situation. I wanted to call Tiffany, but she was in the middle of her own crisis, so I called Silas instead.

"Hey, California! What's up?" Since I had been home, Silas and I had texted a few times, mostly about nonsense, but we hadn't talked at all. He sounded happy to hear from me though, and just hearing his voice calmed me down.

"I got a D in Contracts," I told him without bothering with any pleasantries.

"Oh. That's rough. How did you do in your other classes?" Okay. Silas didn't seem to be getting the point.

"A D. In Contracts. In law school," I repeated slower to him. I wanted to make sure he understood.

Just as slowly as I had spoken, he replied, "I heard you. The first time. That's rough. Other classes?"

I sighed into the phone.

"California, it's not the end of the world, okay? It's a D your first semester. No one died, no one's sick, and you have a whole other semester to do better. You're smart. You'll do better next semester."

He was being so sweet, I almost didn't want to tell him I wasn't certain I would be back.

"When do you get back to school?" Silas asked.

"I'm not really sure yet," I caged. "Why?"

"Because I miss you, why do you think?"

If I didn't go back, I would miss all of my friends, but missing Silas might physically hurt.

I took a deep breath and blew it out before saying, "I don't know if I'm coming back. I don't think I'm cut out for law school."

There was silence on his end of the phone.

"Are you there?" I asked.

"Yeah, I'm here," he responded.

"Well, did you hear what I said?"

"I heard you. I'm just ignoring you. Didn't we have a whole conversation about this?"

I rolled my eyes. "Silas, seriously?"

"Yeah, seriously. It's one grade. You can't decide to leave law school over one class. You're better than that."

Right now it didn't seem like I was.

Silence again.

Then he asked, "What if I promise I'll help you?"

"You already helped me and look how it turned out."

"You got one crap grade, but it doesn't sound like the others are bad. Is this because of Patton?" He paused briefly, waiting for me to answer, but when I didn't, he continued. "Because if it is, Simone, that's dumb as hell. She's hard on everyone. Literally. Everyone. Including me. And be honest, do you really feel like you've tried your hardest in her class?"

I thought about what he asked. I really did feel like I was trying hard in her class. Except that after the incident where I was late and she gave me a verbal ass kicking, it had seemed futile to spend much time on Contracts because no matter what, she was going to grade me harshly. At least that's how it had felt. So maybe I slacked off a little on occasion for the reading in her class, and after the midterm, maybe I'd spent a little less time studying for Contracts than I did for my other classes.

"California, if you leave, you're the only one who'll lose. All Patton's ever really asked is that you try hard and be prepared. Can you honestly say you've done that for her class?"

I hated when he was right.

. . .

I hadn't seen much of River since I'd been home, and I missed her. She called me to go to dinner, and although I was back to couch wallowing, she suggested our favorite restaurant and lured me with the promise of a big hug and a pitcher of sangria. I wanted both. Picaro had the best patatas brava and paella I'd had outside of Spain. I got to the restaurant a little before River and managed to get a table near the window. The vibrant murals outside of the Mission District restaurant made window seats the prime location. They represented the neighborhood itself: vibrant, colorful, and eclectic. After graduation, when River moved back to California from New York, she announced she didn't want to live in Oakland and promptly found an inexpensive studio in the Mission right next to Picaro. We'd been hanging out in the Mission and going to Picaro since high school, so her finding the studio next door was kismet.

Late as usual, River breezed into the restaurant, turning heads as she walked by. When we didn't see each other for long periods, I tended to forget the kind of attention she garnered when she walked into a room. Giving me a tight hug before slinging her purse and jacket across the back of her chair, River said, "Sorry I'm late! I was finishing something for work and lost track of time." Since she was dressed in work clothes, I didn't give her a hard time about the fact that she lived right next door. Her office was closer to the Marina District, and that was much more of a trek to the Mission.

"You're always late." It was true. River was perpetually tardy. It was crazy because she set alarms for everything, but for some reason, they didn't seem to help her get anywhere on time.

"Fair," she said, tossing her hair over her shoulder and tugging at the ends like she did whenever she wanted to talk about something but didn't know how.

Immediately on alert, I asked, "Is everything okay?"

"Yeah, yeah, it's fine," she lied.

"I've known you since we were kids, and whenever you're nervous about starting a conversation, you tug on the end of your hair," I pointed out. "So what's up?" I asked.

She stopped tugging on her hair and met my eyes.

"I need to tell you something, but I don't want you to judge me."

The last time River told me something she didn't want to be judged about was in college when she adopted a puppy only to return it to the shelter a week later when she realized that puppies wake up very early in the morning and she liked to sleep until noon.

"No judgment from me. What is it?" I asked, nervous that I wouldn't be able to keep my promise not to judge.

River took a deep breath and looked around before she spoke.

"Well—" she started, but I interrupted her.

"Let me order a drink first," I said, signaling the nearest waiter to take our order. She was acting a little circumspect and was dangerously close to losing a patch of hair if she tugged any harder. I needed some liquid reinforcement in front of me before she started. Once the waiter brought our sangria and I had taken a generous sip of mine, I told her I was ready to hear whatever it was she had to say.

"So," she started, "obviously I didn't intend for this to happen and it doesn't mean anything, not really, but I've been sleeping with my boss."

Oh God, this again? This wasn't her first go-'round sleeping with a boss, so I wasn't sure why she had expected me to be shocked. She had a thing for power, or at least perceived power, and bosses were her thing. It was an odd River quirk.

"Okay," I said, not pointing out that we'd had this exact conversation about a different boss when she was in college and then again in her very first job right out of college. "Are you into him?"

She sighed heavily and rested her chin in her hands.

"I like him," she said simply.

"Tell me about him," I said. Given her nerves and lack of immediate gushing, I worried he might be married or involved or something. River wasn't exactly the homewrecking type, but she did believe that love should conquer all, and when she was in love nothing got in her way, and one time the thing in her way was a wife.

"He's wonderful. He's funny and smart and interesting and, for what it's worth, a really good boss."

That all sounded great, but there had to be something else.

"Is he married?" I flat-out asked.

"No!" she shrieked. "That was one time and I didn't know he was married at first."

"Sorry! You know I had to ask, though." The waiter came by and took our orders, giving me a moment to think about how I should pose my next question without sounding like a jerk. Deciding it was inevitable, I went for it.

"So what's wrong with him?" I asked.

"Nothing!" she shrieked again, and I wished we were at home because every time her shrill voice pierced the air, the tables nearby turned to glare at us.

"Well, Rivvy, you're being all weird about this so *something* must be wrong with him. Does he have messed-up teeth?" She shook her head no as I continued to go through the list of things that had been dealbreakers for her in the past. "Is he kinda dumb? Is he kinda short? Does he have too much hair growing out of his ears? Does he have a collection of stuffed animals he keeps on his couch that you can't touch? Does his dog hate you?" She continued to shake her head no, then it came to me. "Holy shit, does he have a micro-penis?!" For reasons I couldn't explain, River and I had gotten fascinated by the idea of micro-penises when we had learned about them in health class in high school. I had no idea why our health teacher chose to talk about micro-penises, maybe to normalize it, but as soon as school was over, River and I hauled ass home to look it up online. We spent way too long trying to figure out how people had sex with them and then promised that if either of us ever encountered a man with a micro-penis, we'd tell the other. We were immature back then, but I was certain the pact remained.

I waited with bated breath to hear about his micro-penis. Aside from spending time with Riv, hearing about a micro-penis would make leaving the couch worth it. Disappointment washed over me when she threw a tiny piece of the bread at me that the waiter had put down moments ago and said, "No, you idiot, he doesn't have a micro-penis. His is lovely and regular sized."

"Then what is it? Why are you being so cagey?"

She sighed and looked down at her hands before saying, "I'm not being cagey. It's just—" She paused and looked up at me. "It's just that he's a bit older. A lot older."

"How old is a lot older?" I asked.

"He's fifty-six."

"Is he a young fifty-six?" It was all I could think to ask. If he was a young fifty-six, maybe it didn't matter?

"He's a young fifty-six." She paused, then said, "But his kids are a couple years older than me and refuse to acknowledge I exist. They live at home with him, so I haven't even been able to see where he lives."

Welp. Okay.

"That sounds like bad news. He's old and—"

"Does it matter?" she interrupted coolly.

"And he has kids older than you who won't acknowledge your existence."

"I think I love him, Simone."

I should have read the room better, or the table as it were, but instead, I blurted out, "This sounds like a horrible idea." I covered my mouth, realizing almost immediately that I'd said too much. But it was true! While she was generally good at the whole adulting thing, River still liked to party, had occasional mini-tantrums when she didn't get her way, and not too long ago had asked her parents for $500 because she had spent most of her rent money on two new pairs of Louboutins and a tiny Saint Laurent purse. She mostly had her life together but slipped up from time to time. The only thing I could think was that this old man wanted to take advantage of my beautiful friend because she was young and too trusting for her own good.

"I'm sorry," I said before she could respond to my outburst. "I'm sure he's lovely, but he *is* a little old with a lot of baggage, don't you think?"

She glared at me. I glared right back. The waiter put our food down, and I thanked him without breaking eye contact with River. She wasn't going to win this one. I wanted to eat, but I couldn't cut my food *and* glare at River, so when she finally looked away, I blinked furiously and started eating my food. So did River. After taking a few bites, she set her fork down.

"That's why I was hesitant to tell you. I knew you would overreact and be all judgy. Thomas is nice to me, we enjoy each other's company, and we're not hurting anyone. I'm not saying he's 'the one,' but he might be, and I do like him."

I suspected River was running headlong into a world of hurt, but she was an adult and I had just, *just* promised I wouldn't judge her, and that was pretty much the first thing I did. Gathering my wits and deciding to eat a little crow, I said, "I'm sorry. For real this time. I'm sure you know what you're doing with this guy."

"Thank you, I do. He's a good guy."

I really did want it to work out for her. River wanted so badly what her parents had.

After a moment of slightly awkward silence, River asked, "So, what's up with you?" mercifully moving on from old man talk. I guessed she'd truly accepted my apology.

"Nothing interesting," I said. "School is kicking my ass, I got the first D of my life, and I never feel like I know anything in class. Other than that, same old, same old."

River rightfully looked concerned. It wasn't like me to host my own pity party. At least historically it wasn't though recently that hadn't been the case.

"You want to talk about it?" she asked, tilting her head. I could tell she was worried about me, but I didn't really want to talk about it.

"I don't know," I said. "It's just that school turned out to be a lot more intense than I anticipated. I knew it would be hard, but I didn't realize the work and the stress would be nonstop. I'm trying to work through it, but sometimes it feels like I'm trudging through mud with no end in sight."

I didn't say anything about considering not going back. I didn't want to broadcast my quitter status until I was sure it would be my status for good.

"I'm sorry," River said. "What can I do?"

"Come visit me," I suggested before remembering I might not be there. "You can meet the whole cast of characters."

Having known each other so long, it wasn't until college that we actually had separate friends, and even then, we talked enough that I knew or knew of most of her friends from college and she knew most of mine. Now, my law school life was a mystery to my oldest friend. She'd heard me mention Tiffany and Silas in the few conversations we'd managed to squeeze in between our schedules, but it was mostly in passing, and even though she'd met Silas, she didn't *know* know him.

"You can meet Tiffany and see Silas again. He's been amazing helping me study, making sure I get out of the house and meet people, taking me grocery shopping. He's the best part of law school."

River looked at me curiously, a smile threatening to sneak its way onto her face.

"What?" I asked. She was giving me the same smug look she gave me when I first told her about my ex.

"Nothing," she responded. The smile she had been fighting won the battle on her face. "Aren't you glad I introduced you two?"

"Technically you didn't, but I'm glad you pointed him out."

CHAPTER SIXTEEN

"Simone, someone's here to see you," my dad whisper-yelled into my room. He sounded perturbed.

I rolled over in the bed my parents had put in my old room when I moved out the first time. It wasn't nearly as comfortable as my original bed, but I figured I could get used to it if I had to. Squinting, I reached for my phone on the nightstand to see what time it was. The clock said six thirty a.m., but that couldn't be right. I didn't know anyone who would show up to my parents' house before nine a.m. They all knew my mom stood on convention and didn't believe visitors should drop by her house before she had time to shower, get dressed, and do her makeup. At six thirty in the morning, we were all still in bonnets and pajamas. I hadn't planned on getting up until at least noon like any good soon-to-be basement baby.

"Tell them they have the wrong house. Nobody I know would come over here this early," I informed him, then put the pillow over my head.

"It's that boy from school. The one me and your mom met when we moved you in. What was his name? Saul, Steve, something like that," my dad insisted.

"I don't know anyone with any of those names," I groaned at him, half asleep.

This was getting ridiculous.

"Simone, you better get down there and get rid of that boy. It's early, and I don't have time for this."

I groaned and crawled out of the bed. Who was it and why wasn't my dad telling them to go away?

I dragged myself down the stairs and was met with my dad's glare.

"He's on the front porch," he threw at me before trudging back down the hall.

I peeked out of the peephole and saw the back of a curly head. I ducked down, then peeked out again.

What the hell was Silas doing in Oakland? He was supposed to be in East Lansing or at least Pleasant Ridge. Christmas was in two days.

I opened the door.

"Silas?"

He turned around with a huge, sheepish grin on his face. "Oh man, tell your pop I'm so sorry. I remember what you told me about your mom and visitors."

I was still trying to process the fact that Silas was standing on the porch of my childhood home when he scooped me up into a huge bear hug. I was too stunned to even hug him back, and he mostly squished my arms to my sides.

"I missed you, California. And when we talked, it sounded like you needed a hug,"

"But, but—" I sputtered. "But you live in Michigan. And how did you know where my parents live?"

"I have a credit card, a suitcase, and the internet. Plus, I have River's phone number. I texted her for your folks' address when I landed. After I talked to you, I booked a flight here."

I smiled, really smiled for the first time in days. I stretched up to wrap my arms around his neck and give him a kiss on the cheek.

"Now that's the kind of welcome I was looking for," he said. "Can I come in? Will your folks care?"

"Yeah, but come in anyway. They'll understand," I said and opened the door wider for him to come inside. "Are you hungry?"

"Starving. They weren't really serving food on the flight, and I didn't eat before I left home," he answered, then gave me the dimpled smile he knew would get me to say yes to almost anything. "You want to whip me up one of your Dutch Babies I've heard so much about?"

"Pretty ballsy coming into my parents' house and asking me to cook for you, don't you think?"

"Absolutely, but I'm hungry and you missed me so much, I know you won't say no," he asserted. And he was right. "You can show me how to make some eggs to go with it, and we could have breakfast ready for your folks when they get up."

I pretended to mull it over knowing damn well I would be cooking Silas breakfast. He had flown over four hours to come see me and give me a much-needed reason to smile. I would make him whatever he wanted.

"Come on, you can put your stuff in my room, then we can start cooking," I said, pointing him toward the stairs. "Make sure to skip the third one, though. It creaks and my mom is a light sleeper. My bedroom is the second on the right."

While Silas dropped his gear in my room, I gathered the ingredients. He had asked for something easy, and I made Dutch Baby batter in under ten minutes. I only needed eggs, flour, sugar, and a pinch of salt. I checked the refrigerator, and we had maple syrup and fresh fruit to top it with.

By the time he got back downstairs, the batter was ready and I was heating the cast-iron skillet in the oven.

"It already smells good. What is that?" he asked, sniffing the air.

"Butter. It should be done in a minute," I said.

I took the strawberries and blueberries out of the refrigerator.

"Can you wash these and slice the strawberries," I asked, then added, "without maiming yourself?"

"Very funny. Yes, I can cut some strawberries without cutting myself."

We worked in comfortable silence until the oven timer signaled the pancake was ready.

"If there were no bloody mishaps, can you put the fruit out on the table? We can eat the stuff you cut, and when my parents get up, I'll make them another one and you can cut more fruit if you don't mind."

"Not at all."

Silas sat down at the table and tore off a piece of the large, flat pancake, topped it with fruit, then drenched it in maple syrup. I did the same.

"Damn, this is good," he said.

Footsteps pounded down the stairs, and I turned when my dad entered the kitchen.

He stopped when he saw Silas sitting at the table. Without acknowledging Silas, he said, "Why is this boy in my kitchen eating my food?"

"Dad, be nice."

He stared at me, then Silas, then back at me. "Hm."

"Silas, you remember my dad, Henry Alexander."

Silas stood up to shake my dad's hand. "Nice to see you again, Mr. Alexander."

My dad looked at Silas's hand, then back up at Silas without shaking it. "Uh-huh, you too. Why are you at my house this early?"

Silas cleared his throat, looking a little uncomfortable. "Sir, Simone called me and sounded upset so I wanted to come check on her as soon as I could get a flight out. I didn't consider the time change."

I hadn't told my dad I was considering not going back, so I was happy Silas had the grace not to bring it up.

My dad nodded at Silas, then extended his hand, saying, "I appreciate you coming to check on my daughter. She can handle herself fine, but I'm glad to know she has someone in her corner out there in the sticks."

Silas laughed and said, "I'm happy to do it, sir."

As Silas went to sit back down, another set of footsteps sounded, and before I could warn my mother that we had company she was already in the kitchen wearing her bonnet and nightgown. For unknown reasons, she hadn't noticed the giant man sitting at her kitchen table.

"Something smells good in here," she said, sniffing the air. She walked over to the counter and snagged a berry off the kitchen island. "I missed your cooking, sweetie."

"Mom, we have company," I alerted her. When she turned around and laid eyes on Silas, she let out a small yelp, hands going immediately to her head. She didn't say anything before she backed out of the kitchen and hightailed it up the stairs.

"So you're only here for the night?" I asked Silas. We sat at the kitchen table after we had cleaned up our breakfast dishes and I'd apologized to my mom for the unexpected visitor.

He nodded. "I need to get back for Christmas. Lauren comes in Christmas Eve for a few days, and I don't want to leave my dad to fend for himself," he said, then he stretched across the table to pick up my hand. I admired his perfectly muscled forearms, and I couldn't resist running a hand down it. He smiled and said, "So I only have a few hours to convince you to come back to school."

I'd missed touching him and, more so, having him touch me. "I want to show you around Oakland. Show you some of my favorite places."

He shook his head at my obvious avoidance but said, "I'm down to see Oakland. I've never been here."

"All right, let me get showered and dressed and we can get going. You can wait down here," I said. Standing up, I motioned for him to follow me to the den. "The remote is in the coffee table drawer if you want to watch something."

"I'm cool," he said. "I might take a little nap while I wait for you."

I ran up the stairs, taking them two at a time. If I hurried, I would be able to show Silas a few of my favorite places and make it back in time to take him somewhere good for dinner. One of the perks of staying with my parents was that I had an exceptionally nice en suite bathroom. When they had the house remodeled when I was a teenager, my mom had said she was tired of me using all her expensive face creams and that if I had my own bathroom maybe I would leave her stuff alone. It hadn't worked, but I had loved having my own bathroom. I had gotten to decorate it myself, and my parents hadn't changed it since I'd left, so it was still one of my favorite places in the house.

I jumped in the shower and spent longer than usual shaving my legs and armpits, something I usually only did if someone other than me was going to see them. A girl could hope. When I got out of the shower, I did a quick dry of my body, tossed the towel onto the rack, then moisturized, brushed my teeth, and took off my shower cap. I slipped on my favorite robe and opened the bathroom door. Across the room, Silas was laid out on my bed, arms over his chest, looking at the ceiling.

"Comfortable?" I asked. Seeing him on my bed, my thoughts drifted to all the activities we could do on a bed. Maybe my bed if we were quiet.

"Extremely," he said but sat up as I got closer.

I pulled the sash on my robe a little tighter and sat down next to him. He gently tugged on the loose end and rubbed it between his fingers.

"I like this robe."

"Thanks," I said, scooting a little closer to him. The movement loosened the end of the sash he had in his hand and the robe started to slip off of my shoulder. Silas's gaze followed its slow movement. I flushed and pulled it back up onto my shoulder, tightening the sash again.

"Don't do that on my account. You should feel free to let that robe drop as far down as you'd like."

I grinned. "I missed you."

He reached his hand up to my face and stroked a finger down my cheek. Without thinking about it, I leaned further into him, relishing his touch.

"I missed you, too," he said.

I smiled up at his handsome face and wondered if I was crazy to have given this up. Given him up.

He stood up then, pulling me out of my thoughts.

"Let me go downstairs so you can get ready. I want to see everything that made you, you." He bent down and brushed a kiss across my forehead before heading out the door.

I stayed seated on my bed, trying to collect my thoughts. Everything about Silas felt good, and I couldn't believe he had traveled all that way to dole out a pep talk. Granted, it was a much-needed pep talk, but it was one that could have been done over the phone.

When I was dressed and ready to go, I found him sitting on the den couch. "You ready?" I asked.

"Whenever you are," he replied. "I can't wait to see a little of The Town."

We got into my car, and I did a quick mental checklist of the places I most wanted him to see: Lake Merritt, the view of San Francisco from the Oakland Hills, and Jack London Square. I also wanted to show him Ipsa's. River had texted me a couple of weeks ago and mentioned that she'd heard from one of our friends that Jordan got fired for going full-on Gordon Ramsey and asking one of the line cooks if they were an idiot sandwich. It turned out the new line cook was Julian's cousin or something, and when he mentioned the idiot sandwich thing, Julian did what he told me I should have done years ago: rat Jordan out to the owner and get his crazy ass fired.

I hesitated.

"Do you want to see where I worked before I started school?"

"You know I do," he said.

"All right, we can do that, but is there anything you want to see first? I have a few other places I want to show you, but if there's something you especially want to see, we can do that instead."

"I heard Oakland has insane redwoods. You mind if we check those out?"

"Not at all. That's perfect as long as you have some good

shoes on. We can get in a quick hike before we head to Ipsa's later."

The redwoods were stunning as always, and Silas was surprised to see such incredible hiking right in the city. Sweaty, tired, and hungry after a long day of exploring, Silas and I drove to Ipsa's for an early dinner. As soon as I parked in the lot, my heart started pounding. I hadn't been back since I'd quit.

I didn't recognize the host, and after a quick once-over of the waitstaff on the floor, I didn't recognize any of them, either. Not that I necessarily had a burning desire to see any of them after my spectacularly unprofessional exit, but recognizing someone on staff would have been helpful in getting a table. The waiting area was small, and it was starting to fill up. It was early, but Ipsa's was popular, and we didn't have a reservation. If Jordan was indeed gone, he'd been wrong every time he'd proclaimed that the restaurant would sink into nameless purgatory without him.

"Do you have space for two at the bar?" I asked.

She told us we could seat ourselves wherever we found a spot. The long bar wrapped around the open kitchen, and there were two seats open at the very end.

"Let's grab those," I said, pulling Silas toward the seats. I wanted to see if the rumors about Jordan being gone were true. During dinner service, he tended to bounce between front of the house and back of the house. He rarely cooked most nights, and frankly, his being out of the kitchen had made it run much more smoothly. The staff was more relaxed whenever Jordan wasn't cooking right next to them. Observing the kitchen, I saw a couple familiar faces, but none belonged to him. Interesting. Julian had said on more than one occasion that Jordan was asking for a harassment suit, but I didn't fully believe him at the time. In my experience, people like Jordan never got punished for their bad behavior. I hoped this time I was wrong.

"So you worked here, huh?" Silas asked.

I pointed to the kitchen. "There to be exact. For almost five years."

Silas nodded. "And you just up and quit?"

"Not exactly. Jordan was a straight-up kitchen nightmare. When I'd staged with him for my interview, he was enthusiastic, and I was super excited about working for him, but as soon as I was hired, it was like he flipped a switch. He constantly screamed at the staff, occasionally threw things, and basically told the chefs that everything they worked hard on was trash, even when it was done to perfection. Which, okay, fine. I understood he wanted to make sure the restaurant did well and his job was also on the line if we didn't perform, but his way of doing it was unacceptable."

I shook my head at the memory of him telling me my sauce tasted like cat vomit. I didn't know how he knew how cat vomit tasted, and there was no way I was going to ask.

"Anyway, he was awful. But when I quit, it was something I'd been thinking about for a couple years. I was starting to really dislike the thing I loved the most, which, as you well know, is cooking, and I didn't want that. So yeah."

He nodded, taking it all in.

"I've asked you this before, but I never got a straight answer. Why law school?"

I shrugged, took a steadying breath, and told him about meeting Julian and about loving my philosophy minor. I told him everything right up until the Magic 8 Ball part, which I glossed over.

"So yeah, it was the one other career that came to mind

when I thought about what I wanted to do next, thanks to Julian. I was tired of being broke all the time, and I wanted to do something that involved thinking and problem solving like philosophy does. Helping people sounded awfully appealing, too. And law school checked all of those boxes."

"So has that changed for you?" he asked.

I thought about it, and it wasn't like I hated law school. Most of the time I liked it. It was hard and it wasn't what I expected, but I didn't hate it. And hearing that Julian's firm had finally managed to get Jordan out didn't make me want to go back to Ipsa's. It made me want to do what Julian did.

"No. I guess it hasn't."

CHAPTER SEVENTEEN

The realities of being back at school hit hard the moment I stepped out of the Lyft from the airport. It looked like a blizzard had hit East Lansing while I was gone, and everything in sight was white. Slogging through the snow to my apartment, suitcase in tow, I wished I had worn a pair of the Ugg boots I'd spent so much time mocking before I realized, living in the snow, they were less a fashion statement and more a necessity. My apartment was freezing. The heater hadn't been on in a couple of weeks, and my feet were sopping wet from walking the short distance from the airport to the rideshare area and from the car to my apartment. When I got inside, I turned on the heater, took off my shoes, and started to unpack. I was almost finished when my phone started vibrating. I smiled when I saw Silas's name come up.

"Hey, Cookie," I said.

"Where are you?" he asked cautiously.

"Michigan," I responded. "I'm back!"

I laughed at the slow clap coming from his side of the phone.

"Good choice. How did you get home from the airport?"

"Took a Lyft," I replied, knowing he was about to get pissed off at me.

"Why'd you take a Lyft?" he bellowed into the phone. "I could have picked you up. You should have called me. You know I wouldn't have minded."

I knew he wouldn't have minded, but the drive was far and I wanted to use that time to think. Thankfully my Lyft driver wasn't a talker.

"How long have you been back?" I asked, silently praying I could change the subject without him noticing.

"Don't try to change the subject. Next time you have to go to or from the airport, you tell me, and I'll take you. Lyft is dangerous. I thought you watched *SVU*?"

Ignoring his comment about *Law & Order: Special Victims Unit*, I asked about what he'd been doing since he got home from visiting me.

"Did you do anything for New Year's Eve?" I asked.

He hesitated a moment, then said, "Oh yeah. A friend was in town, and she and I hung out. You?"

My stomach knotted at the thought of him spending NYE with some nameless, faceless woman.

"Oh?" I said, trying to sound casual but pretty sure I was failing.

"Yeah, it was no big deal. We hadn't seen each other in a while and wanted to catch up. You?"

Silas spent New Year's Eve with someone. A female someone. A not-me female someone. New Year's Eve was easily the second most stressful holiday after Valentine's Day for relationships. Or wannabe relationships. Or single people looking for relationships. Or probably just people in general. Folklore said that kissing someone at midnight offered good luck for the rest of the year, and it mattered who you kissed starting off the year. For instance, River and I had spent every New Year's Eve together since we were old enough to grasp the gravity of having New Year's Eve plans. This year, the Dasans threw a huge party at their house, so it took some of the pressure off of finding something to do. We invited a bunch of our mutual friends, drank a ton of champagne, and everyone kissed everyone at midnight as an insurance policy for the new year. But I hadn't had a date and it sounded like he had. I'd also called him at midnight his time and he hadn't answered the phone. I'd hoped he was sleeping, but that didn't sound like the case. It was probably because he was out with someone else.

"Went to a party at River's folks' house. What did you guys do?" I asked. Torturing myself with visions of Silas and faceless woman was not exactly how I wanted to start a new semester, but I had to know.

"We chilled. We actually ended up going to—"

Please don't say La Pergola.

"—La Pergola. She'd read about it on some *Eater* list, and I told her it was solid."

"Sounds fun, but look, I just got home so I need to unpack. Talk to you later?"

"Uh, sure, okay. Everything all right over there?"

"I'm good. I just had a long car ride and want to unpack and rest a little. I'll call you tomorrow," I told him, then hung up the phone.

Who was this friend he had to catch up with? Dinner and drinks on New Year's Eve sounded too much like a date.

I bristled at the thought of him dating someone who wasn't me.

I had pressed pause on everything with Silas, and for what? It wasn't like by spending less time with him I'd spent more time studying. Sometime after Silas left Oakland but before I went back to school, I'd had a come-to-Jesus with myself.

I'd lit a soothing candle, opened my laptop, and looked at my grades again. Outside of Contracts, they really weren't bad. I wasn't at the top of the class or anything like that, but it could have been much, much worse. So what was it about Contracts that defeated me? When I did the reading, I felt like I understood the cases, and during study group I rarely had a problem dissecting them. Yes, Patton graded harshly, but I was still better than a D. So the only conclusion I'd come to was that I was getting in my own way and maybe dialing it in during class because I was intimidated. I started law school lukewarm, and having Patton be my first introduction to this unknown world hadn't helped convince me of my decision, but when I thought about my other classes, I liked them. And while I was scared shitless much of the time, I still wanted that internship at CL&S, and I still wanted to be in law school. It was the first time I'd admitted it to myself, and it felt good. A bad grade wasn't the end of the world, and I had a whole other semester (and two more years) to course correct. And, I suspected, it didn't have to be all or nothing with Silas. At least, it didn't have to be nothing.

I got down the 8 Ball and asked, "Is Silas dating someone else?" Before the haze cleared, I threw the ball on my bed. I didn't want to see its response.

The first day of the new semester flew in like a tornado. Thankfully, my first class back was with Professor Mason. He taught Criminal Law in the fall semester, but in the spring semester, he taught Torts.

"It's nice to see your shiny faces again this semester,"

announced Professor Mason when class started. "I'm happy to see that most of you came back. I worried I'd frightened you off." He winked. We all knew Professor Mason liked to joke with us and did all the time, unlike some of our stick-up-their-asses professors who acted like students were the bane of their existence.

"All right, folks, let's get down to business. If anyone can give me a torts-based hypothetical that shocks me more than my comforter story shocked you all, you'll get immunity from being cold-called for the first month of class, no questions asked. But be forewarned, I make this offer each semester to my Torts classes and no one has managed to shock me yet." He glanced around the class, and his eyes landed squarely on Silas's face, and he squinted before saying, "But you, Mr. Whitman, you just might be the one to do it."

Professor Mason's comforter example was outrageous. Just...outrageous. When he told it, I briefly wondered if he was making it up given the sheer number of details he gave, but the man had been a public defender, so he had seen all kinds of things. He told us the story when we discussed voluntary manslaughter last semester and our class was having a hard time understanding heat of passion as a mitigating circumstance. He was trying to show that it was different than first-degree murder because there was no premeditation. He said a case that happened in the heat of passion that stood out most for him happened early in his career and resulted from infidelity. His client was a woman who was accused of killing her husband's mistress. She had walked in on her husband having sex with his mistress in their marital bed. She screamed when she realized what was happening and told the woman to get out of her house. The woman calmly stood up, grabbed the edge of the wife's favorite comforter, and used it to wipe down her lady bits. As the woman started to put on her clothes, apparently the wife lost it and jumped on top of the woman, tackling her to the floor and strangling her to death. Coming up with something more shocking than that would have been a challenge.

I glanced over at Silas and could almost see the wheels in his head turning. It wasn't because he cared about getting called on in class because he never minded that part. He would want to do something that no one else had done before. So far it looked like Torts was going to be a fun class. I had briefed my cases the night before, and somehow the reading didn't seem to take quite as long as it had last semester. I even volunteered to talk in class—something I never would have done last semester outside of Contracts and that was only for survival. I felt like I understood torts so far. But five minutes before class ended, I felt dread start to kick in. I could tell the thing I would hate the most about Torts class was that it was immediately followed by Contracts. My second go-round with Patton.

Mason let us out a couple of minutes early, and I sat in my seat not moving, not packing my things. Silas banged around on one side of me, putting his laptop and books in his backpack, and Tiffany sat waiting for both of us on my other side. Silas and Tiffany both stood up and stared at me, waiting for me to move.

"What the fuck's wrong with you?" Tiffany finally asked. Over break I never got around to telling her that I'd gotten a D in Patton's class. She would have been devastated for me, and I hadn't needed that kind of emotion around. I was already devastated enough for myself. Hearing her pity would have made it worse.

"You guys go ahead. I'll be there in a second." I smiled

at Tiffany and waved her away. She frowned at me, not understanding why I was acting strange.

"I don't think you're okay," she said, sounding reserved for once.

"I'll be fine. Go ahead, I'll meet up with you in class."

I needed to sit and collect myself for a moment before I walked back into that classroom. Tiffany glanced at her watch and back at me.

"If you're sure…"

"I'm positive. I'll see you in class." I closed my eyes as she walked away, then I heard the seat next to me scrape against the floor. I opened one eye and saw that Silas had pulled the seat out and sat down.

"Thought we talked about this before you got back," Silas said. "I promised I would help you and I will. Did you get my notes for today?"

I had done the reading for all of my classes as soon as I had gotten back, but it hadn't left me any time to meet with Silas before Contracts, so instead, he sent me his notes on all of the cases planned for today so I could review those. Our study group hadn't scheduled a time to meet yet, either, since our schedule this semester was different than last.

"Yeah, I got them. Thanks, by the way."

"You don't need to thank me for anything. Did they help?"

I nodded and tried to smile at him, but I was sure it looked more like a grimace.

"Oookay, so why are we sitting here with," he looked down at his watch, "eight minutes to class and you looking like someone stole your puppy?"

"I'm nervous," I admitted.

Silas reached over and grabbed the bottom of my chair, turning it toward him and pulling it closer so his open knees bracketed mine.

"You're Simone Alexander. A strong, smart, grown-ass woman who isn't going to let a professor make you feel like you're not good enough. You're more than good enough, you're amazing, and we both know it, so get your cute ass out of that chair," he grabbed the hand sitting in my lap and pulled me upright, "and let's get to class."

When he put it that way, I had no choice but to get my cute ass out of the chair and follow him to class.

I pulled my bag off the floor and put it in Silas's outstretched hand. He looped the bag over his shoulder and slung his arm that wasn't weighed down by bags around my shoulder, pulling me in for a tight hug. "You got this."

We made it to class with five minutes to spare, and I had just enough time to take my seat and pull out my laptop with Silas's notes. Tiffany was already in her seat.

"Glad you made it," Tiffany said. "I was scared we'd have another repeat of last semester. Are you ready?"

I nodded and faced the front, waiting for Patton to get to the room. I glanced at the clock on my computer and saw that she had two minutes to get to class or she would be late. Something about the thought of her walking in late made me smile a little. Hopefully someone would have the balls to call her on it if she was late, though no one would. That old woman was scary, and I doubted any of my classmates would be willing to cross her and incur her wrath. I sure as shit wasn't.

The classroom was eerily quiet, which even in Patton's class was atypical. If I listened hard enough, I might literally have heard a pin drop, so when she stepped into the room, I heard her footfalls well before I saw the beast herself. I glanced at my clock again, and she was exactly on time. Figured she would be.

"We're officially in the second part of your Contracts course. Based on the quality of work I saw, most of you need to be back in Contracts I. We're supposed to curve your grades, and even though I don't believe in giving grades that weren't earned, the university makes me. In this class, there were only a handful of people who earned a grade above a B."

The only thing that really registered was that everyone in the class had done degrees of not well, and I wasn't the only one. Sure, I had done particularly poorly, but it helped to know that other people struggled, too. That it was hard and not just hard for me.

"For those of you who got below a C-," she looked directly at me as she said it, "I suggest you come to my office hours. It's obvious you need the extra help."

She was probably right. I needed to figure out how to do better. Uncharacteristically, Patton seemed to take pity on the class and didn't make anyone cry. It seemed like she was in a decent mood, so I gathered up all my courage and decided to check out her office hours. I despised her, but I hated having a bad grade even more. I told Tiffany where I was headed, and she wished me luck and godspeed. I waved at Silas and made the "I'll call you later" sign with my hands. If I waited too long to go to her office hours, I feared I would chicken out. There was a two-hour break between Contracts and Civil Procedure when I usually hung out with the crew, but I hoped I wouldn't run into anyone on my way to her office. The right distraction and my bravery would be shot to hell.

"Simone!" I heard Rafael calling my name, but I ignored

him and kept walking.

"Hey! Simone, wait up!" he called again. What did Rafael want? He and I rarely hung out unless we were with everyone else, so I couldn't imagine what he possibly needed from me now. I didn't turn around and hoped he would go away so I could continue my mission... He didn't. Instead, I felt a tap on my shoulder.

"Oh, hey, Raf. What's up?"

"Damn, Simone, I've been calling your name for like a minute. You didn't hear me?"

I chose to ignore the question because I didn't want to lie to him. I also didn't want to talk to him, but that wasn't an option without being out-and-out rude to my friend.

"How was your break?"

"It was all right. Went home, caught up with my boys in the Bronx, did some meditating...the same old, same old. Yours?"

"Good, good. It was nice to be home for a few weeks. Hey, I'm in a hurry. I'm trying to get up to Patton's office hours before everybody rushes up there." I started walking toward the stairs, and Rafael followed close behind, still talking.

"No, it's all good. Real quick, though, did Tiffany say anything to you about her break?"

I stopped walking, now curious. I hadn't gotten a chance to catch up with Tiff about break yet, and I didn't talk to her a whole lot during break.

"Uh, no. We haven't had a chance to catch up yet. Is she all right? Did something happen?" I felt like the worst friend ever. If something bad had happened to Tiff and I didn't know about it because I was caught up in my own shit, I would never forgive myself.

"Shit. No. She's fine. I just—" He paused and looked around the stairwell like he was searching for inspiration. "It's, uh—"

He stopped again, and I was starting to get frustrated. He said she was fine, so what did he want?

"Spit it out, Rafael," I snapped, sounding much harsher than I meant. My nerves were already frayed, and he wasn't helping.

"Ugh, I'm sorry, Simone. I don't want you to miss office hours. We'll catch up later. It's all good." Rafael gave me a quick peck on my cheek and walked away. And suddenly I felt like a posting in Reddit's Am I the Asshole. All signs pointed to yes, I was in fact the asshole, but I would apologize to Rafael next time I saw him.

As I walked up the stairs, I also made a mental note to ask Tiffany about it later. With only one flight of stairs between me and Patton, I took a deep breath and walked up the last flight with a confidence I didn't feel but was happy to fake. She was unlocking her door when I got to her office.

"Hi, Professor Patton." My voice squeaked in a way I didn't know was possible. It sounded like a Frankenstein cross between Minnie Mouse and Betty Boop.

Thank you, body, for betraying me at the exact *wrong* moment.

I cleared my throat and tried again, hoping I wasn't giving Elizabeth Holmes vibes. "Hi, Professor Patton." This time I sounded like an adult.

"Oh. Hello, Ms. Alexander. I hoped you would make it to my office hours. Please, come in," Professor Patton said as she opened the door, motioning me forward.

Now this was a surprise. She wasn't smiling or anything to denote a sense of warmth, but her tone certainly didn't fit her demeanor. She seemed genuinely pleased that I decided to stop by. And her office wasn't anything like I'd expected. The woman herself was terrifying, but her office was downright cozy despite its vast size. She had a small couch in the corner flanked with decorative legal-themed pillows, and she even had one with Ruth Bader Ginsburg's face on it. Photos and degrees covered her walls. Coincidence to end all coincidences, like me, she had gone to Berkeley for undergrad and had graduated *magna cum laude* from Stanford Law. No shocker there.

I stood gawking at her degrees and photos until I heard her say, "Surprised to see I have a family?"

I turned, embarrassed because that's *exactly* what I was thinking. The people in the photos ranged from babies to folks that looked about her age. In one, a very dapper older man with a thick Santa Claus beard had his arm wrapped tightly around Patton's shoulders, and she grinned from ear to ear. There was a gorgeous beach in the background. In another, a younger woman, about my age, crouched next to Patton, and they both smiled at the camera.

"That's my eldest granddaughter, Eliza. I had hoped she would be joining me here next year, but as young people do, she changed her mind and decided to take a year off to travel the world. I'm disappointed but so very proud of her moxie." A hint of a smile hit her face as she spoke about her granddaughter. "Please, Ms. Alexander. Have a seat. Can I offer you some tea or coffee?"

I nodded stupidly and settled into the nearest chair facing her desk.

"Which would you like, Ms. Alexander, tea or coffee?"

Too stunned to think about which one I wanted, I said tea since it seemed like the easiest, fastest thing to make in the moment. Patton reached beneath her desk and handed me a mug and a box full of at least ten different types of tea.

"Help yourself. There's a kettle behind you."

I took the mug from her hands and reached blindly into the

box, pulling out a tea bag. I opened the package and placed the teabag in the mug, noting that I had pulled out Earl Grey tea. I'd never tried it, but there was no time like the present to discover something new. I stood up and walked to the kettle on the other side of the office.

As I poured the water, Patton started to speak. "I assume you're here to discuss your abysmal grade on my final exam?"

And she was back. I knew it was too good to hope that perhaps she would be human in this meeting. I finished pouring the water for my tea and walked back to my chair, not responding.

A sneer of anger covered my face, but I couldn't do anything to stop it. Plus, anger fueled action and was better than fear.

My face must have looked pretty annoyed, because she asked, "If you're offended at my calling your grade abysmal, you shouldn't be. I presume you wouldn't be here if you had aced my final, correct?"

"Yes, correct. I want to do better," I replied.

Patton nodded, leaving no room for questioning, and said, "Okay then, now we can have a real conversation. We both can agree your grade on my final was awful, and I imagine you want to improve your grade even more than I want you to improve, correct?"

I nodded. Where was she going with this?

"Then let's discuss how we can do that." She reached into her desk drawer and dug around until she pulled out a thick stack of paper and handed it to me. "This is your final exam. I printed it out this morning in the hopes that you and the others who did poorly would come to my office hours. Kudos for being the first."

"Thanks. You know what they say about the early bird and all."

"You're welcome, Ms. Alexander. Let's dig in here and start at the beginning."

An hour later, I had a much better understanding of where I went wrong on Patton's final and a follow-up appointment to meet with her the next week. Unlike in class, during our session she was endlessly patient with my questions and made sure that I understood a concept before moving on. The meeting wasn't bad, and I realized I didn't completely dread our meeting for next week.

CHAPTER EIGHTEEN

The first month back hadn't been so bad, and that included Contracts, and even if Contracts had been terrible, having Mason for Torts would have made up for it. He made talking about negligence almost fun. Mason swore up and down that when people were having fun, they learned better, so he always tried to make his classes entertaining. It helped that he also chose classes that could be made fun even if the material wasn't super sexy.

It was Thursday night, and I'd been sitting on my couch for three hours reading contracts. My brain hadn't completely turned back on from vacation mode, so I kept having to remind myself to pay attention. After my last class, I had caught up with Tiffany to see if she wanted to do something, but she had said she wanted to stay in and meditate on her first month back. I'd never known that girl to meditate on anything. That was more Rafael's arena. I thought about asking Silas if he wanted to get a drink or something, but I'd be seeing him tomorrow to study and I didn't want to make him feel weird if he and this NYE girl were a thing. He would tell me if they were a thing, though, right? We were good friends, close friends, and that was the kind of thing very good friends shared with each other. So anyway, I had decided not to see Silas and instead focus on Contracts.

Second semester of Contracts was focused on the Uniform Commercial Code, and so far, I wasn't impressed, so when my phone buzzed, I was beyond grateful for the distraction. I saw it was Silas and answered, saying, "You've reached the UCC-only zone. Simone is unavailable but try back in May assuming she doesn't die of boredom. Beeeep."

"Why are you studying on a Thursday night?"

"The same reason you probably are. I'm a law student, and if I don't study tonight, I'll be five weeks behind all of a sudden."

Silas's deep chuckle warmed my insides. I loved hearing him laugh.

"Don't be ridiculous, California. You could be out having fun right now."

"I could say the same of you!"

"True, but I'm also not studying anymore. I've got plans tonight."

"Oh?"

I waited for him to elaborate, but he didn't, and silence ticked by on the phone. Usually he was bursting to share information with me, so I didn't understand why he was holding back tonight. When he still didn't say anything in explanation, I gave into my base nosey instincts.

"What are you doing tonight?"

"A buddy of mine is coming to hang out for a few. No big deal."

A buddy? Did that mean a guy or did he call everyone buddy? He'd never called me buddy, but that didn't mean anything. He might call me buddy when he talked *about* me but not to me.

"I'd invite you over but—"

"No, no, hang out with your friend. I'm studying anyway."

He breathed a loud sigh that sounded like relief.

"You should go out. I'm sure folks will be out doing something. Did you call Tiffany or anyone else in the crew?"

It was funny to think that just a couple months ago I had no friends at school. If he hadn't dragged me out of the house, I probably still wouldn't know anyone outside of him and Tiffany, and now I had a whole crew.

"Tiff's staying in tonight, but I might call Rafael. He was trying to tell me something earlier this month, but I didn't have time to talk, and I think I was a little short with him."

"You might want to avoid Rafael for a minute. He's having some kind of woman trouble and is mopey as fuck."

"Oooh, thanks for the warning. I don't have the headspace for hearing about his relationship issues tonight."

I had my own relationship issues, or non-issues, that I needed to deal with. Specifically, why the hell I was fixated on who Silas was spending his time with when he wasn't with me.

Silas kept talking, but I tuned him out.

Shit.

Did Silas find a cuffing partner? I really, really hoped not because I didn't know if I could handle seeing Silas walking around the law school with some girl knowing that it should have been me. Though maybe it was the friend he spent New Year's Eve with. He'd said she was in town, but he didn't say whether it was for the holiday or more permanently. I did not like the idea of Silas spending *more* time with this woman I knew nothing about who was probably some genius bombshell because only a genius bombshell would be good enough for my sweet, handsome Silas.

"Simone, you still there?" Silas's voice shook me out of my thoughts.

"Yeah, I'm here."

"So will you do it or not?"

I hadn't heard a word he said, but since Silas said "no" to me so infrequently, saying "yes" to whatever he had asked seemed like a no-brainer, so I said, "Of course I'll do it!"

"Oh man, California, you're a lifesaver. I'll bring you the money tomorrow at our study session, and if it turns out you need more, I'll pay you back after."

What?

He continued, "I was terrified I would have to go on a date with some rando."

A date?

S ilas strode through my front door a little before one p.m. It drove him crazy that I kept my front door unlocked even though I had tried to explain on numerous occasions that it wasn't always unlocked, that I only unlocked it when he was coming over, but he still complained about it, and today was no different.

"Why do you insist on leaving your front door unlocked?" he asked, frowning at me when he found me in the kitchen cooking.

"Why do you insist on asking me this every time you come over?"

"Because I hope eventually you'll listen to my advice. Any stranger off the street could walk in."

"But lucky for me, it was you."

"California, why do you insist on driving me crazy?" he asked as he sauntered over to my couch and sat down.

I was cooking for Silas again as a thank-you for helping me study. I had pored over my old cookbooks the night before to find the perfect recipe for him. I'd cooked for Silas at my parents' house when he'd come to comfort me, and the time before that, we'd almost kissed, so I hoped that the third time cooking for him would be the charm. For what, I didn't know.

Silas was sitting on the couch, but he hadn't taken his Contracts book out of his backpack yet, which was fine with me because I wanted to talk to him about whatever it was I had agreed to last night. I didn't want him to know I hadn't heard a word he'd said, but I also needed to know what I might have gotten myself into. Given that the only pieces of information I had were something about a date and money, I proceeded cautiously.

"So, how much do you think this thing is going to cost?"

"Not really sure, to be honest. A couple 2Ls said in the past they've paid anywhere from $20 to $150."

"And so, does that $150 cover the whole date or—?"

Silas gave me a funny look, which made me think I had asked the wrong question.

"The money doesn't cover the date. It goes to the organization. The people going on the date pay for the date."

"And the daters will be from the organization?" I asked. Silas gave me another look.

Yeah, that didn't seem right, but using my deductive reasoning skills wasn't helping, so I tried again.

"So this should be fun?" I finally said.

Silas shook with laughter and said, "Give it up, California. I know you have no idea what we're talking about."

Not yet wanting to admit defeat, I replied, "Yes, I do. We're talking about the thing for charity and—" I stopped. There was no point in trying to prove I knew something that

I so obviously didn't. "Fine, you're right. Just tell me what I agreed to. I promise I won't back out."

Silas proceeded to tell me that the law school did a date auction every year to raise money to buy books and clothing for kids at the local women and children's shelter.

"Some students volunteer to be auctioned off and others are nominated."

"Let me guess which one you were?" I asked, sure of the answer.

Silas looked a little embarrassed but proud and mumbled, "Yeah, I was nominated a couple times."

"A couple times?"

"Ten, actually," he admitted.

The women of the law school *were* awfully fond of Silas who, I saw, had turned such a dark pink his face looked almost purple.

"Yeah, so that's where you come in," he explained. "I don't want to end up on an awkward first date with some random girl, so you're going to bid on a date with me and you're going to make sure you win me."

Hmmm, this seemed like some sort of fresh torture. Bid to go on a fake date with your kind-of-but-not-really ex. This sounded like a Sartre play.

"Why are you asking me to bid on you when there are at least ten people who so obviously want to date you?"

Silas's eyes smoldered when he said, "Because I want my date to be someone I want to kiss at the end of the night."

"Oh," I said on an exhale and bit my lip. Silas's eyes drifted down to my mouth, and suddenly it felt like my mouth was full of cotton.

Okay, so maybe he wasn't *dating* dating New Year's Eve woman. Maybe they were hooking up. Ugh, I didn't want to think about that, either.

"Well, in that case, I'm your girl."

We stared at each other and the temperature went from comfortable to hot in seconds. I didn't want to wait for our maybe not so fake date. I wanted to kiss him now. Right now. I leaned close to him and closed my eyes, waiting for him to close the distance between us. Silas was a breath away, and half an inch more, our lips would be touching. Except that I never felt the warm pressure of his lips against mine. I opened one eye, then the other, and found him leaning back against the couch.

"Hey, what happened there?" I asked. Had I misheard him? I could have sworn he said he wanted to kiss me.

"When we kiss again, and we will, I want it to be at the right time with the right circumstances. It's not going to be this start-and-stop bullshit."

Well, okay. But what did the right circumstances mean? Because this felt like the absolute right circumstances to me.

He shifted his body, pulling his leg up onto the couch so that his knee was almost but not quite touching my thigh. He propped his arm along the back of the couch, leaving his hand dangling between us.

"And anyway, you're gonna be paying good money for all this." He gestured down his body, grinning. "So you'll just have to wait, but I promise, it'll be worth it. This will be the real deal, California. Trust me on that."

"Do I get a say in what we do?" I asked, excited.

"Nope. It's gonna be a surprise, but I promise you'll like it. Just make sure that you win me at the auction. Deal?"

"Deal."

CHAPTER NINETEEN

River's flight was due to land soon, which meant she would be at my apartment in a little under three hours. It had been nonstop studying for weeks, and I was beyond ready to spend the weekend with my best friend. Her flight couldn't get here fast enough as far as I was concerned. Silas and I had had two more two-person study sessions, and I had met with Patton a few more times as well, and finally, Contracts wasn't quite as daunting. And as a bonus, since I met with Patton outside of class and showed her I was sincerely trying, during class she was significantly less brutal to me. At least it felt that way. I supposed it also could have been the fact that I was actually participating in class and volunteering to answer her tough questions whenever I could. It was definitely one of the two, though.

My apartment was freshly cleaned, and I'd changed my sheets since we would be sharing my bed. I hadn't had the Contracts sweaty night terrors at all this semester, but I still wanted to give her clean sheets. Silas had taken me grocery shopping, and I had a fully stocked fridge along with some decent wine so we wouldn't have to eat out every night she was here. I couldn't afford to eat out every night anyway, and I didn't want River trying to treat me. Plus, River loved my cooking.

Standing in my living room, trying to view the space from someone else's perspective, I'd made my little hovel into a pretty cozy space. Even though I still had the university-issued furniture that wasn't going anywhere, I'd finally hung pictures of my friends and family from home, put up a few non-law books, and added some knickknacks to make it feel homier. And it did. Pleased with my makeshift decorating skills, I lay on the couch to cuddle with my new fuzzy pillow when my phone rang.

"River here yet?" Silas asked, as usual not bothering to announce himself.

"Not yet. She should be here in a couple of hours, though." Silas had offered to take me to the airport to pick up River, but I had declined. I didn't even like the idea of having him pick *me* up at the airport, let alone my friend.

"Cool, cool. I'm looking forward to seeing her again. I bet she has some good Simone stories I can convince her to tell me."

Of course she did, but knowing Silas would be trying to get all in my business, I'd sworn River to secrecy about anything more than level-one embarrassing. Knowing someone since childhood gave them the uniquely awful privilege of having a tome of stories to share at the drop of a hat. River would never share anything that would hurt my feelings or mortify me beyond recovery, but even without those caveats, she had an arsenal of stories to pull from.

"Good try, Cookie. I've sworn River to secrecy, and she won't be telling you a word." I smiled to myself, smug in the knowledge that my secrets were mostly safe.

"You don't give me enough credit. I'm a master of persuasion, and I don't know if you've noticed, but I've got dimples that would make a nun blush."

Oh, I'd noticed. I'd noticed a lot given that me and those nuns he spoke of reacted the same way to his flawless dimples.

"All right, dimples, just make sure you bring your 'A' game at the auction tomorrow. I don't want to be bidding on some schlub in dirty jeans and a Yoda T-shirt."

"Hey, I thought you liked my Yoda shirt?" he exclaimed.

I smiled at his outburst. His love for *Star Wars* knew no bounds.

"Calm your tits, Cookie. I *do* like your Yoda shirt. It's just not date auction worthy. The whole point is to raise money for charity, and I don't see Yoda bringing in the big bucks."

"Whatever. I wasn't planning to wear Yoda anyway, and trust me, California, my outfit is going to knock you on your ass."

"In that case," I said, "I look forward to the bruise it leaves."

First my doorbell rang, then it was followed by repeated pounding on the door. I must have dozed off when I got off the phone with Silas because the doorbell scared the bejesus out of me. There was no question it was River at my door. She had never learned to knock on a door like a normal person. Instead, she rang the doorbell, then pounded on the door several times, and if the door didn't open immediately, she started the process again. It usually drove me nuts, but at this moment it was such a welcome familiarity I smiled to myself.

"It's open, Rivvy. Stop banging on my door!"

I wiped the drool off my chin and straightened my clothes. I was still sporting the sweater and leggings I'd worn to class. She opened the door, dragging a gigantic suitcase behind her. As usual, she looked stunning. She also looked sorely underdressed for the weather. I pulled her into the living room and gave her a big hug.

"I can't believe you're actually here," I said, giving her another squeeze before pushing her away. Then we both spoke at the same time.

I asked, "Aren't you freezing?" at the same time she said, "You really shouldn't leave your front door unlocked like that."

We burst into giggles.

"I'll go first," I said. "Given that your bag is the same size as the one I used to move here, I can only assume you packed some warmer clothes. If not, you're going to freeze your ass off." She started to speak, but I interrupted before she could get the words out. "I rarely leave my door unlocked. I only do it when Silas comes over and tonight because I knew you were coming so no need to get on my case about it. Silas does it enough for you both."

Around her laughter, River said, "I knew I liked him."

We dragged River's suitcase into my room where she insisted on unpacking everything. She had brought enough clothes to last a full two weeks without repeating any outfits. We were almost finished unpacking her clothes when I pulled a sweater out of her bag and several packets of condoms spilled onto the floor. Gathering them up and tossing them back into her bag, I asked, "Does this mean things have cooled off with the old man?"

"Oh. Yeah. We broke up a week ago," she answered without pausing in her unpacking.

So that's what she'd been calling me about. She called while I was meeting with Patton, and when I tried to call her back, she hadn't answered. We'd been playing phone tag again. It was a wonder we'd managed to organize her trip here.

"I'm sorry, Rivvy. You seemed to really like him. What happened?"

River looked everywhere around the room but refused to meet my eyes.

"Riv?"

"Not a big deal. Turns out he was married. They're in one of those living-apart-together marriages, and he started enjoying his apart time too much and forgot to mention he had a wife."

"Oh, Riv. I'm so s—" I started, but she interrupted me.

"I'm fine, Simone, really."

"Yeah?"

"Yeah," she answered, then added, "This trip is the perfect time for me to get over him and under someone else." And thus, the condoms.

We finished unpacking River's clothes and got into our pajamas. Our plans to go out got waylaid by our ever-growing interest in wine and a good night's sleep, so we popped open a bottle of red and watched bad stand-up comedy before heading to bed. Even though I was tired, I couldn't fall asleep. Between school and Silas and wanting to make sure Rivvy had a good trip, my brain was in full on workout mode. Not wanting to wake River, I tiptoed to the living room. I thought about making a snack, but I worried too much banging around the kitchen might wake her up. What I really wanted to do was call Silas and see what he was up to, but when I picked up the phone to call him, I realized it was too late. He'd already be knocked out in bed. So I did what any self-respecting insomniac would do: lay down on my couch, turned on the TV, and scrolled through Instagram. As my thumb glided up my phone, I stopped when I saw Silas had posted a photo. I checked the timestamp, and he'd posted it only five minutes before. He was probably still awake. I thought about it for maybe half a second before I pulled up my favorites list and clicked on his name. The phone rang several times, and I was about to hang up when he answered.

"Is everything okay?" he asked. His voice was huskier than usual, and it sounded like he was lying down.

"Shit, were you asleep?" I responded.

"No, what's up?"

"Nothing. River got in earlier this evening."

"Glad she got in all right. Did you guys get into anything tonight?"

"Not a thing. Had some wine and watched a little TV. What are you still doing up?"

"I could ask you the same thing. Isn't it past your bedtime, sleeping beauty?"

He was right. It wasn't often I was up past midnight.

"Had a lot on my mind and couldn't sleep. Your turn," I said.

"Same."

"Care to share?" I asked. Easygoing Silas was rarely fazed by anything. The most upset I'd ever seen him get was when his mom had called, so I wondered if something had happened with Lauren.

"Yes, but not tonight. You?"

I wanted to tell him everything that was rolling around my head, most of which was largely about him, but I needed to figure out what I wanted to say. "I like you, you like me, let's do this thing," didn't feel like quite the right thing to say. Neither did, "We kissed once, I said we couldn't do it again, but now I can't stop thinking about what's under your briefs." So anyway, saying nothing yet seemed like a better choice.

"Same," I answered. Then I had an idea. "Want to watch a movie?"

"Right now?"

"Yeah, right now. Why not?"

"River's asleep, it's cold outside, and while I'll do almost anything to see you, right now, putting on pants isn't one of them."

I burst out laughing. "All good points, but leaving either of our houses wasn't what I had in mind," I explained. "We both have access to every streaming service known to man. Let's pick a movie and talk while we watch it."

For the next fifteen minutes, we went back and forth trying to decide on whether we wanted to watch a thriller or something more lighthearted. We ended up settling on neither when we discovered our mutual love for *Frasier*. Around episode four, Silas admitted that as a teenager he had the biggest crush on Roz.

"She was sexy. When you're a horned-up thirteen-year-old, any woman detailing her sexual exploits is hot," he explained. "You had to have had some strange crushes as a kid. Everyone does."

"Oh, for sure. Do you remember the animated version of *Robin Hood* with the foxes?"

He laughed for a full minute before he composed himself enough to talk. "No way, you were hot for Robin Hood?"

"What's funny?" I asked with feigned indignation. "He was the textbook definition of swaggy. And I liked his little hat." The laughter I was trying to stifle bubbled to the surface. "Don't tell me you weren't a little bit hot for Maid Marian?"

"I mean, of course I was, but that just makes sense. She was sassy, always giving Robin Hood shit and flipping her little tail around. But Robin Hood? He was obviously your classic fuckboy."

I must have fallen asleep at some point because the sound

of water running, then the feeling of water dripping on the back of my head, jolted me awake. Still on the couch, I looked around, trying to work out where the water was coming from. Thinking the ceiling must be leaking, I rolled over and found River standing over me with a damp paper towel in her hand steadily dripping water on my head.

"Good morning," she announced with more energy than seemed necessary at this ungodly hour, whatever the hour was.

"Why are you up so early?" I croaked. My voice, like most of my body, hadn't quite woken up yet.

"It's ten o'clock and time for you to get up and study so we can go out tonight. Silas called me and he's on his way over here. You might want to put something on over your—" The door handle jiggled then the doorbell rang before she could finish. For once the door was still locked when Silas came over. Not thinking about what I had worn to bed, I rolled off the couch to answer the door. The cold from outside hit me like a semi.

"Morning, come on in," I grumbled to Silas, still not fully alert.

He didn't move. He stood in the doorway staring at me, his mouth hanging slightly open. His eyes raked me from head to toe and his gaze got heavy before he turned away, seeming to realize he was staring.

What was his problem?

"Are you coming in or what?" I asked, confused about his behavior.

"Oh. Yeah. Uh, did you want to put something on or..." He trailed off, trying his best not to look at me and failing.

River came out of my bedroom carrying a robe she handed to me before giving Silas a quick hug.

"Morning, Silas. Forgive her. She just woke up and hasn't

processed that she's only wearing—"

"Arrgghhh, why didn't you assholes tell me I don't have any pants on?" I screamed as I pulled the robe on and tied it tightly around me. Silas saw me in my underwear. Which was not to say I didn't want him to see me in my underwear. I very much did. But I wanted that underwear to be something red and lacy or some cute boy shorts, not my formerly white, currently grayish granny panties. I must have gotten hot in the middle of the night and taken off my pajama pants. I didn't usually wear underwear under my pajamas, but I thought it might get hot sharing a bed and I would need to take my pants off, which was exactly what happened, except I wasn't sharing a bed. And thank God for small favors. If I hadn't worn underwear under my pajamas, I'd have answered the door completely bottom naked.

River doubled over laughing while Silas stood in the living room looking everywhere but at me. I scowled at River. It was the crack of dawn, and she looked like she'd had a full night's sleep followed by full glam. Meanwhile, I probably looked like River had dragged me in by the hair from the outside. I touched my hair to see if it felt as bad as I guessed it looked. I winced when I got to the side of my hair that was smushed flat against my skull.

Pulling my robe even tighter around my body, I asked, "What are you guys getting into today?"

Silas finally looked at me. All of me. His eyes took in my silk robe–attired body from head to toe, and even though he couldn't see anything specific, the robe left little to the imagination. Also, he'd just seen me almost naked, so I was sure he didn't have to imagine much.

I popped my hip out and cleared my throat. "See something you like?" I said.

Without skipping a beat, he met my eyes and held my gaze. "Every time I look at you."

My mouth dropped open at his unflinching response, and like clockwork, suddenly that robe felt too warm on my skin. I stared at him, not moving, not saying anything, and he stared back, flexing his jaw. I didn't know how long we stood staring at each other, but finally River cleared her throat. "If you two need to be alone, I'm sure I can find a hotel somewhere."

I blinked and shook my head a little.

"Funny. You have everything you need?" I asked.

"All I needed was my escort for the day and here he is, so I'm ready to check out everything East Lansing has to offer a gal."

"Don't get too excited," Silas piped up. "East Lansing isn't really the pinnacle of entertainment, but I can promise I'll show you a good time." He crooked his elbow for her to take and led her out of the front door. I stood in the doorway waving at them like someone's grandma as they drove off.

I studied for a few hours, then called it quits around three thirty. River and Silas still weren't back from wherever they went, and I hadn't heard from either of them all day. I assumed that meant they were having fun. After reading my favorite cooking blog on my laptop for a while, I looked down at my phone. It was already five p.m. I started to text River to check in but decided against it. They were fine. Most likely they were sitting in a cafe somewhere while Riv regaled Silas with tales of our semi-feral childhood.

As I wondered if River had told Silas about the time I thought I could use a golf umbrella to glide off the roof Mary Poppins style, I heard voices getting louder outside. I peeked out of the front window as they walked up to my front door. I unlocked the front door and scrambled back to the couch to sit as nonchalantly as I could given that I was slightly out of breath. I made a mental note to check out the gym. One of them knocked on the door and, without waiting for an answer, turned the doorknob and nudged it open. River walked in first, her head turned away from me.

"Dammit," she said, digging into her purse. She pulled out a $5 bill and held it out to Silas.

He took the bill from her and shoved it in his pocket. "I told you, even though she swears she locks it at night, whenever I come over the door is unlocked."

"It was locked this morning," I pointed out.

"River already told me she locked it last night."

Not this again. I rolled my eyes but decided not to comment. If I commented, it would give them reason to keep harping on me.

"Welcome back. Everybody have fun?"

Silas closed the door behind himself as he followed River into the apartment.

"We had a good time," River said and smiled over at Silas.

"Yeah, I showed your girl all East Lansing has to offer."

"Oh. In that case, what took so long?" I asked, half joking and half wondering what they had been doing for the past several hours.

"We had lunch, walked around campus and downtown. I took River over to my spot for a little while, then we came back here," Silas said.

Caught off guard, I asked Silas, "Your place?"

"Yeah," he said as he settled himself on the couch next to me. River had walked into my bedroom. "Kevin met up with us, and we ended up playing Xbox for a couple hours. Why didn't you tell me Riv was such a gamer? She kicked both our asses at *NBA2K22*."

"Yeah, she's a huge gamer. Always has been but you'd never know it. She keeps that part of herself firmly hidden away. Could you imagine what those geeky guys would do if they knew someone who looked like River was one of them?" I chuckled at the thought. They'd lose their nerdy minds.

"Kevin said almost the exact same thing now that you mention it," Silas said.

"Kevin was exaggerating," River piped up as she came out of the room having changed out of her day clothes into more form-fitting evening attire. Specifically, she had on jeans that fit her like a second layer of skin and a long-sleeve crop top that stopped about four inches from the top of her pants.

"No, he really wasn't, Riv. Those boys would lose their minds over you," I assured her.

She rarely lacked confidence, so I didn't know what this odd modesty was about.

"Whatever. Anyway, Simone, you need to get dressed for tonight. We only have an hour until we have to leave." Her eyes flicked from me to Silas, and she said, "You too, slick."

CHAPTER TWENTY

McNally's was crowded as usual. Every inch of the pub was occupied by law students and their guests. Signs announcing the date auction plastered much of the wall space, and there was an elevated platform off to the side decorated with balloons, a podium, and a big banner that read, "Date for Charity: Trust Me, I'm a Lawyer."

I couldn't see Silas anywhere, but I spotted Tiffany and Rafael off to the side. I waved to them and motioned toward the bar so they would know I was getting a drink before heading over to them. They both waved back, but neither smiled. In fact, they both looked pretty glum. I wondered what that was about. River and I clambered through the throng of students. At the bar I ordered a beer and River ordered a scotch on the rocks.

"Something you picked up from the old guy?" I asked, joking. What twenty-something woman drank scotch on the rocks? I'd certainly never seen Riv do it.

"It is not, thank you very much. I've wanted to try scotch for a while now, and being on vacation is the perfect chance to try new things." I didn't want to annoy her after she had come all this way to visit me, so I took a hearty sip of my beer instead.

"Come on." I grabbed her arm after she took a tentative

sip of her scotch. "I want you to meet Tiffany and Rafael."

By the time we reached Tiffany and Rafael, Kevin, Jack, and Alison had joined them as well. I gave hugs all around and introduced Riv to everyone except Kevin, who she gave a big hug.

"You guys got your cash ready?" I asked, feeling for the lump of cash Silas had given me. He told me to spend as much as I needed to win the date.

"Sure as fuck do," Tiffany said and produced a thick wad of money. "Pierce volunteered to participate, and he gave me $500 to use to bid on him."

"Thinks pretty highly of himself," Rafael snorted under his breath with no trace of amusement on his face.

Tiffany cut her eyes at him but didn't say anything.

"Do you guys know who else is in the auction?" Kevin asked.

"Other than Silas and Courtney, I have no idea. Is one of you bidding on Courtney?" I asked. "Kevin? Rafael?"

"I'll probably bid on her if it looks like she isn't getting enough bids," Kevin said.

"That's so sweet of you," Riv responded.

"I assume you're bidding on Silas, Simone, right?" Rafael confirmed.

"Yes," I answered, "but why would you assume that?"

Everyone in the group, including River, laughed.

"Why's that funny?"

"Let's call it a hunch," Tiffany answered when no one else did.

My friends were absurd sometimes. Not wrong, obviously, but absurd nonetheless. Out of the corner of my eye, I saw someone walk onto the platform up front, and a moment later a deep voice cleared its throat into the microphone. "Good evening, law students. Are you all ready to spend some money for a good cause?"

It was Professor Mason. I should have known he would want to be involved in this. The bar roared with applause at seeing him, and it was good to see everyone liked him as much as I did.

"I'm sure I don't have to go over any rules, but we're all lawyers and future lawyers here, so I will." The crowd laughed. "Each volunteer has chosen the music that will play when they enter the stage. The bidding will start at $10 and go up in $5 increments from there. I will say, 'Going once, going twice, closed,' and that will be the end of bidding for that person. Payments for the date will be made as soon as you win. You can pay via credit card or cash. Folks being auctioned can do almost anything to increase their bidding amounts. The only things off-limits are nudity, unsolicited touching, and harassment. Everything else is fair game. I trust that I don't need to say this, but this is for charity and for fun. If you don't like someone on the stage, keep your feelings to yourself. No booing, hissing, name-calling, or otherwise juvenile behavior." He looked around at the crowd, appearing to make sure everyone was listening. "If we're all on the same page," he said and produced a gavel from underneath the podium, "let's begin!" As soon as he smacked the gavel on the podium, Mariah Carey's "Heartbreaker" blared out of the speakers I hadn't noticed on the stage.

First on stage, Professor Mason announced a 2L I didn't recognize. She came out wearing a stereotypical Britney Spears–type schoolgirl outfit that the guys, and a few of the girls, ate up. She bounced around doing what I was sure she thought was dancing, and her bidding skyrocketed. By the time Mason yelled closed, she had raised close to $250 for the charity and won a date with Mr. Aarons. Of course, the schoolgirl thing would do it for him.

Polar opposite of the 2L girl, Courtney came out next, sporting her college soccer uniform and carrying a soccer ball. When she dropped the ball on the stage, Beyonce's "Who Run the World (Girls)" started playing. She juggled the ball from foot to foot among cheers and constant bidding, never breaking focus, never dropping the ball. Her badassery earned $325 for the charity and a date with a very hot 3L I knew she'd been eyeing.

Three more students I didn't know followed Courtney, raising $150, $225, and $310 respectively. Mason announced we were halfway through the auction and exceeding expectations. He said so far with the money we had raised we would be able to buy several outfits for the women and children at the shelter as well as buy more books for their library.

"Let's keep the momentum going, folks!" Mason said. "Next we have a 2L who's moonlighting in the building next door, earning his MBA. This student is—" I knew before he finished that the student was Keith. Of course it was Keith. When Mason finished his introduction, "Pony" started playing out of the speakers because of course he would choose "Pony." Keith sauntered onto the stage wearing a snug three-piece suit. He did a turn with his arms out as if to say, "Check me out."

"We're gonna start the bidding at $10." Mason looked around the room and continued, "Do we have anyone for $10?"

Someone in the back called out, "$10."

"Holy shit, that's Keith," I turned to explain to River. I had told her about Keith when I first met him and mentioned that I'd gone to his apartment after my run-in with Patton. Strangely, despite my telling Rivvy almost everything, I hadn't mentioned anything to her about what had happened between me and Silas. Not the kiss, not the pseudo breakup…nothing.

"Damn, he's hot," she responded.

I nodded. Keith was hot as hell, but I couldn't encourage River to go down that road. From the looks of things, he was dating Suzy but was still down to clown. I hoped for Suzy's sake they weren't serious.

Mason's voice cut through the crowd. "$15, do we have $15?" No one bid even as Keith started to do a few awkward hip thrusts toward the crowd.

"$75! I have $75 for him," a female voice screamed from the back. I couldn't see who it was, but the crowd gasped.

"Wow, really kicking it up a notch there." Mason paused to let the price sink in. "Do we have $80? $80 for the future JD/MBA with the *Magic Mike* moves. Any takers?" No one else bid. "All right, then, going once, going twice, closed for $75."

Keith stood on the stage looking apoplectic. He must have thought he would go for more. I scanned the room looking for who had bid $75 on Keith and saw Suzy making her way to the stage, money waving in her hand. Made total sense. What didn't make sense was the fact that Keith was seriously hot and checked a lot of boxes but still couldn't get above $100. I wondered if his low bid indicated he'd broken more than a few hearts through the law school.

Whoever followed Keith had to fare better than he did.

I wasn't a country music fan, not by any stretch, but the first few bars of the song that followed Keith's exit and introduced the next auctionee were as familiar to me as the top of my left hand. When Bonnie's voice belted out through the speakers, Silas sauntered onto the stage and the crowd burst into loud whistles and applause. The only other person that garnered that kind of reaction was Courtney with her ball juggling. Silas danced around the stage in snug jeans, cowboy boots, a cowboy hat, and a striped button-down shirt that hugged his arms and chest in a way that had me hoping fervently he planned to remove it so I could get a glimpse at what was underneath. The cowboy look wasn't usually my kink, but seeing Silas tush push around the stage made me grateful to Mr. Strauss that jeans existed.

Before Mason could formally start the bidding, a female voice from the back yelled, "$50!"

"I guess that means the bidding will start at $50."

Another voice yelled, "$55!"

Shit, I needed to get into this game. I pulled out my wad of cash and yelled, "$75," knowing full well that wouldn't be enough, and sure enough, a familiar voice next to me shrieked, "$100!" I looked over at River waving her hand around. I yanked it down and hissed, "What are you doing?"

She smirked and said, "What? It's for charity. Plus, his ass looks great in those jeans."

They sure did.

"$150." I hoped we were getting closer to the end. Silas had given me $300 to bid, and we were halfway there.

"$175," someone yelled.

When Silas had come onto the stage, I had pushed my way to the front so he could see me bidding. Mere feet from my face, along with his rendition of the tush push, he belted the words to the song, which surprised me because whenever we were in the car and a country song came on, he said he couldn't stand that whiney shit.

My favorite part of the song was coming up, and I looked at the stage to see Silas staring directly at me singing the words I loved by heart. The lyrics seemed to speak directly to me when they mentioned thinking about someone every day and dreaming about them every night.

I held my breath and his gaze while he sang. My heart pounded in a way that wasn't completely familiar and the crowd disappeared. Silas was singing to me. Just me. And as far as I was concerned, no one else existed. He smiled down into my eyes then, and suddenly my breath was shallow like I'd just ran a 5k. I melted into the stage, eating up his attention.

"Girl, he's singing to you," River said, nudging me and breaking the spell. I looked around at the myriad faces gazing up at Silas. Apparently, we weren't alone. My attention moved reluctantly to River, and Silas shifted his eyes away from mine and out into the crowd. The moment was broken, but I would have to be an idiot not to know something more had just happened there. All the things I still felt, he felt them, too.

"$350!" I screamed, hoping that would be enough to seal the deal. I was willing to go higher whether Silas paid for it or not. Maybe I could sell my hair or something. No one else was getting that date with him.

It was the highest bid of the night. I waited anxiously to see if it would be enough.

"Going once. Going twice. Closed!" Professor Mason announced from the front of the room. I had won the date.

Silas jumped off the stage and ran over to me, winding his way through the crowd of revelers congratulating him. When he finally reached me, he gripped me around the waist and lifted me off my feet. I threw my arms around his neck as he swung me around.

"Holy shit," he said, returning me to my feet. "I got scared there for a second when I didn't hear you bidding."

"I promised I would bid on you, and I'm glad I won. You're a hot commodity. It looked like every woman in here wanted a crack at you."

River leaned over, joining our conversation. "But the best

woman won, right, Silas?"

I chuckled at River, still playing matchmaker.

"So what's this big date you have planned and when are you taking me on it?" I asked.

"You gotta wait and see. I promise you'll like it, but you have to give me a full Saturday."

Silas and I had spent plenty of Saturdays together, mostly doing nothing, so the fact that he had a plan already made it feel more important.

"This one," I said, too excited about the date to be cool. "Let's do this Saturday." The one and only date we'd been on had been one of the best, and I couldn't wait to see what he would do this time.

Someone tapped me on the shoulder, and I tried to shrug it off. Silas's dimples peeked out as he fought off a grin and pointed over my shoulder. I turned and found River peering over my shoulder, grinning.

"Hi, best friend. Might you have forgotten something? Or someone?"

Oh. Right. River would still be in town. Oops.

"It's all good. I need some time to solidify the plan anyway." Silas chuckled, then said, "You're gonna love it."

CHAPTER TWENTY-ONE

"So, are you excited about your date with Silas?" River asked me over breakfast the next morning. We had stayed at the bar for a few hours after the date auction was over, then went to get some late-night Mexican food with Silas and the rest of the crew.

"I am," I admitted. "I'm excited to see what he has planned."

"Is that all you're excited about?" she asked, raising her left eyebrow in an inquisitorial way that I had wished I could do since we were kids.

"Shut up," I said, throwing the balled-up napkin next to me at her.

"What?" she insisted. "You know you're hot for Silas. I know you're hot for Silas. I think the only person who doesn't know you're hot for Silas is Silas."

"I am not hot for—" I started to protest, then stopped. Who was I kidding? "Yeah, I'm hot for Silas, but it doesn't matter because I said we'd cool things off and just be friends. Except I think that was a mistake. Also, he went out with someone on New Year's Eve, and I'm not sure if they're a thing."

Before the date auction, I'd told Riv about my and Silas's date, but I had refused to admit out loud that I still wanted him until right that moment.

"Well, did you ask him if he's seeing her?"

"No."

"Has he mentioned her again?"

"No."

"Have you seen him with anyone that looks like she might be a girlfriend-type person?"

"No, but—"

River leaned across the table and gripped my forearms with her freakishly strong hands. It kind of hurt, so I knew she was serious. River looked me in the eye and without blinking said, "Don't be stupid, Simone. He's a good one, and he likes you, too."

When I didn't respond, she loosened her grip on my arms, then let go altogether. She shook her head and got up from the table, saying, "Give him a chance. Open yourself up a little. You might be surprised at what you let in." She walked to the bathroom and took a shower.

River and I didn't see or mention Silas for the rest of her visit, but as she was getting into her cab to the airport, she hugged me and said, "Don't forget what I said." I promised her I wouldn't as she climbed into the backseat of the taxi. I waved as my best friend disappeared around the corner. I missed her already and she hadn't even left the state.

I had another Contracts review session with Patton, and I found that I no longer dreaded meeting with her.

"Come in, Ms. Alexander. Have a seat. Would you like some tea?"

"Yes, please. I'll take the peach oolong."

"You've been here enough, Ms. Alexander. You know where to get it. I'll put on the water."

Since that first meeting, I'd been to her office several more times, and each time my opinion of her improved. What I couldn't understand was why she was still such a beast in class. Not necessarily to me, but to people in general. No one had cried yet this semester, but it was still early and she had plenty of time to cause psychological trauma.

"What are we here to discuss today, Ms. Alexander?" Patton said, settling behind her desk with her own steaming mug of tea. I'd learned that she preferred mint tea and almost always drank it during our meetings.

"I'm having some trouble understanding remedies. I mean, I think I understand on a basic level that the plaintiff needs to be made whole, but I'm not quite understanding how it works."

"You understand that there are several types of remedies for breach of contract, yes?"

"Yes, I understand that. I think the one I'm having the most trouble with is specific performance."

"All right. Tell me what you think it is?"

I thought for a second before answering. "Well, I think it's when the breaching party has to take action to correct the breach."

"That's correct. And why might specific performance be more appropriate than, say, compensatory damages?"

I wasn't completely sure of the answer, and I didn't want to give her the wrong one. Yes, she was better outside of the classroom, but I still feared her wrath. "Uh, I don't know?"

"Ms. Alexander, I thought we'd gotten past this. For one thing, are you asking me or telling me that you don't know? For another, I think you do know what the answer is. Dig deep, Ms. Alexander. It's clear you know more than you think you know."

Encouraged by her words of faith in me, I said, "I think it's because sometimes monetary damages won't properly or adequately compensate the non-breaching party."

"Do you think, Ms. Alexander, or do you know?"

"I know."

"Good. You're right. Now give me an example of an instance where specific performance would be the appropriate remedy."

I wracked my brain for an example while she waited quietly behind her desk sipping her tea. She didn't seem to be in a hurry, but I couldn't take all day.

"Um, what about, like, with a one-of-a-kind antique?"

"Go on," she said. Since Professor Patton hadn't rolled her eyes or heavily sighed at me, I figured I was on the right track.

"An antique would be something unique that likely couldn't be replaced. If someone reneges on a promise to sell you the antique, compensatory damages wouldn't be enough, because even if someone paid you the value of the thing, you wouldn't be made whole with that exact item, so the only thing that would make you whole in the case of a breach would be getting the antique." I looked at her hopefully and silently prayed that I was right.

"Well done, Ms. Alexander. I knew you knew."

I looked down at my fingers and smiled, pleased with myself for getting it right. I glanced up to see Professor Patton watching me. She wasn't smiling exactly, but her usual scowl was conspicuously missing. That seemed like progress as far as I was concerned.

"I presume you're here because you want to be a lawyer, yes?" Professor Patton asked after a moment.

A few months ago, I wouldn't have known how to answer

because I'd gone to law school as a bit of a hail Mary and didn't know enough about it to be certain if I wanted to be a lawyer. Things were different now. There were some things I loved about law school like Torts and Criminal Law, but Contracts was killing me, though less so now, and Civil Procedure wasn't something I enjoyed. Now, though, I could pretty confidently tell her that yes, I wanted to be a lawyer.

"Yes, I do."

"Well, then, remember this. You're still a woman and a woman of color at that. I hate to say it, and I hate for it to be true, but we have to work harder to prove ourselves in this world. I'm not tough on my students to be a bitch, as I know I've been called numerous times. I'm tough on them to prepare them for the world. Despite your rocky start, you've shown you can do the work needed to overcome. You've got promise as an attorney. You're smart, that's clear to see, but you need to be more assertive. And I think you know by now preparation is key. Be prepared and know what you know. Don't let anyone tell you otherwise. Do you understand what I'm saying?"

I nodded dumbly without saying a word. Patton was a woman of color? With that pale skin and blond hair I realized, on further inspection, was dyed, I'd always assumed she was white, but I guess she could be a person of color?

"Speak up, Ms. Alexander. You have questions written all over your face. What did I just tell you? Be. Assertive."

I started to speak and then stopped. How do you ask someone what kind of people of color they were? It was simple. You didn't, so instead I started with the simpler question while I figured out how to formulate the other. "You think I have promise?"

"I do. If I didn't, I would be honest with you. Brutally so, as I've been told on countless occasions. The question now is whether you want to use what you've got to the fullest. And only you can answer that."

"So—" I said, then paused and tried again. "How are you—" Nope, that wasn't it, either.

"I'm Mexican. Is that what you wanted to know?"

I sighed and nodded, relieved that she saved me from having to ask an awkward question.

"As you might be able to tell from the photos, my husband is a gringo, but my given last name is Juarez."

"Why the blond hair, then?" I blurted out, then covered my mouth with my hand.

For the first time, Professor Patton laughed a full-out belly laugh. "My husband asks me the same thing, and I'll tell you what I tell him: blondes have more fun!"

I burst out laughing.

CHAPTER TWENTY-TWO

Silas was supposed to pick me up at nine a.m., and I wasn't anywhere near ready. I couldn't decide what to wear since he wouldn't tell me what he had planned for us. I had tried again to pry the date plan out of him, but he was utterly tight-lipped about it. The only thing he said was to dress comfortably but to bring a change of clothes and any other toiletries I might need. So a) what did "dress comfortably" mean and b) what specific toiletries did he have in mind? And that's why there I was at eight forty-five a.m. still in my bra and panties with half my closet on the bed. The change of clothes was easy—I had packed that the night before, since a dress with the right jewelry and makeup could be dressed up or down. Just in case, though, I had packed three dresses: a mini, a midi, and a maxi, plus a pair of tights in case I decided on the mini or midi. It was still freezing out. The toiletries, on the other hand, were a mystery. Did I need to bring a toothbrush and dental floss? Were we spending the night somewhere I would need to bring face wash and all of my evening skin care products? Would I need a bath towel? Did I need to bring my satin bonnet or shower cap or both? I didn't want to be underprepared, so I packed everything I thought I might need for the day/evening. And that was a lot. When the clock hit eight fifty and I was still virtually naked, my only consolation was that at least my makeup for the "dress comfortably" part was done.

"Fuck it, it's Silas," I said out loud.

Even as I said it, I knew I was lying to myself, but a little self-delusion never hurt, and it got me to rally so I could get dressed. Jeans, a Fair Isle sweater, and my snow boots would do. I checked my hair in the bathroom mirror, crunched my curls a little tighter, and reapplied the red lipstick I wore to give me a boost of confidence. By the time the doorbell rang, I was dressed and ready to go. When I opened the door, I knew I'd dressed correctly. Silas and I could have been clothing twins.

"Was it actually locked this time?" Silas asked with no other greeting besides a hug.

"As a matter of fact, it was, so there," I said and stuck my tongue out at him, making him chuckle. "Are you ready to tell me what we're doing today?"

"Nope."

"You've got to be kidding me. Don't you think the day of the date would be a good time to tell the person who's joining you on the date what they're doing?"

"Not if you want it to stay a surprise."

I rolled my eyes, feigning annoyance, but I loved that he wanted to surprise me.

"Just be glad I'm not making you wear a blindfold."

Hm. Being blindfolded by Silas didn't sound so bad.

"All right, I'm ready to go. Let me grab my purse."

In my bedroom, I took a deep breath, attempting to calm down. I reminded myself that this was Silas, my friend, my study buddy. The man whose lips had damn near kissed me to heaven. I took a few more steadying breaths, and on the last breath, I hooked my purse onto my arm and went back into the living room.

"I thought you got lost."

"Shush," I said as I moved past him to the front door. "You coming?"

"I wouldn't miss it."

W e drove for over an hour before stopping in front of a nondescript building with a blue sign in front.

"Is this the date?" I asked, excited. "Can I get my bag out of the back now?" When we'd gotten to the truck, I tried to take my bag from Silas so I could put it into the covered bed of his truck. The back was never covered, so I knew he was hiding something in there.

"Nice try," he'd said and hustled me into the passenger seat.

"You don't need your bag yet," Silas said as he opened my door. He held out his hand to help me step down, same as he'd done many other times, but this time instead of letting go of my hand when my feet touched the ground, he entwined his fingers with mine and pulled our joined hands to his mouth, giving the top of my hand a kiss. I hadn't paid enough attention to his hand before. They were always so gentle on me, I thought of them as also being soft, but they were just the opposite. Against my own, they were rough and masculine.

Spacecat V-stro was as cute and nondescript inside as it was outside.

"This place is cute. Should we get a table?"

"We're ordering food from here, but we'll get it to go."

Silas tugged me further into the restaurant so we could place our order. He let go of my hand to snag a menu.

"I thought we could get a bunch of things and share it all. Does that work for you?" Silas asked.

I hesitated.

"Are you good with sharing?" he asked again when I hadn't responded.

"Of course I don't mind sharing, but don't worry about getting only vegetarian things just for me. Get whatever you want."

"Don't worry about it. Everything here is vegetarian or vegan. I wanted to make sure you'd have enough options. This date is for you, remember? You won it fair and square."

No one, not even my family or River, had ever voluntarily gone somewhere vegetarian with me so that I could eat everything on the menu. It was a thoughtful change of pace. When it was our turn to order and Silas suggested I do the choosing, I pointed at everything that sounded good. Silas smiled as I pointed to item after item on the menu.

It took a bit over half an hour for them to prepare our order, and when the host brought out our food, there were five to-go containers for the two of us.

"One more stop and then we're off to the main event." We went to a wine shop a few doors down from the restaurant, and instead of asking what I wanted, he reached for my favorite bottle of champagne. Either he'd guessed really well, or he and River had been colluding. Assuming Silas wasn't suddenly clairvoyant, I sent a silent thank-you to my friend.

Back in the car we drove another ten minutes before pulling into a parking lot full of cars. There were no buildings around, just hills and hills of snow.

I climbed out before he could come around to help me and beelined it to the back of the truck. I had a feeling I knew what he had planned, and if it was what I thought, I couldn't wait.

He sauntered around to the back of the truck, taking his time. "Are you ready for the surprise?"

I nodded, doing everything I could not to bounce from one foot to the other. I was an adult for goodness' sake.

"Are you sure you're ready?" Silas teased.

"I'm positive. Now open it," I exclaimed.

He laughed and uncovered the truck bed, revealing exactly what I hoped I would see...sleds.

"How'd you know?" I shrieked. I'd always wanted to try sledding, but whenever we went to the snow, I skied.

"One of the times at Meier when we passed the sled display, you said you'd never done it and asked if there were any big hills close to us."

I couldn't believe he remembered that.

Silas dragged the sleds out of the bed of the truck and put them on the ground between us. "Do you want your own sled or should we ride down together?"

Of course I wanted to share a sled with Silas. Was that even a question?

"What? Scared to ride with me?" he asked.

I edged closer to him and stopped an inch away from his chest. His jaw clenched when I wrapped my arms around his neck and pulled his face down to mine. "Far from it."

Then I pulled away from him and grabbed my own sled. "But first, I want to race!"

It had snowed the night before, and the ground looked like it had been littered with bottle after bottle of baby powder. The snow in this area was untouched. The only evidence of life was the footsteps we left behind as we trudged out of the lot. I walked next to Silas and he pulled the sleds. We stopped at the top of a deserted hill, and he handed me the leash from one of the sleds.

"You ready to get your butt kicked, Cookie?" I asked Silas.

"Oh please. There's no way you're beating me. I'll even give you a head start."

"That's very gracious of you, but when I win, I want it to be fair and square, got it?"

Silas put his hands in front of him as if in surrender. "I'll tell you what, Ms. Confident. Let's place a little wager on this."

"I'm listening." I couldn't turn down a good bet. I rarely gambled money, but I loved making a wager. A bet was how I ended up with my one and only tattoo on my ribcage.

"If I win, I get to dare you to do something I choose, and if you win, you can dare me to do anything. Deal?"

I didn't even think about it before I blurted out, "Deal."

"We can get down the hill however we want as long as all body parts stay on the sled after the initial push off. You can't use your hands or feet to propel you along," Silas announced and pointed down the hill. "Whoever makes it past that bush first wins. You ready for an ass kicking?"

"That's pretty big talk for someone who's about to lose, don't you think?"

He laughed at my bravado and held onto the back of my sled so I could position myself. I jammed my heels into the snow to hold it still until Silas was on his as well. He lay on his stomach, and I stayed sitting on my butt.

"We go on three," Silas said. "Ready? One, two, three!"

As soon as he said three, I yanked my feet onto the sled and pushed off on the snow behind me. I glanced to the side to see Silas do the same. The hill was steeper than it had seemed on the way up, and I flew down the hill much faster than I'd anticipated. Sledding was fun! I peeked over again to see Silas still next to me but gaining speed. His body was arrow straight on the sled, and it looked like his sled and body had converged into one entity.

Crap.

He was going to win, and I was going to have to do whatever he dared me to. He wouldn't do anything mean, I knew that, but I had no idea what he would have me do. And then he pulled ahead. Way ahead. No amount of contorting my body allowed me to catch him. Evidently, he was a sledding pro. I watched as he sailed past the tree and put his foot out to slow himself down. I passed the tree a couple of crucial seconds later and let the sled stop at his feet. He was already grinning that dimpled grin, and he had a glint in his eye that told me he had my dare planned.

I lay back on the sled and covered my eyes. "Give it to me straight, Cookie. What do I have to do?"

"Nervous?" Silas asked, pulling my hands away from my eyes and reaching out a hand to help me to my feet.

"Nope," I responded. "Let's hear it. What do I have to do?"

His dimple quirked and he said, "Ride with me."

"That's it?" I asked. Sharing a sled with him wasn't a dare. It was the prize.

"That's it," Silas said, then paused. "Well, that's it, but you have to ride down my way."

I knew there was a catch. We abandoned my sled and dragged his back up the hill together.

"And how is that?" I asked when he made it to the top, maybe holding my breath a little waiting to hear what he would say.

"I'm going to ride down the same way I did the first time... and you're going to ride on top of me."

"But—" I started, then stopped. I was about to say that wasn't a real dare. But then I realized it was. Me and Silas. Alone. My body nestled snugly against his. We hadn't been that close since the night of our date. I'd kept my distance, at least physically.

"Ready?" he asked, but I could sense the question he wasn't asking: *Is this okay?*

He lay stomach down on the sled and held it still with his arms.

"Climb on up."

I took a deep breath and lay gingerly on his back, both touching nothing on him and everything at the same time. My breasts and hands pressed flat against his back and my pelvis lined up perfectly with his baseball-player ass. I was enjoying every muscled inch of it pressing into me.

"Is that all you got?" Silas threw over his shoulder, interrupting my appreciation of his body. "Hold me tighter. I don't want you slipping off."

The teasing in his voice also rang of a challenge I was all too ready to accept. I tightened my grip on his shoulders and tried to wrap my ankles around his, but I was a few inches short of reaching them, so I wrapped my feet around the bottom of his calves, then tucked my chin into his shoulder right by his ear. "Better?" I asked.

"Much," he said, digging his hands into the snow. His shoulders and back flexed beneath me, sending a thrill straight through me. I didn't know what my dare would have been, but I was certain this was much better than anything I would have come up with.

"Hang on," Silas yelled, then we were zooming down the hill. Riding a sled alone was fun. Riding a sled on top of Silas was otherworldly. We skidded to a stop at the bottom of the hill, and I bounced off of him like an over-sugared five-year-old.

"Let's go again!"

We zoomed down the hill sandwich style several more times, and my sled remained abandoned at the bottom. Once I'd tasted the thrill of riding down on top of Silas, there was no going back, but it started to get cold around the tenth run, and we agreed to go one more time before moving on to the next part of the date. At the top of the hill, we got into position and Silas pushed off. Gliding over the snow and picking up speed, he leaned his body side to side, making the sled zigzag down the hill. Neither of us noticed the rock jutting out of the snow. Before we could register what happened, the sled went one way and we tumbled into the snow the other. I rolled a few times downhill before landing on my back. Wind knocked out of me and a little stunned from the tumble, I closed my eyes and struggled to catch my breath.

I didn't notice Silas next to me until I heard, "Simone. Simone, are you okay?" My eyes were still closed, and I heard scrambling next to me.

"Simone, open your eyes. Are you okay?" I opened my eyes at the command and found Silas bent over me, inches from my face. His brows were furrowed, and his green eyes looked frantic.

I smiled weakly at him and huffed out, "I'm okay. Just a little surprised to be in the snow, you know?"

He exhaled sharply when I spoke, and his brow relaxed. He cupped my cheek in his hand and the warmth told me he'd taken off at least one of his gloves. "You almost gave me a heart attack. I thought you'd cracked open your skull on that rock or something." His thumb stroked the side of my face as he spoke, and I closed my eyes, leaning into his large palm, enjoying the sensation of his rough hands on my cheek. "You can't go scaring me like that, California."

"Sorry," I said, still a little shaken from the fall. "I really am okay, though. Just cold." I started to sit up, and Silas moved his hand off my cheek, taking all that warmth with him. He jumped up and reached for my hands, pulling me gently off my butt and out of the snow. Once I was on my feet, he wrapped his arms around me and rubbed my back, warming me up. I counted to ten in my head, promising I would pull away when I got there, but he beat me to it. Silas took a step back, releasing me from his grip, and I felt the loss in every part of my being.

I liked a lot of things about myself, but my lack of a poker face was not one of them. My face must have displayed the disappointment I felt because Silas stepped toward me again, frowning. "Are you sure you're okay?"

I was okay physically. Emotionally? That was another conversation.

"Do you have a girlfriend?" I blurted out. So I guessed it was going to be this conversation.

"W-what?" he sputtered.

I really wanted, no needed, to know where we stood. "Do you have a girlfriend?" I asked again.

After a beat, he said, "Why do you ask?" Well, that wasn't a no.

"Because," I said, trying to lace my voice with as much indignance as I could muster with a slightly wet butt and teeth that were starting to chatter, "we keep almost kissing, and if you have a girlfriend, I need to know so I can stop hoping for some follow through."

"And you think my girlfriend is the reason we haven't kissed again?" he shot back.

"I don't know. That's why I'm asking. So are you seeing someone or not?" When he didn't answer right away, I figured I'd gotten my answer, for better or worse.

"Never mind, it doesn't matter. Let's just go back to the

truck." My voice was thick with emotion, and I was trying my best not to cry.

"Simone, you're obviously cold. Why don't we gather up these sleds and we can talk about this in the truck. Okay?"

He was avoiding answering the question. I knew it. He had a girlfriend. I wrapped the leash of the sled around my hand and started pulling it back to his truck. I was mad, and I didn't have any right to be. I had put us on ice, not the other way around. Nonetheless, I continued toward the truck without looking back. If I got there in enough time before him, I could take a few deep breaths and calm myself down before he got there. I didn't want to ruin our day, and I feared I was well on the way to doing just that. Unfortunately for me, I underestimated the length of his legs and his lifetime of walking in the snow. Both put me at a distinct walking disadvantage, and I was barely off the hill when he caught up to me.

"Uh, what happened back there?"

"What do you mean?"

"You know what I mean. What's your deal?"

There were times when it's the best thing in the world having someone know you so well. This moment was not one of those times.

"It's nothing," I answered. "I probably banged my head too hard or something."

He gave me the same disapproving look he did whenever he walked into my unlocked apartment.

"Okay, fine." I had to figure out how I was going to explain myself without sounding like a scorned ex-girlfriend. Technically I was neither scorned nor an ex-girlfriend. "Okay," I started again. "We're just friends now, and I know I have no right to be hurt that you're dating someone, but I am. I broke us, and it's my fault you moved on, but I don't have to be happy about it."

"This isn't fair of you, California. You said you didn't want to be with me."

"No, I didn't. I said I didn't think I *should* be with you. I said I needed space. There's a difference."

"You and I both know those are semantics. The end result is that now we're friends and nothing more, so you can't get mad if I'm seeing someone else, right?"

I knew it. I *knew* it. He was seeing someone else.

"Oh no, I'm mad," I said truthfully. "I don't have a right to be, but I am. I guess I thought you'd wait longer for me."

"And how long was I supposed to wait? Three months? Six months? Until you decided you wanted me again? You didn't ask me to wait for you."

Message received.

"Let's go back to the car. I'm cold." I wrapped my arms around myself and continued to the parking lot.

"California," Silas shouted to my retreating back. "Simone, wait up."

He caught up to me easily and grabbed my arm to turn me around.

"I'm fucking with you."

"Excuse me?" I asked, confused.

"I'm fucking with you. I'm not seeing anyone. I told you I wasn't going to give up on you so easily."

The relief spread through my whole body, top to toes, like a warm bath. "You're not seeing anyone?" I asked again to make sure I heard him correctly.

"I'm not," he said. "And for real, you think I'd be trying so hard with you if I was seeing someone else?"

I smacked his chest. "Mean! I can't believe you did that!"

He laughed. "I'm sorry, I couldn't help it. You give me no credit, girl. I never stopped wanting you."

CHAPTER TWENTY-THREE

"Now that you're done being ridiculous, can we go on to the second part of our date? It took me ages to plan this, and I can't have you go ruining it with all your head trauma–induced emotions." He wasn't smiling, a rarity, but I could hear the humor all over his words.

"Shut up," I said, and he grinned at me. "Where to next?" The sledding was such a perfect surprise, I couldn't wait to see what else he had planned. Our food had disappeared somewhere around the fifth run when we took a break to eat in the lodge I hadn't seen when we first arrived, and given that I had thought that was the second part of the date, I had no idea what to expect.

"Are you hungry?" Silas asked as he started the car.

"Not yet."

"Good, because we have a few hours until dinner."

"I can wait a few hours, but whatever we do, I need to get out of these wet clothes." My butt would have been frozen if not for his heated seats. It was still wet, but at least it was warm and wet. I took a peek in the visor mirror to see if I looked as raggedy as I felt. And yes, yes I did. My lipstick was smeared across my mouth, my hair was sticking out at every angle possible, and my mascara was smudged underneath my eye. Not a good look for me. "Get out of these wet clothes and retouch my makeup," I amended my previous statement.

"I got you covered."

"Where are we going?" I hoped it was somewhere I could change clothes and re-do my makeup, but a hotel seemed excessive.

He squirmed a little in his seat. "Actually," he began, "we're going to my dad's."

His dad's house? On our date? I wanted to meet his dad—he sounded great—but this seemed like a strange time to do it. Though we did need somewhere to change clothes.

"Sounds like a plan, Stan." I cringed as soon as it was out of my mouth. The only person I'd ever heard say that was my dad.

"California, we're going to see my dad, but that doesn't mean you have to break out the dad jokes. I'm sure he'll like you even without them," Silas said as he smirked.

His dad's house was only about a fifteen-minute drive from the sledding hill, but the moment we got to his neighborhood, it was clear we'd stepped into a ritzy area. The houses weren't quite mansions, however they were whatever would be considered a step below a mansion.

"Whoa," I said, gawking at the houses getting bigger and bigger the farther in we drove. "You never mentioned your parents were rich," I commented, taking in all the houses.

"They're not," he replied with a grimace. "Well, my mom is. She shoots for all of the major women's magazines: *Vogue*, *Elle*, *Cosmopolitan*, and for the past several years she's shot the Swimsuit Edition for *Sports Illustrated*."

We pulled into the winding driveway of a house that was at least double the size of my parents' house back in Oakland… and their house wasn't small. The house had a wraparound porch with a swing on the side. There were several trees on the expansive front lawn, and I could tell that during the summer and fall the trees would be full of color-changing leaves. There were two cars in the driveway, and even from our distance I saw that they were both expensive. As we pulled farther into the driveway, I recognized the unmistakable emblems on each car that identified them as a Tesla and a Mercedes respectively.

Silas parked the car and swore under his breath.

"What's the matter?" The whole energy in the car seemed to have changed in a matter of seconds.

"My mom is here. I thought she was still out of town. She was *supposed* to still be out of town."

Right. That fraught relationship with his mom.

Silas's discomfort was almost palpable. "We don't have to stay," I offered. "I can change in the car. No big deal."

"It's all good. I'm not going to make you change clothes in the car. Just because she's here doesn't mean we shouldn't be," he said, then turned to me with an intense look in his eyes. "Can I say in advance I'm sorry for whatever she says to you and please, please don't take any of it personally?"

Shit. What could this woman possibly say to me in the time it took to change clothes that Silas felt like he had to prematurely apologize?

"Uh, okay. You're scaring me a little here, but okay."

"Okay. It'll be fine. We won't hang around long."

"Sweetheart," the woman I assumed was Silas's mother gushed. "I didn't know you were coming by today."

She was tall, not as tall as him, but taller than me—at least five foot ten by my guess—and she looked like a softer, female version of Silas. She had his same green eyes and curly, dark hair, though unlike his, hers was cut short.

"Hi, Mom," Silas responded without enthusiasm. He leaned down to plant a kiss on the cheek she had turned toward him.

"And I see you brought a friend." She turned her intense, green gaze toward me and held out her hand. "Hi, honey, I'm Lauren." Her tone was welcoming, but when she smiled, it never made it to her eyes.

"Nice to meet you. I'm Simone Alexander. Silas and I are classmates."

"Oooh, so you've decided to waste your time in law school as well. At least Silas has some company during his second little flirtation with school."

Wow, she was coming in guns blazing and we hadn't even gotten inside the house yet. I didn't know how to respond, so I smiled wanly and said nothing.

"Mom, stop," Silas snapped and pushed past her into the foyer. I followed him, not knowing what else to do.

Lauren closed the door. "What, sweetheart? I'm sure Simone knows it's a waste of time, don't you, honey?"

Whoa, what was this woman's deal? She didn't even know me.

"Lauren, stop harassing those kids. Just be happy to see your son," boomed a deep voice. I looked up to see a slightly round man with glasses descending down the stairs. He had an irrepressible smile on his face that warmed the chill Lauren cast over the room. Hearing the voice, Silas's shoulders dropped and he unclenched his hands.

"Pops," he said, moving quickly to wrap his father in a tight hug.

"How's my oldest son?"

"Oldest and only." Silas grinned. Their back and forth was

easy. A marked difference from that with his mother. "Pops, there's someone I want you to meet."

Silas motioned to me, and I ambled across the foyer to where he stood with his arm draped across his father's shoulder.

"Dad, this is Simone Alexander. She's over at MSU with me."

"Hi, Mr. Whitman, it's nice to meet you," I said, holding out a hand to shake.

"We're huggers in this family," Silas's dad said before enveloping me in a bear hug. "And I'm only Mr. Whitman to children. We're all grown folks here. Call me Daniel."

I laughed, liking Silas's dad immediately. "Nice to meet you, Daniel."

"Let's not stand here wasting time with pleasantries. Come on now, let's move into the kitchen," Lauren announced. Apparently, greetings and introductions, along with law school, were a waste of time. Go figure.

"The queen has spoken," Silas retorted in an uncharacteristically snarky way.

"Silas," Daniel warned. And Silas looked appropriately chastened.

We all followed Lauren, and I was in awe at their house. Everything in it looked buttery and expensive, from the creamy white leather sofa in the sitting room (yes, they had a sitting room) to the oriental rugs that graced many of the floor's surfaces. It was very clear there was no room for Ikea in this house.

"Lauren, your house is beautiful," I remarked, hoping that was the right thing to say to soften her frigid demeanor.

"Oh, hon, you must not see places like this very often, do you?"

Okay, I didn't want to dislike Silas's mother, but she was

making it exceedingly difficult to warm up to her.

"I didn't realize there were places like this in Michigan. In California, sure, these are commonplace, but in a state like this I had no idea." My comment was bitchy, and I didn't even mean it, but this woman was bringing out the worst in me. I had a feeling I wasn't the first person she'd rubbed the wrong way.

Lauren scoffed at my remark and turned back around to continue parading us to wherever we were headed. Her footsteps now took on a much heavier sound, and I couldn't believe this adult woman was seriously stomping mad through her house. I hoped we wouldn't have to stay here too long.

The kitchen, like the rest of the house, was a showpiece. It was nicer than some of the commercial kitchens I'd cooked in except that this kitchen looked like Martha Stewart had personally come in and blessed every surface. Fresh flowers sat on each counter next to glass canisters labeled flour, white sugar, brown sugar, cereal, and cookies. The cookies were stacked in a circular pattern that screamed "decoration only," so I was shocked when Silas reached in the container to grab a couple.

He held one out to me. "Want one?"

I glanced over at Lauren to see if she was going to say anything to Silas about eating the decorations, but she stayed quiet, walked over to the pantry which, when I looked inside, was as large as my freshman-year dorm room, and took out a pack of cookies. She moved across the kitchen and promptly replaced the ones Silas had taken out. Silas rolled his eyes at her action and moved away from Lauren to stand on the other side of the room. He motioned me toward him, and I hastily joined him. I was equally eager to get away from Lauren. I was afraid staying near her, some of her nastiness might rub off on me, and I didn't need that kind of karma. The energy in the room was giving serious bad vibes, and we'd been in this house less than half an hour.

"What are y'all's plans for tonight?" Daniel asked in a sweet attempt to break up some of the tension. It didn't break it exactly, but it forced Silas to look away from Lauren, who he'd been glaring at since the cookie incident.

"We're grabbing a bite to eat after we change here."

"Don't let us hold you up, son. If y'all want to go get changed, go right—"

"Have dinner with us," Lauren interjected, interrupting Daniel.

Silas froze next to me.

"Uh, no thanks. We already have a reservation, and it took a while to get it so—" Silas stammered toward an explanation.

"Don't be silly, Silas. Reservations can be changed. I'm only here for another night or two, and you and Simone can go to dinner together anytime. Isn't that right, Simone?"

Dammit, why did this she-beast have to involve me in their family mess? I looked at Silas, and "no" was written all over his face.

"Mom, no," Silas said more firmly this time.

"Simone, I rarely get to see my son. I'd like to have a nice family dinner to catch up with him and get to know you a little better. That's not too much to ask, is it?" There was gentle pleading in Lauren's voice that I doubted happened often and wondered about the genuineness of. She sounded almost vulnerable, but vulnerability didn't seem to fit her. Still, it wasn't my place to decide whether we should stay or not. This was family business, and I wasn't anything close to family.

"Why don't we go upstairs, get showered and changed, and we can decide from there? Does that work for you?" If we got some distance from Lauren, Silas could take some time to think and not have a knee-jerk reaction.

Silas nodded slowly like he wasn't quite sure he wanted to think about it. "All right. I'll show you where you can get showered and changed."

I trailed behind Silas, taking in the rest of the house, and was amazed it was where he had grown up. The paintings on the walls looked like signed originals, and more oriental rugs lined the floors. The hallway we walked down was wide enough for us to walk side by side without touching, and when he stopped in front of a door and opened it, I sucked in a breath.

"You can get dressed here." Silas led me through the door and gave me a quick tour. The room reminded me of the time River and I had gotten upgraded to a honeymoon suite in Vegas because we had told the host we were getting married that weekend. The only thing missing was the hot tub in the middle of the room. The king-size bed, the couch, the giant picture window, and the sixty-inch television screen all brought back memories of the fancy hotel. Everything in this house screamed wealth and privilege, and Silas was so…normal. He was down to earth, and hearing about and then meeting his father told me Daniel was the same. Lauren was the outlier in the family.

"The bathroom is over here if you want to shower or whatever." Silas walked me across the room and opened a door that I hadn't originally noticed because it blended so seamlessly into the dark wood on the walls. And I found the hot tub. Screw the bedroom, the bathroom was really the showstopper with the jacuzzi bathtub and the rain showerheads. Obviously, I wouldn't be getting my fresh twist out anywhere near that showerhead—it wasn't wash day and we didn't have time for all of that anyway—but I couldn't wait to shower in it. The wall had a panel of switches, one of which controlled the lights, but the rest were a mystery.

"What are all these switches for?" I asked Silas.

He pointed at the switches one by one and said, "Floor heater, jacuzzi tub, window shades, fan, and TV." TV? I didn't see a TV in the bathroom. Silas noticed my questioning look and flipped the TV switch. The wall turned around and revealed a small built in television screen.

"Towels are in the chest at the foot of the bed and toiletries are under the sink if you need them. If you need anything else, I'll be right down the hall." Silas started to walk out.

"Hang on," I said. "We haven't talked about whether we're staying for dinner or not." I pulled him over to the couch and sat down, dragging him down with me.

Silas let out a big sigh and propped his elbows on his bent knees, cradling his head in his over-large hands. He was quiet for a minute. Then longer than a minute. And when he still didn't respond, I rubbed his back and felt the corded muscles there. He was beyond stressed.

"Want to talk about it?"

Silas shook his head no but started talking anyway. "I can't stand being here when she's here. She's a classic narcissist. She comes into this house and tries to manage everything and everyone in it even though she's barely around. She comes back here maybe, *maybe*, once every two or three months and expects us to act like that's normal. She's done that for as long as I can remember." His body was still tighter than it should have been, but talking seemed to be loosening him up.

"She breezes in and out of here on a breath and acts like we should be grateful for her company when she *is* here." He lifted his head out of his hands and grasped for my hand.

"Fuck, and the way she came at you. Simone, I'm so sorry. She had no right to say that to you. She's usually on better behavior around company."

"Always good to know it's you that brings out the worst in someone," I joked with Silas. He didn't laugh, but the corner of his mouth quirked slightly upward. At least that was something.

"Silas, I'm fine. It's really not a big deal. Your mom wasn't the most pleasant person to be around, but she wasn't the worst I've encountered, so there's that. But what's her deal? I mean, why is she like that?" I tried to ask as delicately as possible since there was no good, polite way to ask why someone's mother was a shrew.

"She's self-absorbed and judgmental. Like the whole law school thing. She makes it sound like she hates me being in law school specifically, but she hated me being a management consultant, too. She'd have preferred I be an artist like her instead of a 'corporate drone' like my dad. Her exact words, by the way.

"Let's forget about her, though," he said, jiggling our entwined hands to get me to look up at him. When I did, he was gazing intently down at me. He had a look on his face like the one he'd had when he sang the Bonnie Raitt song at the date auction. Like he was searching for an answer to a question he hadn't asked.

"She's already forgotten." Any other words seemed like they would be too much and would diminish the moment.

Neither of us said anything for several seconds. Then Silas took a deep breath. Then another.

"How has this semester been for you so far?"

That wasn't the question I anticipated, but okay.

"Uh, fine. Much better than last."

"And you feel like you have a handle on everything, workwise?"

"For the most part, yeah." Where was he going with this?

"So, I think we need to give us another shot. Try again, you know. You've got a better handle on school," he said. "And we've established that I'm still single despite your best efforts to prove otherwise," he teased.

Got it. That's where he was going with this. He clearly had a plan for this date and nothing, not even his awful mother, would change that.

"We're good together, and it doesn't have to be me or school. You know I respect the shit out of your goals. I won't get in the way."

The bedroom door cracked open a little, and Lauren poked her head in. Her timing was impeccable, just like everything else in the house.

"Silas, honey, I knocked on your door and no one answered, so I rightly assumed you'd be in here. Sweetie, I do hope you've decided to stay for dinner. I went ahead and called the caterer and they're already making enough food for four. It would be such a waste for the two of you to leave."

Silas shook his head in disgust.

"Whatever. We're in the middle of something here. We'll talk about it when we come downstairs."

"Sure, sweetie, no problem." How did someone with so much vinegar in them manage to sound so saccharine sweet? It was disconcerting.

"Sorry about that. We don't have to stay."

"I don't mind staying if that will keep the peace. I get the sense she's not going to go down without a fight on this one."

"You've known Lauren all of an hour and you already get how she is." He rolled his eyes. "Thank you, though. My life will be much less complicated if I can get this dinner out of the way. If we leave, I'll never hear the end of it." He paused and took another deep breath. "You're not like anyone I've ever met before. You're quirky, a little neurotic, funny, smart, and like that wasn't enough, you're gorgeous. Simone, I adore everything about you, and I've tried to respect your decision to be friends, but I'm over it. I don't want to just be your friend."

Then he closed the bit of space between us and kissed me, hesitantly at first and then with all the pent-up emotion of the last few months. And my brain shorted out momentarily, making the only thing I focused on the warm, soft pressure of his lips on mine. His strong hands cradled my face, and when I opened my mouth to let out a sigh, he traced my lips with his tongue and let it slip inside my mouth. I moaned at the contact and my fingers curled into his chest, gripping his shirt and pulling it out of his waistband. His hands tangled in my hair as he pulled my head back, offering better access to my mouth.

Then—because she could sense happy and was sent to destroy it—a sharp knock pierced the charged air, and Lauren poked her head into the room again. We reluctantly pulled apart at her intrusion. Silas's breath was coming hard and fast, matching my own.

"Oops. Sorry to interrupt again." She didn't sound the least bit sorry. "But since you all haven't left, I assume you'll be staying for dinner."

Without taking his eyes off of me, he said, "We're staying, and we'll be down shortly. Go."

"Wonderful news, sweetie. Dinner should be here within the hour." She turned to leave and then threw over her shoulder, "Simone, dear, in this family we dress for dinner, so hopefully you brought something a bit nicer to wear." Then she hauled ass out of the room before Silas could lambast her for being insulting.

CHAPTER TWENTY-FOUR

Dinner was an unmitigated disaster. When we'd walked down the stairs to join his parents, Silas had warned me the climate in the household would get colder, but foolishly, I thought how much worse could it get. The answer: much, much worse. Lauren was already terrible and had been since we'd walked in the door. In my naive mind, there was nowhere else to go but up. And to be fair, she didn't get nastier toward me or Silas; she kept that at baseline rude. She turned all of her loathsome ire on Daniel who, to his credit, took it like a champ. From belittling his job to belittling him as a human being, she held nothing back...guest and her son at the table be damned. The best part of the evening after our kiss was when Silas unlocked his truck and opened the door for me so that we could get in and go home.

We rode quietly for a while with only background music to break the silence. Then Silas spoke.

"I hate that once again I have to apologize for Lauren. I'm sorry you had to see that."

I shrugged even though I knew he was focused on the road and not looking at me. "Every family has their stuff, you know?"

Even though the dinner was something of a second

date disaster, it helped me understand Silas's compulsion to please Patton. The armchair psychology I picked up from *The Sopranos* and that episode of *Sex and the City* when Carrie dated Jon Bon Jovi was that because he could never please his mother, he sought out acceptance from another powerful woman in his life. Either that or he just wanted to do well in Contracts and had crappy impulse control when it came to answering questions. I never took psychology in college.

His knuckles gripping the steering wheel were white. I hated seeing him like that.

"My family has more than their share of stuff. It's so fucked up they're still together. By all appearances, my mom seems to despise my dad."

"How did they end up together?" I asked, genuinely curious. They were so different I wondered how they even met.

"I'm not supposed to know this, but Mom was crazy in love with some other dude. I found some old love notes he'd sent her. He didn't want to get married, so to spite him, she started dating my dad and ended up getting pregnant. She never really wanted kids, but her parents guilted her into having me and marrying Pops, so she's been making our lives miserable ever since. The one thing she cares about more than anything else is photography, and when I was younger she loved taking me on shoots with her, but as I grew up I wasn't interested anymore and she's made it her job to punish me for it." He looked over at me briefly. "So that's Lauren David in a nutshell."

"That must be so sad for her, but how awful for you and your dad," I said.

He shrugged and said, "She's the reason I promised myself that when I met someone I thought could be the one, I'd do my best to hang onto them."

Was he saying he thought I was the one?

"But," he said and hesitated, "there's something I need to tell you. I debated whether it was worth mentioning, but I want to be completely transparent before we start anything together."

I braced myself for whatever he was going to admit.

"I hated the food at Ipsa's," he said, a grin beginning to break through his face's serious facade. "It was too fussy for my taste, and with those little plates, I was still starving when I left."

My laughter filling his truck was part relief, but mostly unbridled happiness. I adored this man.

I rested my hand on his thigh and said, "Pull this truck over so I can kiss you."

Silas dropped me off at my apartment and gave me a slow kiss at the door.

"Do you want to come in?" I offered.

"You know I do, but I need to check on Jackson. I had a new farrier go over to shoe her this morning, and he claimed she wouldn't pick up one of her feet, so I need to check on her."

Disappointment must have been written all over my face because Silas lifted my chin and gave me a quick peck.

"Hey, I want nothing more than to come inside with you, but if I don't check on Jackson, I'll be worried about her and distracted, and that's the last thing I want."

I loved that he loved his horse so much.

"I'll see you tomorrow?" he asked.

I nodded and wrapped my arms around his waist. He bent down to kiss me, and I meant for it to be a peck, but when he slid his hand around the back of my neck and let his tongue flick across my bottom lip, I couldn't help but bite his lip. He groaned at the sharp pain, then deepened the kiss, letting his hands move up the front of my sweater and roam over my belly. When his thumb brushed the underside of my breasts, then made its way over my nipple, I arched into him, wanting more. I felt his hand fumbling behind me, opening my front door, and then he was nudging me into my apartment. With willpower I could only assume was sent from the ancestors, I put my hands on his chest and backed up a step.

"Go check on Jackson. You won't forgive yourself if she's not okay," I told him.

"She'll be fine," he said, moving my hands off his chest and pulling me close again. He nuzzled my neck and inhaled deeply. "How the fuck do you smell this good?"

I closed my eyes and let myself enjoy the feel of his scratchy beard on my neck before I pulled away again.

"Seriously, go take care of your horse," I said with more conviction than I felt. "I promise, I'm not going anywhere."

He tipped his head back and groaned again.

"Fuuuuuck. I hate it when you're right," he said, adjusting himself. "Tomorrow. Me, you, and no interruptions."

"Aye, aye, captain," I said, giving him a fake salute. He kissed me on the forehead and walked out before either of us could forget our good intentions.

But seriously, screw that horse.

I called River to tell her the good news and distract myself.

"Guess what?" I said when she answered the phone.

"You finally figured your shit out with Silas?"

Wait, what? How did she know?

"Have you talked to Silas or something today in the two minutes since he dropped me off at home?"

River laughed. "No, nerd. I remembered today was your and Silas's date, and he told me he was planning to tell you how he felt."

"Wait, wait, wait...you guys talked about this?"

"Of course! What do you think we talked about all day the day we hung out?"

Good point.

"Well, damn. You kind of ruined the surprise, but yes. He and I decided to give it another shot. We're checking things out. Seeing if we fit."

"I'm happy for you guys, Simone. Really. Silas is a nice guy and is crazy into you."

"Get this. I also met his parents."

"Whaaat?" River squawked at me. "So soon?"

"I think he only meant for me to meet his dad, but his mom was there, too. His dad's great, but his mom's a real piece of work."

"How so?" she asked.

Before I could answer her, my doorbell rang. God, please let it be Silas saying Jackson was fine and he had to have me right now.

I dropped the phone, screaming to River that I would call her back, and ran to answer the door. Grinning, I flung the door open without looking through the peephole. My grin faltered then faded as I took in the person on the other side of the door. It most definitely was not Silas.

Standing at my door, looking like he'd lost his brand-new puppy, was Keith. His usually warm face was drawn. Without thinking, I opened the door wider, ushering him in. Almost midnight, it was too late for unexpected visitors of the not-Silas variety. I wasn't looking for the offerings most late-night visitors usually came with—at least not from Keith—but it also didn't look like he was at my door for an impromptu booty call. He looked flat-out miserable.

He walked in, head hung lower than low, and flopped on the couch head in his hands. I closed the door behind him and joined him on the couch.

"What happened to you?" I asked. Keith and I didn't have the kind of relationship where he came to me with problems and I helped him solve them. We were friends, but him showing up at my house in the middle of the night was unusual.

"Suzy broke up with me," he mumbled.

"I'm sorry. What happened?"

"She said since I wouldn't officially commit to her, she wasn't going to waste her time waiting for me anymore."

Smart girl.

"Was it serious? How long had you been together?" I asked.

"Yeah. We were together almost three years."

What the fuck. I took it back. Maybe she wasn't so smart. Three years was two and half years too long to wait for someone to commit to you if that was what you wanted from them.

"I mean, not to rub salt in your wounds, but do you blame her? What makes you think she should wait around for you to figure out if you want her enough?"

"Because I love her," he said, then heavy-sighed and hung his head even lower if that was possible. This guy was all kinds of messed up over this. Hypocrite.

"Let me ask you this, Keith. If you love her, why won't you commit to her? What's the issue?"

"Because when women who look like you come around, I want the chance to explore my options."

Oh, stop. This mofo.

He spread his fingers and glanced at me through them.

The man had the nerve to have a small twinkle in his eyes.

I think if I had rolled my eyes any harder they would have gotten stuck in my head. "Keith, go find Suzy and talk to her. Sitting over here trying to flirt with me is going to get you nowhere. Be better."

He groaned and lowered his head again, resting it in his hands.

"I know. I'm sorry," he said, then stood up and let me give him a big bear hug.

"Now get out of my house and go find your girl so you two can work it out," I told him.

To help him along, I walked him to the front door and flung it open only to find Silas standing there, hand poised to knock.

"Silas!"

"Hey, Silas, man. What's up?" Keith said casually like he hadn't just been bellyaching on my couch.

Well, this was awkward. I knew it looked bad, Silas coming back to my place thirty minutes after dropping me off and finding Keith there looking smug as all hell. Not at all how Keith had looked when he first walked in.

"What are you doing here?" Silas asked. He sounded relatively calm except the spark behind his eyes and his clenched jaw gave away his irritation.

"Keith stopped by because—" I started to say before Keith interrupted me.

"I stopped by to visit my girl, Simone. I was in the building, and I wanted to see how she was doing."

This motherfu—

"Keith, don't be stupid," I said and turned to explain to Silas, making sure my back was to Keith.

"Suzy dumped him, and he came over here basically in tears." I glared over my shoulder. "I was opening the door to send him groveling back to Suzy."

Silas nodded, clenching and unclenching his jaw.

Silas stepped around me and walked toward Keith. He didn't look menacing exactly, but with his massive size, clenched hands, and the determined look on his face, Silas wasn't someone I would mess with. Keith read his body language the same way and backed up as Silas moved closer to him. Silas reached him right before Keith backed into the wall and slid his arm around Keith's shoulders.

"Dude, it's time for you to go. I don't give a shit why you were here, but you need to get. Out." Silas ushered Keith to the front door and didn't pause until he was on the other side of it. Silas closed the door with more force than he normally did and, as usual, locked it.

"Idiot," he muttered under his breath before turning back to me. "I gotta get back to Jackson, but I'll give you a call tomorrow, Simone."

"Wait, are you okay? You know nothing's going on with Keith, right?" I started to feel panicky, like I couldn't quite catch my breath.

"Yeah, yeah, I'm cool," he said, then turned around and walked out the door.

I stared at the closed door, trying to comprehend what had happened. Was Silas pissed at me? There was no way he thought anything was going on with Keith, did he?

I waited the appropriate amount of time I thought it would take him to get to the stables, then called him. It went straight to voicemail.

I sat on my couch and turned on the TV to watch something stupid to distract myself, but when it didn't work, I picked up my phone to text Silas.

An hour later, I still hadn't heard anything from him, and

I was starting to freak out. He couldn't possibly be mad that Keith showed up at my apartment. Yes, it looked really strange, but I had explained what happened and it wasn't a big deal. At least it wasn't to me.

Two hours later when I still hadn't heard from him, I called Tiffany. I needed some advice, and even though Silas wasn't her favorite person, she'd be honest with me.

"Damn, you fucked that up," Tiffany said when I explained the situation to her. "Also, I *knew* you and Silas had something going on. Wait until I tell Rafael."

"First of all, there might not be anything to tell Rafael after tonight, and second, how did *I* fuck it up?" I asked, surprised. "I didn't know Keith would come knocking on my door in the middle of the night."

"No, but you let him in," Tiffany explained. "And Silas knows his friend. Even though Keith was there to whine about Suzy, coming over at midnight was a real bad look, and so was letting him in that late."

Right. She was completely right. I shouldn't have let Keith in, but he looked so sad and he was still my friend.

"So what am I supposed to do? I called him and texted, and nothing. He said he was going to check on his horse, but he should be back by now, shouldn't he? Should I go over to his apartment?"

"Bitch, no, you shouldn't go over there tonight. Give him some time to cool off. Call him tomorrow, and if he still doesn't answer, we'll gather the crew and get it figured out, all right?" Tiffany said. I loved that she was so logical. I also wanted a second opinion because what if she was wrong?

"Thanks, Tiff. You're probably right."

Tiffany and I talked for a little while longer, and as soon as we got off the phone I called River. When she picked up the phone, I didn't even bother to say hi.

"After he dropped me off at home, Keith came over wanting to talk about Suzy and how he messed up with her, so I let him in, but then Silas came back over and saw Keith at my place. He left, and now he's not answering his phone or texting me back. Should I go over tonight?"

"You one hundred percent should not go over there tonight. Maybe his phone died. Maybe he fell asleep. Maybe he left to kick Keith's ass, but going over there tonight is a bad idea."

"Tiffany said the same thing. She was slightly less delicate than you, but the message was the same," I confessed to River.

"That's why I like Tiffany. If I can't be there to keep you from going off the deep end, at least she can."

I felt uneasy about how things had gone with Silas but hoped with the morning came some sort of clarity or at the very least a text message.

When I woke up the next morning, the first thing I did was check my phone.

Nothing.

It wasn't like Silas not to respond to me, and I was worried. I had told Tiffany and River I wouldn't go over there last night, but I hadn't made any promises about today. I checked the clock. It was eight a.m. I would give him until eleven a.m. to respond to me, and then I was going over there. If he was that upset about Keith being there, I had to do something big. Something to show him that Keith meant nothing, and he meant everything to me. I sat on my couch and stared at my phone, willing it to make a sound, any sound, that would indicate I had a notification. The stupid phone pinged all the time, and the one day I was waiting for a phone call it stayed library silent. By ten thirty, the only notifications that had come through were email spam and a text from Beckett. I had to do something, but I didn't know what, so I called Rivvy again.

It was seven thirty a.m. at home, but this was important, and I didn't think she would mind.

"This better be the emergency of your life, Simone, or I swear on my favorite hair dye I won't speak to you for a week."

River made the same threat any time I woke her up earlier than noon.

"I swear, it's an emergency. I still haven't heard from Silas, and I need to go over there and do something," I whined.

The sleep was evident in River's voice, and I felt a little bad for waking her up so early, but I was desperate. "What kind of something? Why don't you just go over there and talk to him?"

"I'm going to, but I also want to do something big. Something he'll remember, you know?"

"Cook him his favorite dessert and take it over there," she suggested.

It was a good suggestion, and I would probably do that, too, at some point, but I wanted more.

"Or what if I re-enacted his performance from the date auction?"

"You mean dress up like a cowboy and sing?"

"Yeah."

River laughed so hard I thought she might hyperventilate. At least she sounded more awake. "Absolutely not, don't do it. I hate to break it to you, but have you ever heard yourself sing? You sound like a beached whale."

She was right, it was awful. I had recorded myself once

to see if it sounded as bad as everyone told me it did, and it was way worse.

"It's Silas. He'll think it's hilarious assuming he answers the door."

She quieted her laughing, but I could tell she was still smiling. "I'm sure there was some kind of miscommunication between you two, but if you think that's what you need to do, go for it, girl. Maybe wait until tonight, though. Give him a full day to respond. Plus, if anyone decides to record your declaration of love, at least it'll be dark."

"I'll let you know how it goes. With my luck, someone's going to film it and it'll end up on a TikTok what-not-to-do list."

"Love you, girl. Good luck!"

I thanked her and hung up the phone.

I didn't know how I was going to occupy myself until the evening if I didn't hear from Silas. I was caught up on my reading and briefing and wasn't in the headspace to try to get ahead, though having it as an option was a welcome change. With nothing to do but wait, I putzed around my apartment, checking my phone every twenty minutes.

As soon as it started to get dark, I went straight to my closet and found a pair of tight jeans, a flannel shirt, and the most cowboyish boots I owned. They weren't very cowboyish, but Silas would get the idea. I cued up my phone to Bonnie Raitt, and before I could consider how ridiculous I would look, I flounced through the door, laser-focused on Silas's apartment.

It was the longest five-minute walk I had ever taken. I thought about turning around to wait for him to call me, but this thing with Silas was good, and I didn't want to be a bystander to my love life or any other part of my life. The least I could do was try, and if it didn't work out with him, it wouldn't be because I didn't put forth the effort.

When I got to his house, his window coverings were drawn shut. It was early in the evening, so he couldn't be asleep. I tried to peek through the curtains, but they were drawn tight and I couldn't see inside. I turned and did a quick once-over of the parking lot. The Vespa was there, and so was the truck, which meant Silas was likely home. I stood at the front door taking several deep breaths before knocking. When I heard footsteps getting closer to the door, I started the music. I wanted him to get the full weight of the song, so I played the instrumental version and sang over that instead of trying to sing over Bonnie.

"Hey, Simone, what are you—" he started but stopped when he heard the sounds coming out of my mouth. I sounded terrible, and the sheer horror on Silas's face told me it wasn't my imagination. It was as bad as I thought, but I kept going.

Silas let me screech and muddle my way through the entire song, never interrupting, but visibly cringing every time I tried to hit anything that resembled a high note. My whole body was on fire from the embarrassment, and the only thing that made it less awful was the fact that it was dark and no one else could see me.

When the song ended, Silas clapped. To his credit, he didn't immediately burst out laughing. Instead he said, "Well, that was something."

"It was supposed to be, you know, a romantic gesture," I said. "Like an apology."

"An apology for what?" he asked, wrinkling his brows.

"For Keith being at my apartment when you came over. Aren't you mad at me?"

To my surprise, Silas laughed. "No, I'm not mad at you. You're hot and Keith can be a little skeazy, especially when he thinks he's backed into a corner. Of course he would try a little late-night driveby. I need to put his ass on notice that you and I are officially together."

I swooned a little in my boots. He wasn't mad. But then why hadn't he called or responded to my texts?

"If you're not mad, why didn't you text me back?" I asked.

"You didn't get my email?" he asked. I shook my head. "Shit, now I see what this getup is all about. I lost my phone somewhere between leaving your place and the stables. I came to your apartment to see if it had slipped out of my pocket, but I got distracted seeing Keith there. Anyway, I ended up finding it on the ground at the stables, but the screen was all busted up and I haven't gotten a new one yet. I sent you an email when I got home so you wouldn't freak out. Clearly, you didn't get it."

Oh.

"So we're good?" I asked.

"California, we're more than good. I hated leaving you the other night, but I needed to get out of there or I would have punched my best friend in the face for trying anything with you."

He smiled at my stunned face and pulled me inside.

"I didn't like leaving you. I never like leaving you." Then he bent down and kissed me. I stood on my tiptoes and wrapped my arms around his neck, kissing him back with everything I had. His arms tightened around my back, then loosened as his hands moved under the back of my shirt. I shivered when his hands glided over my waist, settling on my hips and pulling me that much closer to him. I loved how tall he was, but at this particular moment his height was making it difficult for me to get as close as I wanted. He must have felt the same way because he picked me up and carried me to his couch so that when he sat down, my thighs straddled his.

"Better?" he asked.

"Much," I said and pulled his head back down to mine.

Silas's hands made quick work of my clothes as they explored my body, first unsnapping my bra, then doing away with the whole shirt. He stopped to stare at my breasts, and my nipples puckered under his gaze.

"Perfection," he said and lowered his head to kiss them, then stopped. "I want you and I want this, but not on a couch. I want you in my bed so I can watch you writhe underneath me."

I didn't think it was possible for me to get any more turned on, but Silas had proved me wrong.

I wrapped my legs around his waist and let him carry me to his bedroom.

CHAPTER TWENTY-FIVE

I woke up with a big, hairy leg draped across my naked thighs. I sat up quickly, glancing around in a gentle panic, then settled back into bed as I remembered the events of earlier in the night. Holy shit. Me and Silas. I hadn't meant for us to move quite so fast, but it was Silas, and when his lips grazed my neck and his hands slid into the back of my shorts, stopping became near impossible. And God, he was amazing. Silas had done things to my body I'd only read about in books, and he'd spent the whole night showing me how talented he was.

Inch by inch, I rolled over onto my back, trying my best not to wake Silas. A quick peek at my cell phone on the nightstand told me it was still the middle of the night. I wanted a repeat performance, but Silas needed to sleep. So did I, but the thought of Silas's big body covering mine again made the need for sleep secondary.

"How long have you been staring at me?"

I jolted at the gravelly, sleep-tinged voice. Silas's eyes were closed, but apparently, he wasn't asleep.

"And don't even try to deny it, California. I can feel those pretty eyes boring into me."

He looked as hot sleeping as he did when he was awake.

"Fine, you busted me. I didn't get to look at you as much

as I wanted last night, and I was making up for lost time."

Silas leaned up on his elbow and turned to the side to look at me. "Last night was amazing."

I nodded my agreement, playing with the ends of his hair.

"But I want to be clear. If we're together, we're together. No stopping and starting and no just friends. Are we on the same page here?"

I yanked the covers down and climbed on top of him, straddling his hips.

"Same exact page," I promised. Then we stopped talking.

I went home early Monday morning with a kiss and the promise that we would go to campus together later, so the knock on my door was no surprise.

"Ready to go?" Silas asked after planting the kind of kiss on my lips that made me want to say screw class and jump right back into bed, dragging him with me.

"I'm ready—unless you want to play hooky?" I raised my eyebrows like Groucho Marx. I was only half kidding about playing hooky. But if he said yes, I would strip down immediately.

"Tempting. Too tempting. If I hadn't already missed the max number of classes, I'd say fuck Contracts and throw you into that bed."

Truth be told, going to campus and going to class really wasn't so bad these days, and even Contracts couldn't ruin my buzz from the weekend. Plus, I was prepared for Patton. I understood her so much better now and why she was so hard on everyone. And I did feel tougher since starting law school. Not that I wasn't tough before, I was, but I felt stronger somehow. Like nothing could break me down.

Silas and I walked into Patton's class holding hands. It seemed we had both forgotten that our friends had no idea we had gotten together over the weekend. You would have thought they were a bunch of seventh graders the way they hooted and hollered when they saw us.

"Ahhhh, shit. When did this happen?" Rafael yelled in our general direction from the front of the room. He was perched on the desk next to Tiffany's seat.

"Good, you got it figured out. Everybody's been waiting for you two to make it public," Tiffany added.

I rolled my eyes at them but grinned. I was too happy to care or even be that embarrassed by their display. Silas gave me a peck on the cheek, squeezed my hand, and let it go so that we could sit in our respective seats before Patton walked in the class. She and I were on better terms, but I didn't doubt she would still happily eviscerate me if I stepped a toe out of line.

Precisely at nine a.m., Patton walked through the door, cane in hand as usual, except now my heart didn't thud out of my chest at the sight of her. There were a few residual nerves that I was starting to realize were purely part of being a law student, but beyond that, I felt okay. Better than okay. I felt great.

"Good morning. I trust you all had a good weekend and spent it preparing for my class?" Even with everything that happened with Silas over the weekend, we still managed to prep for Patton's class. We were in a romance cocoon, but we weren't stupid. I glanced around to see my classmates nodding. In paying attention to everyone else, I forgot to nod and, of course, Patton zeroed in on my static head, not nodding like everyone else. Before she even said my name, I had a feeling she was going to call on me.

"Ms. Alexander. I know it's not your turn to go, but let's shake things up a bit this week, why don't we?"

I was ready.

"Yes," I said and proceeded to brief the hell out of the case, answering each of the questions she threw at me with ease. Patton rarely gave compliments, and it was even more rare that a student impressed her. When the corners of her mouth curled up slightly and she asked the class if anyone had anything else to add, no one raised their hands. I waited to see if Silas would interject anything, but nope.

"Nicely done, Ms. Alexander," Patton said before moving on to the next student. I had nailed it. I sat back down, pleased with myself.

Tiffany nudged me and mouthed, "Damn, girl. Good job."

I mouthed back a quick thanks before turning around to see if I could catch Silas's eye. When my eyes landed on him, he was already looking at me and grinning. He knew I'd nailed it, too.

After Patton dismissed class, I waited for Tiffany to pack up and signaled to Silas that I would meet him outside in the hallway. As I pulled up the handle to my wheelie backpack, Patton strolled over to me and Tiffany.

"Ms. Alexander, I'd like to speak with you before you leave my classroom."

I said goodbye to Tiffany, telling her that I would catch her later in Torts, and walked to the front of the room to meet Professor Patton.

"Ms. Alexander," Patton started before I reached the podium. She leaned against it like it was the only thing that kept her upright, but I knew better.

"Good morning, Professor Patton."

"Ms. Alexander," she started again. "Tell me, how do you think you performed this morning?"

"I thought I did well," I said.

"Are you sure?" she asked, raising an eyebrow.

"I'm positive," I said.

"Yes, Ms. Alexander. You did very well. If you aren't able to toot your own horn, who else do you think will do it?"

I blinked at her, surprised.

"I'm very impressed with your improvement this semester."

"T-thank you," I stuttered. Even though I experienced firsthand that Patton had a softer side than she showed in class, it still surprised me to see it.

"No need to thank me. You did the work to get here. If you do as well on the final as you've been doing in class, I imagine you'll be getting an A in my class this semester."

Stunned, I just nodded at her, not sure what to say. "Thank you" didn't seem appropriate, plus she'd already told me not to thank her. I looked around trying to figure out how to respond when I spotted Silas's face at the window in the door. He looked vaguely concerned, so I smiled to reassure him, then turned back to Patton.

"And you've applied to the position with Chang, Lowe & Sanders?"

"Yes, in January, but given my GPA from last semester, who knows if they'll have me?"

"I happen to know they're not making any interview decisions for another couple of weeks. You did well on the midterm, so keep up the good work and I'd be happy to call in my recommendation on your behalf."

I stood there with my mouth hanging open.

"That's all, Ms. Alexander. You may go." I shook off my shock, gave her a quick smile, and started toward the door.

"By the way, Ms. Alexander, you could do a whole lot worse than Mr. Whitman. That young man has a brilliant mind and a lovely disposition—the same things I loved in my husband."

The blush from her words creeped from my face down to my chest and into my hands. My legs suddenly felt hot as well.

"I'll, uh, I'll keep that in mind," I stammered and hightailed it out of her classroom.

Silas had moved away from the window, but when I pushed the classroom door open, it bumped squarely into his chest. He jumped out of the way.

"Everything all right?" he asked.

"Everything is better than all right. Patton basically told me I killed it in class today and she said if I keep doing this well, she'll recommend me for the position at CL&S." I had a hard time containing my excitement.

Silas scooped me up in his arms and spun me around. "That's my girl! I knew you had nothing to worry about."

Then he kissed me right there in the law school hallway, and not just a peck, either. There was passion and adoration and maybe love? Neither of us cared that students took up almost every inch of the hallway as they exited their respective classrooms. I couldn't speak for Silas, but I barely even noticed. He lowered me down until my feet were back touching the ground and he did it all without breaking our kiss.

"Damn, you guys didn't get enough of each other this weekend?" Tiffany's voice broke through our daze.

Silas put me back down on the ground and gave Tiffany the stink eye.

"On that note, I'm gonna give you ladies some time to catch up." He leaned down and gave me a peck on the cheek before moving easily through the crowd of students. I couldn't help but watch him as he walked away.

"Hey, snap out of it. That's gross. You look like a lovesick puppy."

I turned my attention back to Tiffany, annoyed at her interrupting my Silas ogling.

"Speaking of lovesick puppies, what's been going on with you lately?" She'd been MIA and hadn't really divulged what she'd been up to.

Tiffany rolled her eyes. "If I ever saw you, you'd know already."

Got it. She was irritated at me.

"I know, I know. I've been a crappy friend. Let me make it up to you. We can do a girls' night in kind of thing and I'll cook for you. I'll even go to your place. Okay?"

Tiffany sighed. "Fine, but it better be a damn good meal to make up for abandoning me all semester."

CHAPTER TWENTY-SIX

"Why haven't you been doing this all semester?" Tiffany demanded after dinner. I had made her a vegan meal I knew she would love even though she wasn't strictly vegan given that she loved leather and bacon. Black bean and sweet potato enchiladas with cashew crema was one of my favorite meals to cook, and I figured my fellow California girl would appreciate it.

"That's right, I never told you about Contracts," I remembered. "I bombed it last semester. I got a D."

"Fuck. I don't know if I would have come back to school after that." Now I recalled why I hadn't told Tiffany. I loved the girl, but her grade anxiety was the very last thing I had needed when I was just barely hanging on.

"Yeah, well, that's why you didn't see much of me outside of study group. When I wasn't in class, I spent most of my time reading or in Patton's office."

Or thinking about Silas.

"I'm glad you came out of it all right. I saw you talking to Patton after class. You didn't run out in tears, so I figured it must have gone okay."

"It was better than okay," I told her, explaining what Patton had said about the summer position.

"So you decided to go corporate, too? Good for you. Make that money, girl." Tiffany mimed making it rain. "And I heard Silas got a job in Wayne County?"

He had? He hadn't told me about it.

"I don't know, he hasn't mentioned anything to me about it."

"Oh yeah, he told Rafael and Rafael told me. Rafael really wanted to be in Wayne County, too, but it looks like he's going to end up in Ingham."

It hadn't occurred to me what would happen to me and Silas over the summer. We were so new, I hadn't thought that far ahead, but he and I needed to talk about it. I applied to the San Francisco office of CL&S so I could be in the Bay Area for the summer and start building my legal network there. It seemed important since I planned to practice there when I graduated.

"Simone?" Tiffany said after I didn't respond.

"Rafael didn't get into Wayne County?" I asked, checking back into the conversation. "Wait, how do you know so much about what Rafael's doing?"

Tiffany and Rafael were friends, just like the rest of us, but I hadn't realized they were that close. Had I been missing something?

Tiffany blushed a deep red I had never seen on her face. I didn't think she was capable of blushing. Or embarrassment.

"Tiff, is something going on with you and Rafael?" I didn't know how I hadn't noticed before. I really *had* been in my own world.

"No, no. We're just friends." That line sounded familiar.

"Uh-huh, what kind of friends?" I asked.

Tiffany blushed even deeper if that was possible.

"The kind that kisses sometimes but hasn't slept together because one of them is a virgin."

"You're a virgin?" I joked.

"Not since summer camp one year, but Raf is. Imagine my surprise when I thought we were heading to my house to bang and he dropped that bombshell."

"Crazy. Since when?"

She looked at me like I was an idiot.

"Right, yes, since always. What I mean is, when did you find out he was a virgin and how long have you guys been playing kiss-face?"

She explained that they had kissed one night after study group when Rafael had walked her home.

"Wow. That's so...sweet," I said, charmed by the story.

"Fuck you, I know. It's too sweet. I had to call Pierce after and invite him over after to fuck some sense back into me. But I had to stop sleeping with Pierce and can't seem to stop kissing Rafael."

Huh. Tiffany and Rafael. It didn't make sense on paper, but what did I know? I was dating a pickup-truck-driving, floppy-haired Michigander that pre-law school Simone wouldn't have looked at twice.

S ilas leaned against the wall by my front door waiting for me when I got home. He must have left as soon as I texted him I was on my way home from Tiffany's.

He straightened with a cute little half smile as I approached him. "I checked the door to make sure you weren't crazy enough to leave it unlocked while you weren't home."

"And?" I asked, knowing the answer.

"It was locked."

"Of course it was." I grabbed his hand and yanked him off the wall to follow me. "Now come inside so we can talk about this job you got in Wayne County that you didn't tell me about."

The little smile dropped from his face, and he paled at my words.

I leaned up and wrapped my empty hand around the back of his neck to pull him down for a reassuring kiss. "Don't worry, I'm not mad. I just want to talk to you about it."

He relaxed into me and tried to deepen our kiss, but I pulled away. "Let's talk first."

He groaned as he followed me into my apartment. "Fine. Is this going to be a long talk? Because if so, I need to order some dinner. It's late, and I haven't eaten yet."

Whether the conversation would be long or short depended on Silas. It seemed easier to jump right into the conversation than to beat around the bush. "Yeah, order some food, but I'm good. I ate at Tiffany's. I'll take some dessert, though."

"Tiffany told me that Rafael told her that you were offered a position with Wayne County for the summer at the PD's office. Are you taking it?"

"Nope."

"Why not? That's your dream job."

"I don't know if you know this, but there's this girl I kinda like, and she doesn't plan to be here for the summer so..." he said, then shrugged. "I hear Bay Area summers are pretty nice."

"Silas. No. You absolutely cannot turn down your dream job to come with me to California. That's nuts. We just got together, and it's way too soon to be making huge life decisions around each other. Take the Wayne County job. I'm not going anywhere. It's only a summer. We can survive a summer."

Amusement drenched every one of his words, and he

smiled as he said, "Wow, California. Are you done yet? I haven't ordered the food, so if you'd like to continue, can you take a pause while I order? I really am starving."

"I'm serious," I exclaimed.

"So am I. I've never been to California in the summer."

"Silas. No." I gave him a "stop screwing around" look.

He started laughing. "Okay, fine. I did turn down the position with Wayne County but not expressly to follow you for the summer." Silas took my hand and held it between both of his. "I applied for the position with Littleton & Henry back in December because I wanted some law firm experience before I ventured into the public sector forever. Littleton was at the very top of the list of firms I wanted to work at this summer. They have an outstanding defense practice, and with my interests, it was an ideal fit. They do have a Detroit office, but the partner I want to work for sits in the SF office. You being there is a perk I hoped would matter back when I applied."

Relief spread through me, both at the knowledge we would be close this summer and at the fact that he wasn't changing his life plans based on mine.

"I'm clerking with Wayne County in the fall when we're back at school. It's early days with us, and I don't doubt we're real, but I'm also a grown-ass man and this isn't my first rodeo. I know the risks involved, and I've thought about them all, and at the end of the day, I want to be with you. I'm falling in love with you, and I want to give us a serious try. You're everything I've been looking for, and I'd be stupid to throw it away without even seeing what could happen. Does that sound okay to you?"

It sounded more than okay. It sounded like everything I wanted.

"So California, you down to give it a try with me?"

I climbed onto his lap and held his face between my hands.

"More than you know," I said.

Then he kissed me.

EPILOGUE

I had already decided I wouldn't be living in the same apartment when I came back after summer break. It wasn't a terrible place, I'd grown to even almost like it, but I hoped after spending a summer together Silas and I might be ready to cohabitate when we got back to school. It was woefully premature, but I had faith in us. Finals were thankfully over, and I was spending the day packing my things so that Silas and I could take them to the storage unit I had rented. I really only needed to travel with a few items of clothing. Not many of the clothes I had in my current wardrobe were appropriate for going to a corporate office.

I got the job at Chang, Lowe & Sanders.

The plan when I got back to Oakland was to shop for more professional clothing than the one suit I had in my wardrobe. Silas and I had rented a van to transport my belongings to the storage unit and, more importantly, to drive us to the Bay Area. We offered to let Tiffany join us on our road trip, but she'd said she'd rather puke bile for a week than drive cross country with a brand-new couple. I was secretly happy Silas and I would be able to spend so much uninterrupted alone time together. It would test our relationship, but I felt confident we were strong enough to handle it.

I looked at my phone and saw that Silas was supposed to pick me up in five minutes. My suitcases and boxes were stacked by the door, and the apartment had been cleaned. The only thing left for me to do was open the last of my mail. I seldom received anything worthwhile, but opening the mail before you left an apartment seemed like a thing people did as a final farewell. As usual, there was nothing interesting in the first several pieces I opened. There was one plain white envelope mixed in with everything that had my name and address on it without a return address. I opened it, and when I read it, I teared up. Silas wasn't here yet, but I couldn't wait to read him the note. I heard someone drive up, and I knew it was Silas without even looking out of the window. He'd pulled onto the lawn again and honked before jumping out of the van to help me with my bags.

"Doesn't have the same effect as the first time, Cookie. Are you losing your touch?" I yelled down to him.

"You know better than that. If I had the truck right now, you'd be swooning just like that first time," he said as he kissed me on the top of my head.

"Uh-huh, sure. We'll have to test that out in Oakland one day this summer. See how swoony I get when one of the neighbors comes screaming out of their house threatening to call the EPA on your big-ass truck murdering the lawn." His truck was being shipped to California so he would have a vehicle for the summer, then we planned to caravan back with my car.

"Can't wait to see it, California. Now grab a bag so we can get going. I can't wait to introduce you to my music. You're gonna love it."

The van was already packed with Silas's things he would need for the summer. He had moved everything out of his apartment into his parents' house since he didn't want to stay in his apartment, either. I had a feeling we were on the same page about living together, but neither of us had brought it up yet. It didn't matter, though. We had the whole summer to talk about it. When everything was loaded, I stopped Silas before he put the van into drive.

"Hang on. I want to read you a note I got from Patton."

"Yeah, okay," he said and turned off the vehicle.

I pulled the note out of my pocket and started reading:

Dear Ms. Alexander,

I hope this note finds you well. I heard through the grapevine that you accepted a position with the Chang, Lowe & Sanders SF office. What a wonderful choice! I'm certain you will do an excellent job. You have proven to be one of my most promising students and a budding legal scholar. You didn't give up when many others would have, and you fought your way up from the bottom of the class. You won't have received your grades yet, but when you do you'll see that your final Contracts grade is a B+. While that is a more than adequate grade, I want you to know that you earned the highest grade in the class this semester. If not for your struggle first semester, I have no doubt you would have earned the jurisprudence award for the year. As such, I would like to invite you to TA for my class next semester. Please inform me of your acceptance or declination by May 31.

Ms. Alexander, I applaud your skill along with your determination. It is rare I see a student with your resilience. From one strong woman to another, keep up the fight, and I know you will succeed. Best of luck, Ms. Alexander, and have a wonderful summer.

Warmest wishes,

Jessica Patton

I finished reading her note to Silas and glanced over to see his reaction. The grin on his face told me he was as proud of me as I was of myself.

"So? Are you going to take the TA position?"

"Absolutely," I answered without hesitation. It didn't even cross my mind to ask the Magic 8 Ball.

Silas turned on the radio, and as Prince blared through the speakers, we drove off, leaving our first year behind.

ACKNOWLEDGMENTS

A whole crew of folks worked with me to get this book out into the world and I am, and will forever be, grateful for the endless support.

Desmond: You mean the world to me and I can't thank you enough for allowing me the time, space, and energy to finish this project. You encouraged me when I wanted to stop and celebrated every single win, no matter how small. You've been a patient sounding board with my frequent asks of "does this make sense?" Even when it didn't, you talked it through with me until it did.

Poppy: Kid, you're just the best. Thank you for being patient when mommy has to work. I finished my very first draft of this book when you were two months old and you've been my driving force to keep going ever since.

Mom: When they say she gets it from her mama, it's very true in this case. I learned to write from you and I learned to appreciate writing from you. When I finished this manuscript, then learned it would be published, there's a chance you may have been more excited than me. Thank you for always being my biggest cheerleader.

Dad: You've championed every one of my new endeavors of which there have been many. From law school to book writing and everything in between, you've always told me I can do whatever I set my mind to and I've held that with me whenever I embark on a new challenge. Thank you for being proud of everything I do.

Family (especially Uncle Reggie, Uncle Shaun, Auntie Lenita, Amber, Cynthia, Baba): This book was my quiet project for a long time but when you all found out about it, wow! The excitement and support have been more than I could have imagined. Thank you all for listening to me, encouraging me, and keeping me motivated.

Jenna: You were the very first person to read my entire manuscript. Like literally, the very first. You read the whole thing all the way through before I did. You've read this manuscript almost as many times as I have and the feedback, cheerleading, and general you-can-do-its have been invaluable. Thanks, Wifo!

Lauren and Erin: My fellow romance-loving-friends. Thank you both for your excellent brainstorming, your amazing enthusiasm, and our bookish group texts. They're some of my favorites.

Friends: There are too many of you to name who have been my advocates along the way from encouraging me to pursue publication to preordering my book and convincing your friends to do the same. Thank you all.

To my fantastic agent, Stacey Graham, thank you for keeping me from freaking out and for listening to me when I do. You believed my book had "something there" before I was convinced it did.

Alexander Te Pohe, thank you so much for believing in my book. You took a chance on my #pitmad tweet and were incredibly kind, helpful, and encouraging throughout this process.

Gwyn Jordan, thank you for seeing what my book could be and spending hours talking with me to get it there.

To the Entangled Team: Thank you all for all the things! From my amazing book cover to marketing to editing, it's been a wonderful and wild experience.

Fans of *People We Meet on Vacation* and
The Unhoneymooners won't be able to resist this
witty and heart-stealing road trip tale about taking
the (incredibly) long way round…

Turn the page to start reading for FREE…

CASSIDY

I jolt upright and whip my head left and right. Recognition of my surroundings dawns as my sleepy brain flickers to life. *Airport.* The lights are dim but not out, like a theater just before a show.

And here I was hoping the diversion was a dream.

My attention falls to a foreign bundle of gray fabric in my lap. A tired squeak leaves my mouth as I shove it off my legs. *The heck?*

With a pincer grip, I pluck it off the ground. It has a hood, but no drawstring. The cotton is threadbare and faded. A quick peek inside reveals the tag is missing.

This is the baby blanket of sweatshirts, worn to death.

I lift my chin and search the area.

Of the hundred or so people camping in this gate, there's only one I could pick out of a lineup. And the last thing Mr. *Is This Your First Time Being Right?* would do is offer me a sweatshirt. His dislike of me is so intense he chose to argue with me instead of conceding that I was right about the hotel situation, even after we'd achieved a mutual understanding and respect as our plane landed.

Or so I thought.

That's what I get for attempting to turn over a friendlier

leaf: Luke sass. A glimpse at his ego. I bet if I told him the airport was on fire he'd have to google it to be abundantly sure rather than trust my assessment

So what if he doesn't like me? I didn't like *him* first. I've got squatter's rights on this grudge.

And yet, I have a sweatshirt in my clammy hands.

I spot Luke and his tousled shock of hair across the walkway. It appears he's ransacked it with his hand a time too many. Even the WASPyish among us are susceptible to the harrowing realities of an all-nighter, I guess. He's putting the *lap* in *laptop* as he pecks away at the machine perched on his thighs. His glasses reflect the glow of the screen.

I could ask him. But if it isn't his and belongs to a random good Samaritan who saw I was uncovered—or a random person who intended to smother me in my sleep and failed—I'd be mortified.

Playing *The Sims* until the airline provides an update is safer.

My phone lights up at my touch. *Five twenty a.m.* The drained battery icon winks at me.

I scan for an open outlet. Too many people have fallen asleep body-blocking their charging phones. All plugs are taken except for the top half of one.

The bottom half has been claimed by Luke.

This ought to be fun.

I gather my stuff, cross the crowded space, and approach with my chin lifted and the sweatshirt tucked under my arm. "Can I use the top half of that outlet?"

He looks at me for approximately half a second before returning his gaze to the keyboard. "Sure."

I'm reveling in the ease of this interaction when he adds, "I mean, I don't own it."

"Could've just left it at yes," I mumble as I dig my charger out of the front pocket of my suitcase and plug myself in.

Muscles tight from the plane and sleeping upright, I extend my legs. I've got enough room for a full straddle, but I don't push it far. Just a half. My hamstrings hum in objection, which means it's all the more important I do this to avoid injuries. Even a small one could put me out of work.

"What are you doing?"

I glance to the right as I stretch further. Luke's face is aghast.

I keep my voice low to match his. "I'm stretching my legs."

"*Here*?"

With the scandalized tone of his voice, you'd think I stripped naked and bent over. "Sure. Why not?"

He slides his glasses off his face and buffs them on his shirt. "I've never seen anyone do a *split* in the middle of an airport."

"This isn't a full split, nor am I in the middle of anything. We're on the side of a room where barely anyone is awake. It's not like I dropped down while in line for security." I lean against my elbows, and my muscles sing. "Does this bother you?"

"No."

"Then why do you sound bent out of shape?"

"I'm not." He returns to his computer, peck-peck-pecking.

"Great." I shift even further until my legs are almost a perfect 180, which I had no intention of doing until he questioned me. There's something about his tone—that there are right and wrong ways to do things, and his ways are right— that makes me want to poke him until he snaps. "It's part of my job to be flexible. I'm working, too. Just like you are with your type-type-typing."

The typing ceases. "Your job?"

"Choreographer. Dancer. Professional stretcher, as it were."

He swivels his head roughly ten degrees, runs his gaze up my body, and returns to working. He could weaponize that sharp jawline. "Fascinating."

Heat creeps up my neck. "Astounded by my talent?"

"Moved to tears."

"I'll get out of your way soon enough."

He lets out a strained sigh and scrubs his hand over his mouth. His hoarse voice suggests a lack of sleep. "I didn't say you had to move. Forgive me for asking a simple question."

"Speaking of simple questions." I cross my legs and hold up his sweatshirt. "Any idea where this came from?"

He freezes for a good four seconds. The volume at which his silence yells rails against my eardrums.

I purse my lips and lift it to my nose. The scent is vibrant and refreshing, evocative of California with a hint of citrus, like cold lemonade sipped on a beach. I'd know it anywhere thanks to a summer in high school working at JC Penney and huffing enough cologne to jump-start puberty: Ralph Lauren. "Smells good."

While he continues to ignore me, I lean sideways into his bubble and sniff the air around him.

His gaze remains firmly on his computer. "Did you just smell me, Cassidy?"

"Absolutely not." The delicious scent lingers in my nose as I breathe deeply. "Gosh, it's just the strangest thing. I woke up and it was *on* me. I guess I'll have to go ask every single person in this terminal individually so I can thank—"

"You were freezing." His brow furrows. "Your arms were going to fall off."

I grin, pleased that he admitted it. "So it *is* yours."

He shrugs a shoulder. "It's not a big deal."

I scoot a little closer. At this angle, I get a peek of a color-coded spreadsheet filled with numbers on his monitor. Gag me with a calculator. "That was very nice of you."

The words leave my mouth and heat trickles across my cheeks.

It *was* nice—unexpectedly so.

"Can I do something in return?" I scan the darkened room. "I don't know, buy you a snack from the vending machine or something? You a Doritos guy? Wait—blue bag or red? This is a crucial distinction."

"Not necessary."

"Okay, no Doritos. Soda? Chocolate?"

He pushes his glasses a fraction of an inch up his nose. "You were in danger of frostbite, and I'm not even sure this town has a hospital. Consider it a public service."

"That's actually a perfect comparison. I put out a huge basket of Snickers and Cheez-Its for overworked delivery drivers every December. To thank them for their service. I wish you'd tell me what zero-nutrient crap you like so I could thank *you*."

He eyes me warily. "Not a big fan of snacks. Can we drop this, please?"

"Who isn't a fan of *snacks*?"

His laugh is incredulous. "Have you ever had a conversation that doesn't end in frustration?"

"Actually, my conversations usually reach a satisfying conclusion." My lips arrange themselves in a smile. "Except with you, apparently."

He presses his eyes shut. "And to think, I could've been sleeping this whole time and missed out on all this fun."

I swivel toward him and push up on my knees. He tenses and rears back, hitting his head on the wall.

"I'm not going to smother you with it, Luke." I reach for the suitcase standing upright near his feet, loop the sleeves through his handle, and tie it in a knot. "There. Tiny soldier has returned home."

I catch his eye, and my stomach twists. My neck heats as he studies me.

"You're something else," he says quietly.

I've been on the receiving end of that tilted-head, appraising look before. Like I've rattled off a complex riddle and forced him to solve it against his will.

It's fine being something else—until someone goes out of their way to point it out. It then becomes a judgment. A branding.

I drop back into my seat and angle my body away.

We co-exist in silence long enough that an inkling of color threatens the cloudy horizon. It is the La Croix flavor of sunrise, an almost imperceptible taste. In the interest of letting my battery fully charge, I forgo *The Sims* and dig a notebook out of my purse. I'm halfway done filling the page with pointless doodles when my and Luke's phones light up in unison on the ground between us.

Atlas Airlines JLN to LAX. Canceled. Stand by for updates.

"No." I topple back into my stretch of carpet and snatch the phone off the ground. "No, no, *no*. This can't be happening. How can they just *cancel*? Oh my god, how long are they going to leave us here?"

"That's the airlines for you." His voice has precisely one degree of heat. No urgency.

"This is a nightmare! I can't just wait around here forever."

"Exactly why I'm not counting on a plane." He nods toward a hallway. "The car rental place opens at nine if you're looking for an alternate way out. The desk is near baggage claim."

A few people have stirred in the area, all glaring daggers

at their phones.

Our eyes lock.

In unison, we scramble to gather our stuff.

If this entire terminal is trying to escape, I need to be *first* in line.

We blaze into the quiet baggage claim area, collecting a few looks as we skid to a stop at the back of the rental line.

Luke beats me by a hair.

"I would've been here even faster if you didn't kick my suitcase over," he grumbles.

"You must have me confused me with someone else. I'd never disrespect Samsonite luggage that way."

"Must've been another pint-size redhead with an agenda."

There are eight people ahead of him, and we've still got an unholy amount of time before it opens. My breathing calms as we file in, with two people already queuing up behind me.

Luke's neck hovers just above my eye-line, his perfectly precise hairline hitting like visual ASMR. Smooth and weirdly satisfying. This one doesn't skip his monthly stint in the barber's chair. The strip of tan skin above his travel-rumpled collar brings dull friction to the tip of my finger, like I accidentally traced it.

His physical presence is overwhelming up close. Long legs that perfectly fill a pair of dress pants. A lean but strong back that tests the seams of his shirt. Broad shoulders, perfect for throwing a girl over. For swing dancing purposes, of course—

My phone stirs to life, sending a pulse through my hip. A peek at the caller sounds my internal alarm.

Isabelle, calling at six a.m. her time.

Admittedly my nervous system is hair-trigger sensitive this morning, but this doesn't bode well. "Hey. You okay?"

"Cursdy," she slurs. "You were supposed to call me back!"

I inhale a sharp breath. "Are you drunk?" At six in the freaking *morning*?

"Nope! I slept for two hours. That cancels the drunk."

"Yeah, not how it works. What's going on?"

"This wedding is a *disaster*. I should cancel the whole stupid thing."

My stomach plummets. "Slow down, Bells. Did something happen? Did you and Mikael have a fight?"

"The caterer can't get salmon because of some kind of boat problem, the florist's cooler broke and all my flowers died—*died!*—and I have to go find more and make my own bouquets I guess? Wait, what about the table flowers?" She groans straight into my eardrum. "Mikael's been mostly MIA working on a big, dumb lawsuit. It's like he doesn't even care we're getting married."

"You know that's not true. He's obsessed with you."

"We haven't had sex in three days. *Three*. And two of those were weekend days!" She sucks in a fast gulp of air, a pseudo-hiccup. "Guess he's not attracted to me anymore. I stayed up all night waiting for him to get home from work, and he just passed right out! I had wine and everything. *Gah*, fucking florist, stupid caterer—"

"—Isabelle—"

"—I'm in way over my head with this stuff. And my PTO is *not* time off because my boss is a fuckwad. Mom is useless because she's being so *Mom*, worrying about random stuff I don't care about." She sighs, regaining composure before adding, "I need you."

I saw my lips together. I *knew* I should've come home a week sooner. I could've been attacking the smaller to-do list items, leaving this week free for the more important stuff. But Isabelle is always so meticulous and competent I hardly thought we'd find ourselves in meltdown territory. I never expected we'd be on doubting-our-fiancé's-attraction terrain.

She's losing it. My mother, as a result, is going to lose it. It'll be fire and fury when I get home. The makings of a panic attack simmer at the base of my brain, threatening to alert the rest of my body.

This is my fault. Not much I can do about her tragic three-day sex drought, but the rest of those problems I *must* fix. Somehow.

"Bells, you still got your drink? I want you to put it down."

"But—"

"Down, girl."

I wait until I hear the faint *thud* of a glass. I don't often get to be the boss—little sister problems—but Isabelle needs a firm hand.

"You're going to be okay. We're going to get through this. The wedding is not a disaster. I'll call the caterer and florist today. You need to go back to sleep."

A beat of silence passes. "One more thing. Dad's not coming. Called him last night, which—you know I don't *ever* call him. And...no-sir-ee. No answer. Just a text back. 'Can't make it, Isabelle. It'll be all the better for it.' What does that even mean?"

My heart pangs. "You called him, though. That's the important thing. I'm happy you tried."

"What's it matter if he's not even bothering to come?"

"If you want a relationship with him moving forward, it matters. He's just being stubborn because he's terrified of

Mom's wrath, and he doesn't want to upstage you on your big day."

"He's punishing me for Mom being Mom "

I let my head fall back. It's not the time to have this discussion yet again about our biological father. That's a conversation best left for when she's stone-cold sober and we can give it the unpacking it deserves. "I'll call Dad."

"I mean, I don't want you to *drag* him to the wedding."

"It's clearly important to you. You only get one wedding, and he should be there. Let me handle this, okay? Sleep. We'll talk soon."

"What time is your new plane coming?"

Like the time I borrowed and promptly lost the Ariat boots she bought for Coachella, I have to pick the perfect words to soften the blow. "About that. I'm going to be a bit longer getting there. Having a slight transportation issue. It's looking like tomorrow at the latest. I'm going to get a car and drive straight through."

"*What?*"

"I know it's not ideal—"

"*Not ideal?* Sixty percent humidity is not ideal. You not being here right now is a crisis! I swear, if *one more thing* goes wrong, I'm calling off—"

"Whoa." I jolt at the mere mention of calling anything off, even if it is just tipsy threats. "Don't even say those words, Bells. Everything is always more okay after a good sleep, I promise. I'll make calls to vendors as I drive. I'll even call your boss if he doesn't back off the bride."

"Jack Astaire would drop all the way died"—hiccup—"*dead* if someone talked to him about anything other than profits and numbers."

"Then I'll speak to Jack *Ass*-taire in binary code. Jack Ass

Tear. Wow, what an unfortunate name."

"Promise me you'll be here soon, please? I can't do this without you, Cass."

Determination snakes its way through me until I'm nodding. It's more important than ever that I show up for her. Even if it's just for this week, to check off all one hundred to-dos. To talk her off ledges. To keep my stepfather's side of the family distracted so they don't accidentally perceive Mom's blood relatives and how poor they are, the shame of Mom's existence.

Isabelle, pillar of human perfection, needs *me*. Trusts me to be there for her.

"I'll be there," I say firmly. "I promise."

And when I get there, I'll be the best fucking maid of honor that has ever maided or honored. I may have chosen the wrong flight, but I will do what it takes to get this job done. I want to show Isabelle, Mom, *everyone* that I can be good at this.

Because if I'm not good at the role I've trained for my whole life—standing by while Isabelle shines, helping her look good, and building her up—then maybe I deserve Mom's constant criticism.

We say our goodbyes, and I perch on my suitcase, studying Google Maps for what feels like an eternity, until the desk opens.

When the clerk materializes, she scans the now *long* line of waiting patrons and anxiously fluffs her short salt-and-pepper hair. She receives a lot of intense stare-downs from people awaiting their turn as she works with the first two customers, the kind of impatient scrutiny that would turn me into a blubbering mess. After observing her pace as she hands out the seven rentals in front of Luke, I almost want to climb over the counter and help the poor thing.

She raises her voice to a solid 30 percent intensity when it's Luke's turn. "Next."

Luke lopes to the counter and draws his wallet like a sword. I'm close enough to hear his measured tone. "I'd like a vehicle, please. Something bigger, if you've got it."

She clacks chipped mauve nails against a keyboard.

"Oof." *Clack clack clack.* "This is, um…"

Luke, already gripping the speckled countertop, slides his hands farther apart, bracing himself. "Really, anything will work. Size isn't important."

Her thin, pursed lips and wide eyes suggest she's on the verge of a meltdown. She glances past Luke at the line, catches my eye, and quickly drops her gaze to the computer. "We've only got one vehicle left."

To read more, visit EntangledPublishing.com

AMARA
an imprint of Entangled Publishing LLC